THE FALSE LADY

Under the Shadow of the Marquess Book Three

SUMMER HANFORD

CLAIRMONT
HOUSE

CHAPTER 1

MADELINA GREYDRAKE HALTED AT THE TOP OF THE GRAND staircase in her father's, the former Marquess of Westlock's, London home. Mahogany steps draped in cream and gold carpet curved away before the toes of her slippers, the thick ply a cascade of brightness in the two-story entrance hall. The arc of the wall, mahogany paneling that devoured the glittering candlelight cast by the enormous chandelier, hung dense with gilt-framed portraits. From them, glowering old men and lovely, dead-eyed women stared endlessly outward. Madelina's gaze settled on the largest and newest of the portraits. Her father's over-wide mouth curved in a mirthless smile. Her eyes narrowed in impotent hatred. The marquess had been lain to rest two years past. He was far beyond retribution.

"At least he died ill and unloved," she murmured. Scant comfort compared to the suffering he ought to have endured for his crimes.

Her hands curled, one about the railing to her left, the other creasing the gossip sheets she'd been pursuing before nearby church bells rang out the hour. Any moment, her half-brother, Lord William Greydrake, current Marquess of Westlock, would arrive with his lovely wife, Lanora, to escort Madelina to her first London ball. They would expect her to descend this staircase, crystal-kissed cream

1

muslin rustling and countenance aglow with excitement at her long-awaited introduction to the *ton*. To them, she was a young woman who'd spent over a decade away at finishing school, readying for this very moment.

But Madelina was not that girl, and she could not tread that staircase.

In her mind echoed a scream, the last sound to pass her mother's lips. Though issued nearly a dozen years ago, that fear-wrenched sound reverberated down the steps.

Madelina's slipper-clad feet refused to budge.

She must, as on every other day since taking up residence in her late father's home that spring, take the servants' stair. And do so now, before anyone saw her to ask why. She would await William in the entrance hall.

She turned and gasped. "Aunt Aubrey." Madelina pressed a hand to her hammering heart.

"You let me sneak up on you, child." Her mother's older sister, Aubrey Saint Lawrence, loomed straight backed and tall, both hands resting on the head of her raptor-topped cane. "You know better."

Madelina flushed. She did know better. She'd trained for over ten years, not for concerts and balls and the pursuit of an ideal husband, but as a weapon. She would defend the preyed upon...as did Lord Lefthook. It mattered not at all that he neither knew of her existence nor had invited her to join him in the task. She would prove her value to him when she began protecting those who could not protect themselves.

Madelina licked her lips, opened her mouth, closed it again. No excuse would satisfy Aunt Aubrey. "I was remiss."

Aunt Aubrey slammed the tip of her cane to the carpet, the sound booming despite the thick pile. "You are in danger here in London, girl. Never forget."

"But we haven't even begun." After nearly a month in London, her aunt had yet to permit her to act as champion to the downtrodden, or even to seek out and observe Lord Lefthook. Instead, Madelina had endured a tedious mixture of teas and shopping.

"Sloppiness is the greatest danger."

"Yes, ma'am." Madelina drew her shoulders back and firmed her stance.

"That's better." Aunt Aubrey gave a sharp nod. "Now, go down the stairs."

Madelina met those flint-gray eyes under snow-white hair pulled into a hard bun, eyes so like her own but more at home in her aunt's lined face. "No."

Aunt Aubrey's eyebrows shot up. "No?"

Madelina shook her head. White-blonde curls swished across her shoulders. "No."

"Someday, you must."

"Someday, I will." Madelina strode away from the stairs. She pressed the crumpled paper on her aunt as she passed, pages folded open to that morning's article about the exploits of London's famous vigilante for the poor, Lord Lefthook.

Madelina made her way down the steep back staircase and through the shadowy corridors of the Westlock London home, encountering no one. Though William supplied her with a generous allowance, Aunt Aubrey permitted only a very small, select staff, so the emptiness proved no surprise. When Madelina reached the entrance hall, a glance upward showed that hallway vacant, too, her aunt nowhere to be seen. The nearly deaf young man who served as their butler materialized, Madelina's outerwear in hand.

"Thank you, Wilks," Madelina mouthed, not bothering to add sound to her pleasantry. Wilks would read her lips, and she didn't care to muster the volume required for him to actually hear her words.

He dipped his head in acknowledgment.

Light shifted behind the beveled glass of the leaded front windows. A conveyance approached, carriage lanterns dancing. Those swaying orbs halted without. Madelina would have preferred the candles in the great chandelier overhead be extinguished so she could see into the night to assess any level of danger, but standing in darkness would be too odd even with the excuse of Aunt Aubrey's eccentricities, already liberally employed to explain their lack of staff.

Madelina forced her muscles to relax as she slipped on her gloves. Given the hour, the conveyance must certainly bring her half brother, quite the opposite of a threat. Soon enough, a shadow moved up the townhouse steps. When it reached the stoop, the lanterns there illuminated William, his face carved into a multitude of fragments by the beveled windowpanes.

Wilks glided forward to open the door before the marquess could knock.

As William stepped in, his gaze found her and his smile warmed. "You look especially lovely this evening, Madelina."

She mustered a blush, as any naive young miss would upon receiving her first compliment. "Thank you."

William's attention traveled the entrance hall while Madelina studied him. He stood tall and comely, clad impeccably in black breeches and a tailcoat offset by a white shirt and cravat. The deep green of his waistcoat would match Lanora's eyes. Outwardly, her brother appeared to be everything a lord of the realm ought to be.

And he was. Upright. Dependable. William had protected Madelina—made certain their father didn't harm her—although he'd hardly been a man on the night of her mother's murder. He'd hidden Madelina until the old marquess had agreed to send her beyond his reach.

If only William could have done the same for her mother, but Mother's death had been beyond prediction. She'd deliberately goaded the old lord.

Madelina's gaze slid to the base of the curved steps. If her mother hadn't been distracted, attention caught when some other person in the hall that night gasped, Mother would have seen the old marquess's hands snake forward and push.

A palpable iciness radiated from William, snagging Madelina's awareness. She turned concerned eyes on her brother. It took her only a moment to realize his gaze had found the portrait of their father. William's eyes were flat. His nostrils flared. The muscles along his jaw rippled.

"You should remove that," he said.

Madelina didn't take exception to the harsh edge in William's tone. His hatred wasn't directed at her. "I will." But first, she would walk down that staircase under the weight of her father's gaze.

William refocused on her, his expression clearing save for a dark cast in his hazel eyes. "Your aunt will not see you off?"

"Aunt Aubrey already went above stairs for the evening. She finds steps painful." Because the bullet that ended her career remained lodged deep in her hip. "I told her she needn't come down."

William nodded, but his attention shifted once more to their father's portrait. "You don't have to live here. You and your aunt could come stay with us."

Madelina's smile quavered. "You said you wouldn't offer again for at least a week."

William shook his head. "Apparently, your brother is a liar."

"No, my brother is protective, for which I am eternally grateful. But this is the only home I remember in London, and where I wish to reside, for now." She gave him a shove, something she'd observed siblings do who were close. "Besides, you haven't been married long, and you have your new babes and your newly adopted son. I don't wish to intrude. You need time to be a family."

"That didn't stop our stepmother from living with us before she wed, and it certainly doesn't deter Miss Birkchester," he observed, his tone droll.

"I don't know her well, but I rather think it will take marriage to pull Miss Birkchester from Lanora's side." Madelina suppressed a pang. What would it be like to have so dear a friend as William's lady had in Miss Birkchester? Madelina had her aunt as mentor and guide, but something told her that wasn't at all the same.

"I believe you're correct." William glanced over his shoulder before turning back with a wry smile. "Indeed, you'll find Miss Birkchester is with us tonight, waiting in the carriage."

"Your lady wife secured an invitation for her?" As much as she appreciated William's desire to have more of his wife's attention, Madelina was pleased. Miss Birkchester spoke enough so that no one would notice if Madelina remained silent.

"She did. Lanora wishes to see Miss Birkchester happily wed as much as I do." William offered his arm. "And I shouldn't mind if you joined us in promoting that quest."

Madelina placed a hand on her brother's arm. Wilks opened the door and stood almost hidden behind the edge.

"Not that I don't care for and admire Miss Birkchester," her brother added.

Madelina offered a reassuring smile as they descended to the street. "I would never think otherwise." Waiting at the curb for them, William's coach gleamed, black lacquered, lantern-bedecked, and bearing the Westlock crest.

WILLIAM STOPPED AT THE BASE OF THE STEPS AND TURNED TO LOOK at her, only a few inches taller despite his considerable height. "You're all grown up, Madelina," he said, his smile fond. "You only just returned and now I suppose you'll wed and be off again, but I want you to know, I'm sorry you had to be away for so long and, also...." He hesitated. She could all but see him searching for words. "Also, you can always depend on me. Never forget that. Never feel you can't come to me if you require anything or need someone to talk with."

Madelina smiled, though his words conjured a lump in her throat. There were few people she trusted. This man who, at seventeen, had been willing to thwart the marquess for the sake of a half-sister, counted as one of them. "I know I can. Thank you."

His gaze dropped to the pavement; his features drawn in the wavering lamplight. "I'll never forgive myself for not saving your mother."

"You couldn't have known he would do what he did."

"I knew what he was capable of," William replied, voice hard. He looked up to meet her eyes once more, his stare haunted. "I should have removed her. I should—"

"William? Madelina?" Lanora called from the carriage.

Madelina offered her brother a smile that shook with sorrow, no matter that she willed her lips still. "He's gone," she murmured. "We must leave him in the past." Advice she knew she couldn't follow.

William took her hand and offered a gentle squeeze, then led her across the walk and handed her into the carriage. It didn't escape Madelina's notice that he made no effort to agree with her. She suspected that, like her, William Greydrake would never be completely free of the pall cast by their father.

As she settled into the seat across from Lanora and beside Miss Birkchester, Madelina wondered if their stepmother had escaped the shadow cast by the marquess. Last winter, when Madelina came home for what her family thought was a school break, Madelina had met their stepmother briefly. Cecilia seemed so vibrant, so alive. She'd spent such a brief time with Madelina's father, perhaps she'd escaped unscathed. Newly remarried and newly made Duchess of Solworth, Cecilia lived in Egypt now, under the scorching desert sun. If anything could burn away shadows....

"You look stunning, Madelina." Lanora's bright smile held genuine warmth.

"Thank you, Lady Westlock." Madelina took in Lanora's emerald gown, which complimented her eyes and the hints of auburn in her dark hair. "As do you."

"Lanora," Lanora corrected, as she always did. "Please, call me Lanora."

Madelina nodded, but knew she couldn't. Not with the secret she carried. Even William didn't know, for he'd been sent away all those years ago, thinking his mother dead. As she was, by the time he'd returned.

The carriage dipped slightly as William, who'd been speaking with the driver, climbed in to sit beside his wife. His tiger closed the door. The thumps of the boy clambering up to his perch were muted by thick wood and heavy upholstery.

"Your gown is exquisite, Lady Madelina," Miss Birkchester added. She turned a smug expression on Lanora as the carriage rocked into motion. "You see? The right amount of crystal on a gown augments rather than outshines a lady's beauty. Lady Madelina appears to have been born of magic and dreams, and only now spun to life to grace us mortals." Miss Birkchester let out an envy-tinged sigh and turned to Madeline. "It helps that you're so tall and willowy."

Miss Birkchester's cream gown, trimmed out in a powder blue, accented her eyes but boasted not a hint of sparkle.

"I'd rather have your vivacity than be ethereal and willowy," Madelina replied, seeking the correct mixture of modesty and compliment.

Miss Birkchester tossed chocolate curls that framed a round, rosy face and laughed. "You're only being kind. I am a field mouse compared to you."

"You are both lovely," William said firmly. "Lanora and I shall have our hands full chaperoning you."

Miss Birkchester sniffed. "That day I need chaperoning, especially by Lanora, will be the day the earth turns upside down and we all fall off."

Lanora shook her head. "Grace, you know the earth is a sphere."

"I certainly do not."

"The crown's greatest explorers say it is," Lanora said. "We're near the top, and Australia is near the bottom, which I suppose is why we send criminals there."

"How do they know they aren't simply sailing all the way around the edges?" Miss Birkchester traced a rectangle in the air. "I've seen enough maps and traveled enough roads to know that the earth may be bumpy, but it's flat."

"They have discovered the poles," William said.

Miss Birkchester shook her head. "They've discovered walls of ice they can't cross. Those are what hold the ocean from spilling out."

The argument continued as William's carriage trundled through crowded streets. The *ton* had returned to London from their country seats, bringing light, noise, and crowds. Gentlemen and ladies cluttered the sidewalks, the froth of new dresses on the latter ranging from modest pastels to garish, low-bodiced, and forbidden French silk. As their carriage passed the theater, gentry bubbled forth like foam atop a cresting wave. Carriages choked the roadways. The chatter and laughter of the wealthy and landed rose unfettered into the star-spattered sky.

When they finally arrived and joined the cluster of conveyances turning up the drive of the manor housing the ball, awe wiggled into Madelina's gut. Lanterns lit every surface of the soaring stone mansion, gilding each ornate detail of the towering façade. Eventually, their coachman halted at the front of the line of carriages. Madelina and her companions disembarked, handed down by liveried footmen.

They funneled up the broad steps and into the domed entrance hall. Perfumes, ranging from pleasant to scorching, assailed Madelina's nostrils. Even though she'd been apprised of what to expect by her aunt and other instructors over the course of her training and had attended similar, though much smaller, gatherings in the country, the swirl of people daunted her. Though clad in a gown fit for a princess, Madelina couldn't help but recall that, should the assemblage learn the truth about her, they would cast her aside without a second thought.

They swept through the receiving line where Madelina managed a near-perfect curtsy to the dour old duchess who hosted them. They then continued into the relative safety of the ballroom and stopped halfway across that vaulted space to survey the crowd. Surrounded by so many vivacious young ladies, Madelina hoped to sink unobtrusively into the background. She need simply endure the evening and return to her aunt. Perhaps, after this test of Madelina's social graces, Aunt Aubrey would deem her fit to pursue her real work.

"Who is that?" Miss Birkchester asked, sounding startled.

"Is that," Lanora's voice dipped to a whisper, "Jasper Mclintock?"

"It is," William replied evenly.

A gentleman left a distant window embrasure and approached, apparently unaware of those who melted from his path and then turned to watch his progress. Long strides quickly brought him near and Madelina's gaze collided with the strangest eyes she'd ever seen. A light amber, they seemed almost to glow from within. Rather than sighting anything captured in those tawny wells, she felt the gentleman's gaze reach out to ensnare her.

"Why is he coming over here?" Miss Birkchester squeaked. "I've read about him in the scandal sheets. I will not dance with that man."

"I don't think it's you he means to ask," William said, his tone light.

Askance, Madelina saw Miss Birkchester lean forward to look at her. "Oh dear," Miss Birkchester murmured.

Lanora's head snapped around to face her friend. "Are you certain? But, this is her first event, and he's the very first man to approach."

"I'm always certain," Miss Birkchester declared.

Madelina had no notion of what they spoke. Nor did she care. The way this Mister Mclintock approached them, the way he looked at her, evoked the oddest desire to hide. She stepped closer to William.

"William," Lanora hissed, her voice lower still, "should we really let Madelina meet him?"

"Jasper is an old friend of mine," William said.

Miss Birkchester sniffed. "We all know what sort of friends you used to keep."

Annoyance roiled from her brother's frame. She recalled his earlier intimation that Miss Birkchester living with them didn't exactly suit him.

"Mister Mclintock is also one of my current friends," William said out of the side of his mouth. He stepped forward and bowed to the younger man, which drew Mister Mclintock's attention away from Madelina. "Mclintock, good to see you. Lanora, this is Mister Mclintock."

"Greydrake." Mister Mclintock returned the bow before proffering one to Lanora. "My lady."

Lanora inclined her head.

"I know this is a social occasion, Greydrake," Mister Mclintock continued, his attention now fixed on Madelina's brother, "but have you given any additional thought to that contribution I suggested to my charity? I know what I asked for might sound a bit exorbitant, but—"

"Charity?" Lanora interrupted, her tone touched with surprise.

Disappointment shot through Madelina. She'd been certain Mister Mclintock had intended to request a dance with her, but he hadn't permitted William the chance to introduce her. Not that she wished to dance with the tall, athletic looking, poorly mannered gentleman. She'd no desire to become trapped in his strange amber eyes, or watch the candlelight play off his unruly golden locks. He would prove a distraction to her goal in coming to London, to put her training to use.

Mister Mclintock turned a polite smile to Lanora. "Yes, my lady. I'm afraid I've come begging. Not only for money, but also for support when a certain matter goes before the Lords."

"And you shall have both," William said.

"He shall?" Lanora queried, a deep line marring her brow.

William, too, turned to Lanora. The tall gentlemen, angled away from Madelina as they now were, almost closed Madelina out of the group. Fortunately, she could see over their broad shoulders.

"Yes," William's voice held a trace of amusement. "Mister Mclintock is the one endeavoring to convince the House of Lords to create a special branch of the watch to monitor the most trafficked carriage inns. The posting inns as well, for his cause isn't an atrocity that only befalls the wealthy. He'd like to see a decrease in—" William glanced over his shoulder at Madelina. "In a certain type of crime. He's also begun a refuge for those already affected."

Madelina kept her expression blank, though interest surged through her. She'd bet her left index finger that they spoke of women being snatched from the streets and forced into lives of debauched servitude. The exact sort of thing her aunt had brought her to London to combat. She furtively studied Mister Mclintock's profile. This man, whom so many at the ball chose to avoid, sought to combat that trouble?

"That was your notion?" Lanora said with considerably more warmth. "William has mentioned the cause. Yes, of course, we wish to contribute. If only I'd been more aware of the problem, I should have helped sooner."

"I seem to recall telling you, when first we came here, that it's one of the dangers of London," Miss Birkchester said, obviously not caring that manners forbid her entering a conversation that included a man to whom she hadn't been introduced.

Madelina wished she could be so brash, but she and Aunt Aubrey had agreed that Madelina would attract the least amount of attention, and therefore complication, by portraying a bashful young miss. Deprived of speaking, she studied Mister Mclintock and sought to reconcile his poor manners and unsettling gaze with a man who would organize the protection of the innocent.

"I'm glad you approve, my lady"—Mister Mclintock turned to Miss Birkchester—"and that you understand how dire the trouble is, Miss...." He trailed off and turned a questioning look on William.

Madelina's brother smiled. "Where are my manners? Mister Mclintock, this is Miss Birkchester."

"How do you do?" Mister Mclintock asked, bowing.

Miss Birkchester's answering smile displayed her beguiling dimples. "Rather well, thank you."

Why Miss Birkchester must make herself so appealing when she didn't seem to care for the gentleman, Madelina had no idea, but her behavior rankled.

Mister Mclintock turned, reopening the circle to Madelina.

"And this is my sister, Lady Madelina," William continued.

Mister Mclintock leveled those amber eyes on her. "My lady," he murmured.

His bow reminded Madelina to curtsy. "Sir."

"Will you both dance tonight?"

"We will," Miss Birkchester said. "And we've only just arrived, so we're promised to no one." She offered another bright smile. "You may have any dance you like."

Until that evening, Madelina hadn't appreciated how aggravating Miss Birkchester's outgoing nature and adorable dimples were.

"Then you must promise me the second set, Miss Birkchester," Mister Mclintock said.

"Certainly," Miss Birkchester replied sweetly.

Madelina tried not to gnash her teeth. Really, what did she care with whom the man danced? Her job was to attract as little notice from the *ton* as possible, to hide in plain sight, while she joined Lord Lefthook's battle to eliminate London's greatest evils, of which the abduction of women certainly counted.

Mister Mclintock turned to her. "Lady Madelina, may I be so bold as to request the first set, and the dinner dance?"

She nodded, shocked. To request two dances, that was one step shy of asking William if he could court her. Mister Mclintock watched her for a long moment, amber eyes ensnaring. Madelina stared back, mute.

"Until then," he finally said, then bowed again to her brother, Lanora, and Miss Birkchester. He pivoted and walked away.

CHAPTER 2

Jasper strode from Lady Madelina Greydrake as quickly as his legs would bear him. A tumble of emotions blurred the faces he passed. He'd never, in all his twenty-six years, not even when he'd loved Clementine, been so struck by a woman. Instantly ensnared. Immediately possessed of the need to have her. The feelings coursing through him were madness. Lunacy. Symptoms of a fractured mind.

And unshakable.

Jasper fled to an empty alcove, leaned his fevered brow against the cold of a marble-clad column, and tried to piece his world back together. How quickly, how completely that world had changed.

Upon Greydrake's arrival, his name and title had rippled through the assemblage. Speaking with the marquess and a few other select members of the peerage was the reason Jasper had finagled an invitation to the ball; the reason he endured the derisive looks of his former associates and their righteous womenfolk. Sighting the tall marquess among the crowd, Jasper had set out across the room to secure Greydrake's assistance.

Then, she'd turned. A porcelain goddess dipped in gemstones, though none so bright as her eyes. Those twin pools. Stormy. Deep. If a man could plunge into the depths of those silver eyes, would he come out gilded? Would he be polished free of sin?

Jasper forced down a shaky laugh at such frantic, nonsensical thoughts. He drew in a long breath, seeking control. She was only a woman, after all. Jasper had rather a great deal of experience with women, starting as a lad of not quite fourteen, when he learned how far some of the staff would go to curry favor with the duke's best-loved son.

For a moment, lost in daydreams of Lady Madelina's perfection, Jasper had forgotten that he was a bastard. It mattered not that he was wealthy in his own right, or that his father had given Jasper his name and openly acknowledged an undying love for his mother and a preference for Jasper over his legitimate son.

All the *ton* remembered was that he was a bastard son of the Duke of Aspen. Now, with the duke gone and his title and influence passed on to his son born in wedlock, most of society had no more use for Jasper Mclintock.

Some exceptions existed, like Greydrake. A man who'd been Jasper's friend before his father died and after, evidencing no change in their dealings, save to frequent Jasper's gambling hell, The Black Aspen, less often. That change in habit had everything to do with Greydrake's dedication to the lovely Lanora and nothing to do with Jasper.

But remaining cordial with a titleless bastard didn't fall anywhere near the same realm as permitting a bastard to court one's sister. Especially not Greydrake's coddled, younger sibling, kept sequestered from society and out of harm's way for the majority of her life. Even the fair-minded Marquess of Westlock must baulk at the idea of a bastard courting his sister.

Jasper couldn't afford to alienate Greydrake, one of his most charitable and influential associates. Yet Greydrake hadn't appeared angry. Not that Jasper had paid much attention to the man's reaction to his dance requests. He'd been too busy impetuously courting Lady Madelina.

Jasper let out a harsh chuckle. He truly was mad. Not five minutes in Lady Madelina's company and he'd declared his intentions by selecting two sets, and one of them the dinner dance. He'd meant to leave before supper, but the prospect of dining alongside her overshadowed that plan.

A plan to which he ought to adhere. He straightened, then tugged at sleeves and jacket to ensure order. He had more votes to attempt to sway and more money for which to beg.

Not that he hadn't wealth, he reflected as he strode free of the alcove, his face a polite mask of disinterest. On his death, the duke had left Jasper everything not entailed, including a fortune in investments, a lovely little country estate, and the exquisite townhome in which Jasper's mother resided.

Unfortunately, Jasper's charitable work was exceedingly expensive. On top of that, The Black Aspen proved less profitable than most such establishments, due to what he recognized as unreasonable moral expectations and a horrendous honest streak. Jasper knew that, alone, he couldn't win his battle against the abduction and enslavement of innocents. Especially not the way in which he fought it, retroactively. More must be done to stem the tide of abductions. That was where the city watch came into play.

He stopped to search the sea of hostile faces. Each time he watched a former companion look away or scowl, Jasper worked to keep his expression bland. Inside, every cut rankled.

They'd always known him for a bastard. His father's devotion to his mistress had never been hidden. The duke had lived with them, rarely visiting his wife or the ducal London seat. He'd conducted all dealings, business and social, from his home with Jasper's mother. Until his father's death, Jasper had been accepted by the *ton*.

No longer. Now, he had to beg invitations to their events, and even then, he often failed to gain admittance. Women who once danced with him and batted coquettish lashes now scurried from his path, lest he attempt to speak with them.

Even those men who still came to his club, for the most part, no longer treated him as their equal. They lorded over him or eyed him with pity. In the two years since his father's death, Jasper's whole world had changed.

Music slipped through the room, signaling that the first dance would soon commence. Jasper adjusted his course. He would have to beg for funds later. His set with Lady Madelina was about to begin.

Greydrake and his family remained where Jasper had left them. He cut through the ring of gentlemen who'd gathered before them and offered a nod to the marquess before turning his gaze on Lady Madelina. The impression might be wishful, but he felt that the encircling gentlemen displeased her.

Hoping her vexation didn't extend to him, Jasper offered a deep bow and his arm. "My lady, I believe I requested this dance."

She inclined her head and placed slender fingers lightly upon his sleeve.

He realized he'd yet to hear her voice, the lack an open void in his heart. "This is your first ball?" he asked as he led her to the dancefloor, painfully aware of the buzz of condemnation his attention to her evoked from the assemblage.

"Yes," she said, without a glance his way.

Did she know already? New to society, yet ready to condemn him as they all did? Was her beauty not coupled with a kindness of heart? "And what is your first impression, my lady?"

"It seems a bit ridiculous," she murmured. "The men are like peacocks, strutting about, attempting to stare one another down so they might acquire the best hens. Certainly, there must be a better way to select a mate, and a better use of time and funds."

Jasper nearly tripped. Eminently true, her words were those never uttered. Their very society would crumble should others take up her view.

She darted a glance his way. "I shouldn't have spoken with honesty. My aunt warned me not to."

Jasper walked her to the assembling row of ladies. "I'm partial to honesty," he said before stepping back to fall in line with the other gentlemen. Her gray eyes contemplated him across the void, giving away little.

The lines of gentlemen and ladies exchanged bows. The musicians launched into a quadrille and the dancers sprang to life. Jasper could hardly say what other ladies and gentlemen surrounded him, his attention was so fixed on Lady Madelina. They skipped, kicked, met in the middle, and spun, the dance the same as always. Jasper had executed the combinations a thousand times, but never with such a partner.

Madelina flowed. She glided. When that long, graceful form leapt, she seemed almost to soar.

Once, at a particularly extravagant private party, his host had imported a troop of dancers from the far reaches of the continent. One of the women, as the finale to their performance, had beguiled with a swirling, scandalous dance involving gauzy scarves and a gilded figure. Until that moment, she was the most graceful dancer Jasper had ever set eyes on. Memory of that dark-haired beauty paled before the grace of Madelina's lithe form.

He was aware of the covetous looks of other men, of their stares, and of a rising, almost angry, pulse within him. Jealousy, he realized. An emotion he'd felt for but one woman before. Jasper could only be glad he'd already spoken for the dinner dance.

The quadrille ended, leaving many other dancers panting from their exertions. Women flipped open and employed lace trimmed fans as couples began taking their place for the second dance of the set. Jasper proffered his arm to lead Madelina to hers.

"I'd enjoy hearing more of your radical views on the marriage mart," he murmured as they waited for the other dancers to assemble.

Lady Madelina issued a light, airy laugh. "Oh, I was being fanciful. I thumbed through one of my aunt's bluestocking pamphlets over tea this afternoon."

He cocked an eyebrow, intrigued by the sincerity she projected while making that statement, for he felt certain she regretted her admission and lied to cover it.

"I'd much rather learn more about the topic you broached with my brother," she added.

Jasper shook his head. "It's unfit for a lady's ears."

"Yet, Lady Westlock seemed to comprehend your reference and felt the issue of grave importance. Should I not attend to it, as well? Perhaps I have something to offer to your cause."

"It's not my place to expose you to the sordid side of London." Or to even acknowledge that such a side existed. "You shall have to take the matter up with your brother." Jasper forwent adding that an unwedded miss had nothing to offer to any cause unless part of her allowance was spent on charity. He suspected, for all her poise, that Lady Madelina didn't enjoy being reminded of the restrictive nature of a titled young lady's life.

She frowned slightly. Her lips parted, as if she were about to say more. A gasp rippled through the room. Discordant notes jarred loose from several instruments. Lady Madelina closed her mouth as she looked past him, in the direction of the ballroom's entrance. Jasper turned.

Gowned in sparkling-violet, dampened silk, her auburn tresses falling scandalously loose, Miss Clementine White stood framed in the ballroom's grand entrance. Their hostess's anxious footmen hovered to each side, arms extended to block Clementine's path without touching her. It was obvious they knew she shouldn't be permitted to enter, and equally obvious that they were unsure if putting hands on her was acceptable. Clementine raised a long, white, glove-encased arm, palm up. She met Jasper's gaze and beckoned him, expectant.

Jasper stifled a curse. Though obviously pleased with the opportunity to scandalize the *ton*, Clementine wouldn't be there without good reason. Much as he loathed to, Jasper must leave.

He turned to Madelina with a bow. "My deepest apologies, my lady." He worked to keep his voice light. "I must beg off our second set, and my commitment to Miss Birkchester. My—" He caught back his words. "That is, my business associate requires me."

Madelina's eyebrows winged upward. "Business associate?"

Jasper nodded. Business associate...and mistress. "Shall I escort you back to your brother?"

"He remains where we left him, just over there. He's watching us even now," she said, her cool alto giving no indication of her thoughts regarding Jasper's sudden need to depart. "I daresay, I'll be able to make it to his side on my own and unscathed."

Jasper couldn't ascertain if she meant her words to be amusing or biting. He bowed again. "I reiterate, I am very sorry. I'd looked forward to dining with you."

She inclined her head, expression unreadable, then turned away.

Jasper watched her graceful strides for a moment. Every fiber of his being cried out to follow. If he left now, how could he ever expect a second chance with her?

A buzz filled his ears, resolving into the murmurs of the other guests. The only thing that would cause more talk than the scene he'd already created was running after her. He squared his shoulders and went to Clementine.

Again, his former peers stepped out of his way. Heaven forbid, so much as a hem should come within feet of him. His ostracization might be contagious.

He reached the doorway and glanced at the two footmen, their outstretched arms barring his exit. Ignoring the amusement dancing in Clementine's eyes, Jasper looked back and forth between the two. "Gentlemen, is something amiss here?"

They exchanged a glance. One cleared his throat. "We, ah, were told not to permit this...this lady in, sir."

"Hm," Jasper murmured. "Then why don't you permit me out, and I shall escort Miss White away?"

The footmen dropped their arms. "Thank you, sir."

"No need to thank me. I consider it a privilege to have Miss White on my arm." Jasper offered the appendage to her.

Clementine placed a light hand on his sleeve. He started them away from the ballroom and down the wide corridor to the entrance hall. They walked in silence. Jasper preferred not to discuss his business where it could be overheard.

"Who was that delicate flower with whom you danced?" Clementine murmured. "You seemed loath to give her up."

Jasper mustered a snort. "Greydrake's younger sister. I only hope he doesn't revoke his promise of funds for my dropping her mid set."

"So, you secured a donation from the marquess? Excellent."

Jasper cast her a quelling glance. They neared the butler, who stood ready with their outerwear. Before they could reach him, Clementine halted. Jasper turned to her with a questioning look.

"I'm happy to hear that dance was simply part of a business deal." She slid her arms about his neck. "Even at a glance, I could tell that's not the sort of woman with whom you want to become entangled. Too little fun and far, far too much obligation."

"Unlike you?" Jasper said, wondering what Clementine had seen, or thought she saw, in his attention to Madelina to cause this demonstration of affection. Obviously, she didn't wish to depart without an assertion of ownership. Not that she'd anything to worry about. No matter how tolerant Greydrake had been of Jasper dancing with his sister, Madelina was too far beyond reach for hope.

"Exactly." Long fingers trailed along Jasper's jawline. "I'm all fun."

"And I'd love to explore that further, but you must have come here for a reason." She'd best have, after ruining what was likely the only dances, and only chance to dine with, Lady Madelina that Jasper would ever be permitted. Not to mention... "I did just risk alienating Greydrake to hear your news."

Clementine slid her arm back around his neck. "Always working."

"I try."

"And I try to distract you, for your own good." She layered her body against his. Her lips formed a plush pout.

How many times had they played this game? Always before, that look enflamed him. Any other time, he would have taken her in his arms and kissed her so soundly that the heat of their embrace would have radiated back into the ballroom and seared the goggling butler's eyes.

Jasper captured Clementine's wrists and returned her arms to her sides. "Shall we? I'm positive that whoever had the foresight to send for my coat and hat also called for the carriage."

Her eyes narrowed. Jasper braced for a scene. Clementine could become unreasonable when she didn't get what she wanted.

Her gaze shifted to sultry once more, to his relief. "That was me, on both counts." She patted his cheek with enough force to sting. "That's how magnificent I am." With a whirl of auburn locks, she spun, then sauntered away from him to collect her wrap.

Usually, the sway of those lush hips would captivate him. Instead, it took all his will not to look back at the ballroom in the vein hope of sighting Madelina again. Jasper ordered his legs to carry him first to the butler and then out the door into the night.

The air held a chill he hadn't noticed when he'd arrived. Trailing Clementine, who continued to swing her hips in a way that seemed almost garish after Madelina's contained demeanor, Jasper crossed to his waiting carriage. The black lacquered door displayed the carved and gilded symbol of The Black Aspen rather than the familial crests boasted by those who could claim such adornment. One of Jasper's men, riding tiger, hopped down to pull open the door as Clementine approached. Jasper climbed in after her.

The moment the carriage door closed, Clementine shifted to the other bench, all business as the conveyance rolled into motion.

"While I hope we didn't lose Greydrake's commitment, the matter is indeed urgent," she said. "I have reports that Madam Dequenne has taken two more girls—sisters. She's auctioning them off tonight, along with others, in a warehouse by the docks." Clementine raised worried eyes to meet his. "The younger of the two is only thirteen."

Jasper cursed. "That's the second time in as many weeks. She's growing more brazen."

Clementine nodded. "Why wouldn't she? We're no nearer to catching her than we've ever been."

"We're never going to get in front of this if I keep piping all my funds into buying girls." Not to mention, Madam Dequenne was making a fortune off him.

"I realize that, but until we can gain assistance watching the carriage stops, I don't know what else we can do."

"There must be something." Jasper scrubbed his face with his hands.

"You don't mean to abandon them to their fate?"

"Certainly not," he snapped. How could she think such a thing? He'd sell off everything he owned to keep even one more gently bred miss from ending up in a whorehouse. "They weren't chaperoned?"

Clementine shook her head. "So far as our people can gather, they were put on a coach by their parents. An aunt and uncle awaited them here, but the girls disappeared from the stop before they could be claimed."

"Do we know the aunt and uncle? Are they family to whom we can return the girls?"

Clementine nodded. "It wasn't difficult to find them. They were quite agitated in their search. Our men learned who they are but didn't contact them."

Jasper nodded. Clementine knew what she was about. Best to return the girls with a cover story. It would be up to the girls whether or not to tell anyone the truth of what had befallen them.

He settled back against his seat. "You have men and unmarked carriages ready?"

She nodded. "Of course."

"Good. Let's go get them back before any actual harm can befall them."

CHAPTER 3

M ADELINA STOOD IN HER CHAMBER, DAZED. W ILLIAM AND L ANORA had bustled her from the ball so quickly after Mister Mclintock's defection, it made her head spin. The scandal sheets would be full of the tale tomorrow: *Lady M, dropped by Mister M, flees first ball after being stranded with no dinner partner, when Mister M's mistress beckoned.*

Who else could the woman in the doorway have been? Madelina certainly didn't believe his claim that the woman who'd called him away was his business partner.

Her lips curled in bitter amusement. So much for Mister Mclintock's assertion that he preferred honesty. Or maybe he simply didn't feel the need to reciprocate it.

She'd never seen anyone look so totally and completely like a man's mistress as the woman who'd summoned Mister Mclintock from the ballroom. Only a mistress would exhibit such an extravagant collection of lush curves, auburn tresses, and clinging violet silk. Yes, the woman had a decade on Madelina, but those years didn't diminish her allure. The evidence of her age added confidence, strength, and a knowing look. Imagining that look called forth a blush.

The woman in the doorway made Madelina feel like a lamp post by contrast, and she didn't enjoy the feeling. She'd always been pleased with her body. Proud of muscles honed by hours of training with pistol and sword, gymnastics, and riding. Still, curves exaggerated by dampened silk filled her mind. How could Madelina expect any man to choose her over that? It was like asking if one preferred to dine on a ripe plum or a stick of rhubarb.

"I don't care," she muttered under her breath. "Finding a husband is a façade for the real reason Aunt Aubrey and I have returned to London. And who would want a man so eager to run to his mistress?"

Footfalls in the hall, coupled with the familiar thunk of a cane, caused Madelina to whirl to face her bedchamber door as it slid open. She shook her head. She should have heard Aunt Aubrey's approach sooner.

"Woolgathering already?" Aunt Aubrey asked. "After mere moments at a ball?"

"Hardly."

Aunt Aubrey's lips pursed skeptically. She marched to one of the armchairs before the fire and sat, hands resting on the top of her cane. "You're home early."

"Some gentleman asked me to dance, and then left halfway through the set." Madelina permitted no inflection in her tone. "William and Lanora felt we must leave after that." Her brother had angled a piercing look at his wife, and Madelina had taken in Lanora's nod.

"Some gentleman?" her aunt prodded.

"A Mister Mclintock. Do you know of him?" Could her aunt shed light on why the whole room stared, and why her sister-by-marriage and Miss Birkchester had seemed so alarmed by his approach? Madelina should have made time for more of the scandal sheets than the nearly daily reports on Lord Lefthook.

"Mclintock?" Her aunt's expression grew thoughtful. "One line of the family holds the Dukedom of Aspen."

Madelina shook her head. No title had been supplied when William introduced them. "Not the one I met." Though Mister

Mclintock exhibited the bearing of near royalty that one expected of a duke. Like as not, the actual Duke of Aspen paled in comparison to the man she'd met that evening.

Expression intent, her aunt studied her. "Tired after your ball, girl?"

Madelina shook her head, a spark shooting through her. "No, not at all, and it's early still." With how late balls began, it was already nearly midnight, but that was not late by society's standards, and certainly not too late for Madelina to begin the work that had brought them to London. "Is this the night, then? You'll permit me to begin?"

Aunt Aubrey nodded. "Seeing how you've nothing better to do."

That's all her aunt had been waiting for? Madelina would have declined the invitation to the ball. She tried to keep excitement from her voice. "And what will I be doing?"

"Don't ask questions to which you know the answer, girl." The tip of her aunt's cane struck the floor with a thud.

Madelina nodded, eagerness in no way dimmed by her aunt's prickly nature. "I am to find Lord Lefthook and observe him, to learn his ways and how I might begin to aid him, to gain his acceptance and trust.

"That's better."

Madelina grinned, exalted. Tonight, finally, she would claim her place beside London's vaunted vigilante, Lord Lefthook.

Almost two years ago, when news came of her father's death, she'd wanted to give up her training, her personal goal of ending his life stolen from her. She'd told her aunt as much, not anticipating Aunt Aubrey's disapproval. Impatient with Madelina's despondency, Aunt Aubrey had said, "London is so rife with suffering, what your father did is the least of it," and then Aunt Aubrey had informed Madelina that she must use her skills to help those who could not save themselves and had handed her a London paper, page folded back to the deeds of Lord Lefthook.

"So, where do I begin?" Madelina asked, wanting to bounce up onto her toes but sure that if she did, her aunt would decide her too eager to be permitted to go.

"Where do you think, girl?"

Madelina tried to concentrate through her excitement. "I know nothing of London other than what you have told me." Was deciding where to find Lord Lefthook another of her aunt's endless tests?

Aunt Aubrey's gaze narrowed. "Know nothing of London, do you? Do you not know where the greatest hardships are to be found? Where Lord Lefthook haunts? You stare at the paper long enough each morning, girl. I assume it's because you can read."

Madelina's mind returned to the newspaper, always full of tales of Lord Lefthook. From those reports, she knew what streets he roamed, who he helped. "Practically every day, reports are published of those he's aided, almost always from the same borough. I'll go there and find him."

"Then what will you do, girl, introduce yourself?" Aunt Aubrey raised her voice to squeaky tones that in no way resembled Madelina's, "Oh, Mister Lefthook, I know I'm a slip of a young miss, but I know how to fight. Take me with you on your nightly rounds." Another thump of her cane.

Madelina pulled a face. She rarely enjoyed her aunt's scathing idea of humor. "I suppose I'll need to follow him. I'll need a costume. To pretend to be a man." She let out a sigh, annoyed with the inequities of society.

"Boy," Aunt Aubrey corrected.

"I'm too tall to be a boy."

"A young man, then. For all you don't screech like most girls, you'll never manage too deep a voice."

"Fine," Madelina agreed. "A young man." She flopped down on the edge of the bed, dejected.

"What are you sitting around for, girl?" Aunt Aubrey demanded with a third thump of her cane.

Three raps meant shaky ground, but too much dejection filled Madelina for her to care. She'd thought her aunt had been about to send her out, alone, into the London night. Now, "I suppose I must spend days sewing." Or could she buy men's breeches and a shirt?

"Nonsense." Aunt Aubrey pointed at Madelina with her cane. "There's a locked chest under your bed."

Surprise and elation shot through her as Madelina dropped to the floor, heedless of her gown. True to her aunt's declaration, a large, flat chest rested beneath the bed where she'd never seen one before, positioned beside her own locked case. Madelina pulled it out.

She turned back to her aunt just in time to catch the key, before it hit the side of her head. Madelina applied the key to the latch, though she could have picked the lock. She'd half expected the lock to be another test.

Inside the chest were black breeches and tall black boots. A black shirt and binding for her chest rested on top, not that the billowy shirt wouldn't cover most of her meager assets. A black belt with sheaths rested within, as well, and a scarf for her face, with another for her hair, along with a cap.

"Your pistols and knives are cleaned and ready?" Aunt Aubrey asked.

Madelina answered with a derisive sniff. She crawled back under the bed to pull out the other box, in which she kept her weaponry.

In short order, she dropped her gown in a sparkling puddle on the floor and donned her men's garb. She checked and sheathed her weapons, excitement threatening to make her hands shake. Ready at last, she turned to face her aunt.

Gray eyes studied Madelina for an uncomfortable length of time. "You'll do," Aunt Aubrey finally allowed. Her gaze settled on one of the pistols. "Insidious things. Don't know why you prefer them."

The ball lodged in her aunt's hip had fired from a pistol, though Madelina knew little more detail than that. "I know, you prefer a rifle." Madelina recited, "'Stalk, plan, and engage. A good sharpshooter is more effective than ten men with pistols, and in less danger.'"

"And don't you forget it, girl."

Hardly likely. Madelina had heard the admonishment thousands of times. "Am I ready, then?"

"As you ever will be."

Madelina waited, but her aunt said no more. Likely for the best. Words of encouragement or praise coming from her aunt would have rattled her more than her meeting with Mister Mclintock.

"I suppose I should climb out the window," she suggested, realizing that, even though they'd taken on a very minimal staff, she couldn't very well walk about the townhouse dressed like a highwayman and leave by the front door.

Her aunt shrugged.

Madelina crossed to the large window, banded on the outside by a Juliet balcony, and yanked it open.

"Two things," her aunt said.

Madelina paused, one hand on the balcony's iron railing.

"Lord Lefthook's favorite borough...you can see the whole of it from the old church in the center," Aunt Aubrey began. "And, they say there's a Doctor Carter down on Amber Street who will stitch up any man he deems on the side of right, no questions asked."

Madelina nodded and climbed onto the railing, wondering if that held true for any woman, as well. Nervousness and excitement darted through her frame. She tugged the window closed, hoping her aunt couldn't see her tremble.

The well-worked souls of her boots had just enough thinness and flex to allow her to feel the narrow rail of metal beneath her feet. Surefooted, Madelina turned to face the roof. Ornamental molding spread left and right at chest height and offered excellent purchase. She swung herself up and darted to the roof's peak on light feet.

Townhomes, built touching or nearly touching even in this prominent neighborhood, stretched away before her. A slow smile widened Madelina's lips. She could better understand Lord Lefthook's reputed preference for rooftops. They extended into the distance, her private roadway to wherever she wished to go.

Madelina hastened to a lower portion of roof, not wishing to stand out against the sky. She regarded the churning, low-lying clouds and reflected on the value of the maps she'd studied, for no stars peeked through to orient her. She turned in the direction of Lord Lefthook's favorite borough and set off at a run.

Her world became a blur of slates and gaps, and intense scans of the horizon. Once she left the wealthier parts of London, progress became easier, the streets so narrow and the buildings' overhangs so pronounced, she no longer needed to scale down the side of buildings and scurry across avenues before shimmying up to the rooftops once more. Soon, her goal came into sight: the borough's lone church spire, a dark pinnacle etched against the clouds. The best vantage point for miles.

Madelina scaled the church, its ancient and cracked stone lending easy purchase. The spire proved more treacherous, with rotted wooden slats apt to give way under her weight, but she claimed the summit. One arm wrapped about the pitted copper cross, she braced her feet against the steeply angled roof and leaned out to scan the night.

The moon, a crescent, toyed with making an appearance, until denser clouds swept across the sky. A group of too-thin women clustered about one of the borough's only lighted lampposts and called out their prices to passing drunkards. The next street over, a pride of well-dressed young men sauntered down the middle of the lane, singing, obviously feeling mighty that they caroused one of London's most dangerous neighborhoods. Several members of the watch rode a discreet distance behind. No one wanted the trouble that would follow should any of the fools come to harm.

Madelina continued to scan. Searching, scouring. Some of those below might need her assistance. If she didn't find Lord Lefthook, she would follow the poor wretches around the lamppost to ensure they were treated properly and hand each a few coins. From the coughing that echoed off the walls lining the narrow street, she doubted any of them were long for the world, but perhaps coin would offer comfort for a time.

A flicker of movement above the streets drew her gaze in the direction of the river. She watched a shadowy form jump across street after street, moving away from her and to the right. Exaltation shot through her. She'd found Lord Lefthook. No matter what else happened this night, she would not have to skulk back to her aunt in total shame.

Watching him, Madelina assayed a humorless smile. Here, then, was the flaw in rooftop hunting. Lord Lefthook's movements, though stealthy, were easy to detect. Little else stirred on their makeshift highway above the cobblestones and below the night sky.

Madelina set off after him, balancing speed and stealth. She doubted he would look back until he halted. People rarely did.

Lord Lefthook led her to a warehouse alongside the docks, Madelina's least favorite part of any city. Inevitably, the stench of rotting fish and sewage roiled upward. From her perch several buildings away, she watched him swing through a high window. Inspecting the area, Madelina circled the large, squat structure, keeping to the rooftops when she could.

Her circumnavigation revealed several oddities. For one, though not garbed for dock work, a cluster of burly men loitered in the alleyway beside the warehouse, outside a small side door. Based on those of her aunt's associates who'd come to train her over the years, Madelina felt the lot of them were hired guards. Strong, obedient, armed, and ready to act.

On top of that, a veritable traffic jam of expensive carriages stood before the warehouse's wharf-facing door. All the gleaming carriages were lacquered and boasted well-dressed footmen and drivers. Odder still, none of the servants were liveried and none of the carriages bore crests. Generally, the sort of money that accompanied such a mixture of eccentricity and extravagance went hand in hand with the peerage.

Her scrutiny of the outside of the building complete, she leapt to the rooftop of the warehouse, near the window where Lord Lefthook had entered. She flattened her belly to the pitch and gravel cladding and slowed her breath, focused on the window through which Lefthook had disappeared. A large rat scurried across the cracked tar to her right. Ships and rope creaked on the Thames. The air by the docks, perpetually damp with evening fog, slicked every surface.

Somewhere in the building below, voices rose and fell. Try as she might, she couldn't make out the words. She inched forward. Bracing her legs against the flat, dirty roof, she hinged out over the edge to lower her face in small increments until she could see through the window.

Her searching gaze found beams outlined against a faint light. Somewhere, past rows of crates, flame illuminated an area of the warehouse nearest the large wharf-facing door at the front. Silhouetted against that wavering glow, Lord Lefthook crouched on a beam above the end of the stacks of crates.

Madelina levered her torso upward and slid back onto the roof. Nearly silent, she reversed herself and inched downward, feet first. Her booted toes found the sill. She ducked to fit inside the window, took a deep breath, and jumped to the nearest beam.

She landed firmly and plastered her side to one of the angled trusses. She didn't dare check if Lefthook had heard her. She willed her racing heart to slow, sorting out the voices that played back and forth at the front of the building.

After a long moment, while she still struggled to understand what transpired, she darted her head out to find Lefthook hadn't moved. He still faced away from her. As silently as she could, she took the long strides between the beams. She didn't attempt to reach Lefthook, only sought to get near enough to sort out and understand the words and voices below. One more beam should—

"…are the two I want," Mister Mclintock's voice said. "I assume they are Madam Dequenne's usual price?"

Nearly missing her footing, Madelina grabbed for the support of a truss. What the devil was Mister Mclintock doing there?

"S-she said fifty pounds more than usual for the older one," another man replied in a fearful, halting stutter. "And one hundred more for the younger."

"A hundred?" Mister Mclintock growled. "She's a child."

"M-madam s-said that's why she's worth more."

"I'll pay if he won't," a woman said, voice harsh.

"You already bought all the other six," Mister Mclintock replied.

"Can always use more girls," the woman countered.

"These aren't your usual dairymaids, Madam Ester," Mister Mclintock said. "Your customers wouldn't know what to do with them or want to pay what they're worth."

"Maybe I'm thinking of fancying the place up," Madam Ester replied. "Sweet little virgins like those will bring me better clientele."

A feminine sob sounded somewhere beyond the stacks of crates. A sick weight settled in Madelina's gut. They were selling girls. She'd stumbled upon an auction. It seemed an impossible coincidence to find Mister Mclintock at such an auction mere hours after he'd importuned her brother for money to prevent the practice. Was this what Mclintock really used the money for? Anger kindled in Madelina's gut.

"You'll never get anyone what's not flea bitten in that shack you call a brothel," yet another voice said.

"Flea bitten? Like your arse?" Madam Ester screeched.

Beyond the crates, the voices deteriorated into a squawking babble of argument, in which Mister Mclintock did not engage.

Part of Madelina's mind sorted voices, totaling them abstractly, as one counts church bells after realizing they were ringing out the hour, but most of her thought was taken up with stark, absolute horror. More sobs joined the first, adding to the din.

This was where Mister Mclintock had raced off to. An illegal auction of poor, obviously kidnapped young women. He was...buying them...for...

Madelina's mind revolted. A weighty layer of queasiness settled under the rage in her gut.

"Enough!" Mister Mclintock's firm baritone silenced the squabble. "The two gentlewomen are mine. I'll pay Madam's additional fees."

Madelina's gaze slid to Lefthook. Why didn't he act? Despite her role as an observer, she would aid him. They must charge over the crates, draw their weapons, and liberate the bereft, sobbing women.

Seven, her mind said. She'd counted seven voices, including the auctioneer, and excluding the sobs. Eight guards lingered in the alley. She doubted they'd all been left without. That meant there were likely eight below, plus the ones outside ready to charge in. At least sixteen armed, professional or semiprofessional men. Six brothel owners, at least one of which she suspected could fight, and the auctioneer. Steep odds for two people, let alone for Lord Lefthook on his own, and he didn't know she was there, or on his side.

The bidders had moved on to counting out money. Lord Lefthook shifted. Madelina slipped right, to the outer wall. She layered her body along a truss to watch him pass. Completely silent, Lord Lefthook returned to the window and climbed out.

He must have a plan. From all she'd read, Lord Lefthook wouldn't abandon those girls. She sorted back through the conversation. That madam, Ester, she'd bought six girls, the ones not gently born. Mister Mclintock had purchased two.

Suddenly, Madelina knew Lord Lefthook's plan. He would wait until the auction broke up. Once one of the carriages separated from the others, he would strike. Furthermore, Madelina knew which carriage he would follow. It wasn't a choice anyone would wish to make, but he could be in only one place, and all knew Lord Lefthook's love for the downtrodden. He would value six dairymaids, or whatever occupation the poor country girls had given up to come to London, over two gentleman's daughters.

Madelina headed for the window. She must hurry if she wished to find a vantage point from which she could observe what carriage Mclintock took, yet not be seen by Lord Lefthook or anyone below. With the river bordering one side of the warehouse, that would take some doing.

She knew she'd come out to observe, that her aunt would claim her not ready to intervene, but Madelina couldn't turn her back on those two women. Besides, the best way to gain Lord Lefthook's approval and trust was to mimic his good deeds, and that was exactly what Madelina intended to do.

Not only would she rescue the girls Lord Lefthook couldn't save, but she would also put Mclintock in his place. How dare he saunter into a ballroom espousing charity, as upright and handsome as a knight of old, and then turn around and buy people?

All those gentlemen and ladies who'd shifted from his path were correct. Mister Mclintock was unfit for polite society. As she neared the open window, Madelina's left hand brushed the hilt of one of her pistols. If he resisted her attempt to rescue the two girls too fiercely, he might even prove unfit for life in general.

CHAPTER 4

A PRICKLING SENSATION RAN BETWEEN JASPER'S SHOULDER BLADES. He paused while climbing into his carriage, turned back to the warehouse, then looked up and down the street, before raising his gaze to the rooftops. The night sky had become cloaked in inky clouds, but nothing appeared amiss. He shrugged, trying to shake off a feeling of being watched so strong that he had to force down a shiver. Though he couldn't locate a watcher, the person's malevolence struck like a physical blow. With a second shrug, he alighted, and his carriage started forward.

That malice couldn't have come from the two young woman he'd purchased, he reflected as he settled into his seat. He'd sent them out the side door with Clementine and his men. They should be almost to the second coach now, parked in an alley several buildings away.

Jasper didn't care to take chances. Not with Madam Dequenne's non-existent honor or the girls' still-salvageable reputations. Once, and once only, she'd tricked him by retaking girls he'd bought, under the guise of robbing his coach as he neared The Black Aspen. Now, he snuck the young women out, concealed them amid clumps of men, and had them taken immediately under heavy guard to their waiting relations.

Clementine and his men would have the girls delivered to their aunt and uncle before the churches rang out two. On the way there, she would help them devise a story, likely something about missing the earlier coach when it made a stop and taking a later one, their baggage still on the first. The simpler the better, Clementine knew, and the young women would have ample reasons to keep their secret.

Jasper rubbed a long-fingered hand across his forehead, attempting to ease the pounding therein. What he'd paid for the girls would hardly be replenished by the funds he expected from Greydrake, and Jasper had missed his chance to cajole those few others he'd meant to approach at the ball. At this rate, he'd be forced to sell some of the holdings his father had left him in order to continue.

He required funds on hand to rescue the next innocent, unsuspecting girl grabbed from one of the coach or posting inns. Not to mention, to gain the votes needed to assign more dedicated guardsmen to those areas. Not that every peer whose vote he might win took bribes, but many expected them, and others needed to be met with and persuaded, which required the right clothes, invitations to events, and memberships at clubs. Nearly all the profits from The Black Aspen currently went to making new lives for women already affected. Jasper felt loathe to divert those funds. It would cut him to the quick to have to turn away anyone seeking a new start.

Perhaps if he approached his half-brother, begged Matthew to purchase some of the lands their father had left Jasper, the ones that bordered the ducal estate—

The carriage stopped.

Jasper threw his arms wide, braced against the walls to keep from flying from his seat. His coachman shouted at something, or someone, in the street.

Jasper clenched his teeth. Madam Dequenne. Well, all her men would find this time was Jasper and his driver. He righted himself in his seat and tugged straight his jacket and cravat. It wouldn't do to meet the ruffians in a disheveled state. To command the situation, he must give the appearance of calm.

The carriage dipped. His driver getting down, or someone

climbing up? Jasper forced his expression into a look of boredom. He leaned back against the plush cushions. The carriage bounced on its springs as someone jumped down. Then the door swung open, revealing a narrow figure, rendered little more than a silhouette by the lengthy distance between lighted lamps in that unfriendly corner of London. Jasper made out dark garments and a face obscured by a scarf and cap. In the dark shrouding the man's face, two eyes glinted with distant lamplight.

His first thought was Lefthook, but Lefthook stood at least half a head taller and possessed a bulkier build than this youth. Besides, why would Lefthook halt Jasper's driver so abruptly, or be there, at all? Per their agreement, the vigilante was to rescue the other six women.

And Lord Lefthook never carried a gun.

Jasper forced his gaze not to linger on the pistol barrel the would-be robber trained on him. Instead, he met the lad's gaze with a look of even greater disinterest. "I assume, as you've only one shot and I heard none, that you haven't harmed my driver?"

"I don't harm the innocent," the youth grated out.

So much anger smoldered in the other man's tone that Jasper wondered if he'd personally wronged the lad somehow. "Well then, you and I should get along marvelously."

"I doubt that. Where are the young women?"

Not someone he'd wronged, then, but simply another of Madam Dequenne's lackies. One day soon, Jasper vowed, he would discover the whereabouts and identity of the mysterious madam and permanently end her half-century reign of evil, for no one else seemed able to curtail her villainy. For years now, he'd hoped the old woman would simply die, but she proved too tenacious for that, likely sustained by her wickedness.

"I asked you a question," the youth said.

"I realize it's dark, but I'm sure you can see for yourself that they aren't here," Jasper said. "What did you do to my driver, seeing how we both agree you didn't shoot him?"

The black-clad youth leaned forward to look into the carriage, pistol pointed unwaveringly at Jasper's chest. "Nothing permanent."

Jasper found that hardly reassuring, but doubted he'd get more from the lad. He narrowed his gaze. Would this hired assailant, this lacky, know how to find Madam Dequenne? Early on, Jasper had attempted to locate her through her auctioneers, but they never knew her. Didn't even work for her. They were men she threatened into holding her disgusting auctions, a different man and a different location every time.

The ruffian glared vitriol at Jasper. "Once more, and once more only will I ask. Where are the young women?" The pistol jabbed closer, closing the gap between the barrel and his chest.

Jasper studied the weapon. The pistol wasn't cocked.

"If you've harmed them in any wa—"

Jasper sprang forward, swinging one arm wide. The pistol slammed into the door jam and flew free. It clattered to the cracked cobblestones as the rest of Jasper collided with the youth.

The lean body twisted away, avoiding Jasper's bulk. Jasper flung out a hand to keep his face from meeting the gutter, then sprang to his feet.

The other man crouched low, arms spread wide and fists clenched. Jasper straightened and brushed off his gloves. With a snarl, his would-be robber charged.

At the last moment, Jasper stepped aside. One arm flung out to clothesline his opponent. The youth bent backwards, nearly folding in half in an amazing display of dexterity, and slid under Jasper's arm.

Pain shot up Jasper's side. He spun. For an incredulous moment, he thought the other man had stabbed him, but the hand he pressed to his back came away clean.

A fist flew at his face.

Jasper caught the youth's smaller hand, engulfing it in his. "I've had about enough of this."

"Really? I haven't." A boot collided with Jasper's side, in nearly the same spot as the punch had landed.

Jasper grunted. It took all his will and a tightening of his grip on the lad's fist to hold in a bellow of pain. "The young women are safe. Your madam can go hang."

Confusion etched a line along the young man's brow. "My madam can go hang?"

"You heard me. Madam Dequenne sold the girls. They're mine to do with as I please." Jasper eased his grip. "You can't enjoy working for—"

Hooves clattered nearby. Jasper stole a quick glance. Several streets up, a half squadron of the watch turned onto the street. It galled him that they would patrol near the docks when he needed them least, yet they allowed young women to be plucked from carriage stops the moment they arrived in London.

The fist Jasper clutched twisted free. The young man danced away, dipping down to snatch up his pistol as he passed. He slipped it into a holster. Jasper belatedly noted a second pistol and what appeared to be knife hilts. In moments, the lad's back came to rest against one of the dark, squat buildings that lined the street.

"This isn't over, Mclintock," he warned in a low, menacing voice.

"Somehow, I thought not," Jasper replied, tone deliberately uninterested.

The lad shimmied up the building's rough siding like a squirrel and swung onto the rooftop. Ducking low, he ran.

Jasper shook his head. London grew odder every day. He turned and climbed up the carriage to inspect his driver. One of the watchmen called out to his companions, obviously drawn by the movement. As a group, they clattered forward.

Jasper's man was out cold. He hoped the young fool hadn't inflicted any lasting harm. Jasper had hired his driver, an older gentleman he'd discovered begging and possessed of a lame leg, to better his conditions, not to see his skull bashed in.

"Who goes there?" one of the watchmen called as they neared.

Jasper probed his driver's head with light fingers. He didn't feel any bumps. What had the lad hit him with? The hilt of his pistol?

The city watch encircled his carriage. Jasper's team snorted.

Hooves stomped on the worn cobbles. Well trained as they were, his horses gave no additional evidence of agitation.

"I said, who goes there?" the watchman repeated.

Jasper straightened, standing beside his slumped driver. "Mister Jasper Mclintock," he called. "My driver seems to be unconscious."

The front two men exchanged looks. "How do we know you're Mister Mclintock and not some robber?"

Jasper let out a long, pained sigh and mustered his most cultured, condescending tone, "I am Jasper Arthur Wendell Mclintock, son of the former Duke of Aspen and brother of the current duke, as well as proprietor of The Black Aspen, of which I am certain you have heard, and..."—he looked them over scathingly—"equally certain you have not, nor ever will, enter."

Even in the dark, he saw the first man color. Horses shifted. One of the men cleared his throat. "And your man just up and went to sleep while driving?"

"I did not say he went to sleep," Jasper corrected. "I said he's unconscious. We were set upon by some sort of masked hooligan wielding a pistol."

"Lord Lefthook?" one of the men suggested, tone eager.

Jasper shook his head. "Certainly not. Lord Lefthook doesn't incapacitate innocent drivers or threaten with pistols. Also, this man seemed hardly more than a boy. Perhaps sixteen."

"How do you know his age?" the first watchman asked, still suspicious. "You said he had a mask on."

Jasper considered a second condescending sigh, generally the best way to fulfill men's images of how a duke's son should behave but discarded the notion. "Our would-be robber had a slender build and a light voice, though he's tall and lithe. Obviously, a youth."

"So now we have a Little Lefthook running about," one of the men muttered. "We can't even catch the first Lefthook."

"I told you, he was nothing like Lord Lefthook," Jasper said, offended on Lefthook's behalf. From the brief encounters he'd had with the man, Lord Lefthook was no hooligan. In truth, Jasper would be surprised if he wasn't a gentleman.

"Don't worry, sir, we'll find this Little Hook," the foremost watchman said. "Did you see where he went?"

Jasper's driver let out a groan.

Forgoing more attempts to correct the watchmen, Jasper gestured vaguely over his shoulder as he turned to his man. "He shimmied up that wall and ran off across the roof when he heard you coming."

"Afraid of us, is he?" The watchman sounded pleased. "He should be. We've no place for his kind in London."

Jasper put a hand on his driver's shoulder as the man groaned again and blinked.

"Sir?" his man queried, looking up.

"How is your head? Where did he strike you?" Jasper asked.

"Strike me?" His driver sat up more fully. He looked about, eyes widening when he took in the gaggle of watchmen. "What happened?"

"We were set on by a robber." Jasper dropped his arm. "He knocked you out."

His driver shook his head, then winced. "No, sir, he grabbed my neck. That's the last thing I remember."

The head watchman urged his horse up alongside the carriage. "Can you describe him?"

Jasper's driver blinked several more times. A hand came up to rub the back of his neck. "He wore black, and a mask. Seemed young."

The watchman frowned. "That's not much to go on."

"Well, it's all we have," Jasper replied, then turned back to his man. "I can drive. You go sit in the carriage."

"I couldn't do that, sir."

"You can and you will."

"Do you want an escort, Mister Mclintock, in case that ruffian comes back?" the head watchman asked.

"That's not necessary," Jasper replied as his driver climbed down, movements made awkward by his bad leg. "Your time is better used looking for our attacker." Though not much better, Jasper silently added.

The watchman nodded. "Don't you worry, sir, we'll get this Little Hook."

"Indeed," Jasper said dryly.

His driver climbed into the carriage.

Jasper took his seat at the reins. "Thank you, men, for your assistance. If you'll move aside, we'll be on our way."

"Yes, of course, sir." The lead watchman gestured to his men. They formed up on either side of the narrow street.

Jasper offered a nod and flicked the reins. The carriage rolled into motion, his team happy to be away. Jasper agreed with them.

As he neared the end of the street, he looked over his shoulder. The watchmen had split into groups of two and spread outward, searching the area. He had no thought that they would prove capable of locating his attacker.

He cursed inwardly. The lad might have been persuaded to talk. He may have given Jasper some clue that would lead to Madam Dequenne. Jasper could end so much evil if he found her and got her locked away.

A thread of desperation snaked through him. Even if he sold all of his holdings, secured donations from all of his old acquaintances, he would eventually run out of funds. Ending the abductions at their source was the only way to halt the evil.

In view of his lack of progress and Madam Dequenne's escalating abductions, he might have to do something he'd very much wished to avoid. He had one more source of information. Someone who had likely seen Madam Dequenne firsthand. Someone he knew well.

As much as he wished not to reawaken old torment in her, Jasper would have to seek information from his mother.

CHAPTER 5

MADELINA STOOD IN HER CHAMBER THE MORNING FOLLOWING HER first attempt at vigilantism, thoroughly put out. She slapped the scandal sheets down on her dressing table. Picked them up. Reread them. Slapped them down again. Her attention shifted to the fireplace. Maybe she would burn the offending pages.

She saw her mistake now. In only reading about Lord Lefthook, she'd failed to take in additional information that might be of value. The pages made it obvious why Lanora and Miss Birkchester were dismayed by Mister Mclintock's approach the previous evening. Perusal of earlier editions, scoured for Mister Mclintock's name, had informed Madelina that he ran a gambling hell, The Black Aspen, on the edge of Lord Lefthook's borough. That, then, was probably where he'd put the girls, to rent their favors to his unsavory clientele.

Madelina's gaze refocused on the open page, locating the lines pertaining to her. Her first, and hopefully last, appearance in the scandal sheets. *Lady M, younger sister to the Marquess of W, abandoned halfway through her very first set by bastard son of the late Duke of A, Mister M, when Mister M's mistress appeared at Lady K's ball.*

The content galled Madelina. The attention the words would garner. The confirmation that the gorgeous creature Mister Mclintock had left with was, indeed, his mistress. Not that she didn't expect a man who bought and sold young women like chattel to have a mistress.

Most of all, that single, accusatory, vile word. Bastard. Mister Mclintock was a man born out of wedlock...just as Madelina had been.

She stared down at the word. Those seven letters, so neatly printed, seemed to pulse on the page. Judging.

Now she knew why everyone melted from Mister Mclintock's path. Refused to meet his gaze. Whispered as he passed.

Now she knew, had seen firsthand, how they would treat her if they learned the truth. Even Lanora and Miss Birkchester. Everyone.

Except her brother. William had called Mister Mclintock his friend. Insisted on it.

Not for the first time, Madelina wondered if she should tell her brother the truth. Reveal what she'd overheard that night. The detail that had wrenched a gasp from her father's unseen companion.

But to do so would reveal that William's mother had been alive during his stay in Egypt. Madelina knew her brother. He would blame himself for not realizing, for not returning to England, though only a boy, and saving her. Madelina couldn't add that regret to the burdens of guilt he already carried.

She reached down and slid a slender finger along that word, that label which defined her. Her mother's words, hot with anger, roiled through Madelina's mind.

"I'll bed who I will, when I wish, just as you do, and there's not a thing you can do about it, old man," her mother had spat. "Every time you bring a woman like that into this house, I'll go out and find a man willing to provide me the same service."

Hidden in her bedroom, peering through that sliver between door and frame, Madelina had seen her mother's face. Righteous and aglow, sparkling with candlelight from the great chandelier in the entrance hall. More lovely than the brightest day of spring.

Then her father had laughed. A hard, grating, unused sound. "Nothing to do about it? I'll have you know, I can cast you aside whenever I choose. William's mother still lived when I wed you. You, my dear, are no marchioness. No lady. You're a bigamist and a whore, and your precious Madelina is a bastard."

Someone gasped. That sound that stole her mother's attention. Made her look away just as those two claw-like hands came into view, aimed at her mother's chest. Madelina clutched her hands to her ears, even though experience told her the act wouldn't block out the scream that ricocheted through her mind.

Why had she been so slow in her training? Why had the old marquess managed to die before she could come back and kill him? She'd been certain, so very sure, that his death would seal away that horrible scream forever.

She sucked in deep breaths, slowing the frantic pace of her heart. Her arms dropped back to her sides. Dimly, she heard a faint swish in the hall. The lightest of thumps. Composing her features, Madelina waited for her aunt to open the door.

Aunt Aubrey stopped in the doorway. She eyed Madelina a moment, nodded, then stomped into the room carrying a wrapped bundle under one arm. Her cane hammered a hard rhythm on the carpet until she settled into a chair by the fire and placed the parcel in her lap. She nodded at the table. "I see you've read the paper."

"I have."

Aunt Aubrey stared at Madelina, disapproval visible in her gray eyes.

"I am aware the evening did not proceed optimally. On many fronts," Madelina added, for she'd explained to her aunt last night how she'd not only failed to remain an observer and follow Lord Left-hook, but also failed to secure the girls. "I'll fix it."

"How?"

Madelina had spent the night thinking on little else. "I will go to Mclintock's establishment, likely all but empty by daylight, and almost certainly where he's holding the young women. I will locate them and take them from him." Hopefully, before they came to harm. "Then, this evening, I shall return to the warehouse to seek clues as to the identity of the auctioneer." She'd seen the sweaty, nervous man leave with Mister Mclintock and the others. "Someone must have let them into the building, so someone there will know where to find the auctioneer. He will tell me how to locate this Madam Dequenne who is snatching up and selling young women."

"Not bad, but you won't be returning to the warehouse."

"I won't?" Madelina asked, surprised. A punishment for her failure to observe only?

"No. I'll send someone to nose around. One of my associates."

"They are in London?" Madelina remembered the men and women who had, at intervals, appeared at her aunt's country manor to train her—fragments of a past about which Aunt Aubrey rarely spoke. Some had stayed for days, some for months, but none had given their real name or visited twice. "May I see them?"

Predictably, Aunt Aubrey shook her head. "We're a secretive lot, we who swore oaths to the Crown. I can't ask for much, but searching out a little information is a small favor."

Madelina swallowed disappointment at not being permitted to reunite with old companions or return to the warehouse. Not that it mattered who went, so long as they learned all they could about Madam Dequenne. "Have it your way."

"Certainly." Aunt Aubrey tossed the bundle at Madelina. "You'll need a different disguise for daylight."

Madelina caught the parcel, which emanated a rank odor, relieved she'd be allowed to return to the street. "So, I may act? I am freed from my role as Lord Lefthook's observer?"

Her aunt snorted. "Freed yourself, didn't you, when you got involved. Someone has to save those girls. Either you do, or you go find Lord Lefthook and get him to."

As Madelina both hungered for the chance to prove her worth and had no idea how to find Lord Lefthook in daylit hours, she turned her attention to the parcel. She unfolded a dingy brown shirt wrapped about equally nondescript breeches, a dusty leather vest, a rope belt, a cap, and a once-red scarf that would go about her neck, but could be raised to cover her face when necessary...if she could endure the smell.

"You'll want to make sure your hair is pinned tight and get a good layer of dirt on your hands and face," Aunt Aubrey said. "The trousers should be loose enough to hide your knives, but you'll have to leave those pistols behind."

"Thank you," Madelina said, more in gratitude for the opportunity than for the clothing. She set the bundle on the hearth to prevent the rank odor from lingering on the sumptuous fabrics cladding her furniture. She started on the row of buttons on her day dress.

"You can best show thanks by keeping your head and saving those girls." Aunt Aubrey came to her feet, her movements slow. "I didn't spend years on your training to see you come to harm, girl."

Unprepared for such a sentiment, Madelina stilled her hands. Those words had been almost...warm. "I won't come to harm."

Aunt Aubrey gave a sharp nod before thumping her way to the door. "I'll send the cook to the market," she said without looking back. "You can depart through the kitchen. I left some boots there for you."

Madelina watched her aunt leave, a bit dumbstruck by the display of affection. She shook her head and forced her fingers to resume their work. When the final button released, she stripped off her dress.

The kitchen was silent as Madelina passed through, and the little garden provided more than enough dirt. In short order, she strode down the alley behind the tall buildings that housed many of London's elite. She employed a long, much practiced masculine stride, her steps unwavering and her head high.

The clothing her aunt had provided appeared too nice for a thief or beggar, so the folk thereabouts wouldn't worry she'd come to steal. Should anyone question her presence, she was a lad hired to leave a note or package, and that's how she behaved. No one would look twice. They would see exactly what they were meant to see. Conversely, the odorous garments weren't fine enough to imply she possessed anything worth taking, which would serve her well as she neared Mister Mclintock's gambling hell.

It took longer to reach The Black Aspen than expected, daylight rendering both the rooftops and running too suspicious. Instead, Madelina trudged through increasingly narrow streets until the gleaming black sign, a leafless tree over the club's name, came into sight. Not slowing stride, she passed by with hardly a glance, then rounded the corner.

She paced half the length of the street, along the side wall of what smelled to be a decent bakery, then ducked into the alley that ran behind the row of buildings. Near the far end, past the loading entrance to The Black Aspen, a group of men carried barrels into one of the tap houses. None glanced her way as she strode down the alley, cap pulled low and face angled to the rutted dirt. When she reached the Aspen, her heart set up a more frenzied rhythm as she sucked in a deep breath, pulling two long bits of metal from her belt. She strode to the door and, quick enough to make it seem like she used proper keys, sprang the lock. Without a look in the direction of the men down the street, she pushed open the door and stepped inside as if she'd every right to enter.

She darted her gaze around a dark room stacked with barrels and crates. No one lingered within sight. In the distance, she made out a woman's voice, the words muted beyond understanding but the cadence one of lecture. Madelina crossed the room and put her ear to the door, trying to discern any shuffle or swish of movement beyond the surge of blood through her veins.

The woman's voice sounded far off, so Madelina cracked the door open. An empty corridor extended to the front of the gambling hell. A smattering of closed doors lined the hall, and a narrow staircase rose right outside her door.

Aware that someone could step through a doorway or descend the steps at any moment, she hurried to the first door in the hall and pressed her ear to the wood. Hearing nothing, she peeked inside. Racks of bottled wine filled the room. She pulled the door shut and moved quickly to the next.

A shiver ran down her spine as she pressed her ear to the door. The staircase creaked and she flinched, darting a glance over her shoulder at the empty hall. The impression of being watched didn't leave her.

Madelina sucked in another deep breath, trying to shake the feeling, and returned her ear to the door. No voice or movement sounded within. The tingling in her spine spread through her frame, rendering her movements jerky as she yanked open the door.

The empty room was set up as a parlor and had a connecting door to the final room on that side of the hall. Opting for the shelter of the empty parlor, she stepped inside and closed the door. For a moment, she leaned against it, heart pounding.

If anyone came upon her, she would attempt the bluff of nosy delivery boy. If that didn't work, she'd fall back on violence. Not only was she skilled in hand-to-hand melee, but she also had her knives.

Head clearer and heartbeat less frantic, she crossed to the far door, wiping sweat dampened palms on her trousers as she went. Again, she listened for sound before boldly thrusting her head inside.

An empty and exceedingly tidy office greeted her.

Madelina slipped through the doorway, hurried to a row of shelves and pulled free what appeared to be an accounting ledger. She spent precious moments flipping through the neat pages but could find nothing to lead her to Madam Dequenne, not even mention of payments for the auctioned women. She did find repeated reference to money being funneled into something called Second Hope, which she assumed was Mclintock's so-called charity. She memorized the address for future investigation. Perhaps she could prove to William that Mister Mclintock shouldn't be provided with funds.

She replaced the ledger and turned to the desk. The drawers weren't locked. Fortunate, because her hands shook enough that picking locks would be difficult. She shook her head, resolving not to tell Aunt Aubrey about her shaking hands She didn't need her aunt's censure and doubt.

None of the drawers contained anything of interest. She pulled out stacks of letters and writing tools, then tapped the backs and sides of the drawers, searching for secret compartments. Locating none, and nothing incriminating among the letters, she returned each item to its place.

She closed the final drawer and straightened to look about the dark-paneled room. She could search more. A rather lovely painting of an ancient castle atop a bluff, overlooking a gleaming sea, likely obscured a safe. The stunning Axminister carpet in coffee tones and tawny golds might cover secrets under the floorboards. The leather sofa could hide documents under the cushions.

Too keenly, though, Madelina felt the press of time. She was here to rescue the girls, not rob Mclintock and discover how to dismantle his business. She slipped from what she assumed to be his office, for the painting and carpet choices somehow reminded her of him.

Once more in the hall, she listened for a moment to be sure the woman's voice still instructed somewhere deeper in the building, then crossed to the first door on the opposite side. This yielded a second office, one with enough feminine touches that Madelina wondered if Mclintock's mistress was, indeed, also his business associate.

The tick of time drove her to a hasty search, though she was careful to return all to order. Again, nothing suspicious met her seeking hands and gaze, save a loaded pistol in one of the desk drawers. This, she took. No, she couldn't travel the streets with a gun, but she could employ this one and then toss it away once she left. Feeling bolder with the pistol in hand, she returned the desk to order and slipped across the room to listen at the adjoining door. Hearing nothing, she slid it open.

An oversized, fourposter bed dominated the room. Flowery silk robes and lace garments peeked from the slightly ajar wardrobe; other clothing lay strewn about. Sighting a large dressing table, her fingers twitched with the desire to search, but she'd already lingered overlong in Mister Mclintock's office. Madelina left wardrobe, bed, and table untouched and continued her search for the girls.

At the adjoining door, which must lead to the final room off the hallway, she stopped to listen. Nothing stirred. That all the rooms could be empty seemed too fortunate, though it was the mid of day and the gambling hell a place dedicated to the night. She took a steadying breath, cocked the pistol, and cracked the door open.

Within, she found a second bedroom, the walls and bedclothes decorated in matching umber. As with the first office she'd searched, the room was impeccably neat, which aggravated her. A man as morally depraved as Mclintock, the obvious owner of the chamber, shouldn't be so bloody organized.

Teeth clenched, she stepped inside, inhaling cedar and cloves. Nor did a man as vile as he have any right to such an alluring combination of scents. She ignored the urge to search through his possessions, it being obvious the two young women were not present, and passed through the room to the hall door.

Pistol held low at her side, Madelina slipped from his chamber and back into the hallway. The woman still spoke somewhere near the front of the building, so Madelina crossed to the staircase and ascended. Another hall ran the length of the building, with more doors than the first. On silent feet, every nerve alert, she approached the nearest closed door. Anyone could be inside, or come from one of the rooms, or ascend the steps. The unnerving tingle crept up her spine again. As long as she held the gun, there was no way her guise would permit her to explain her presence.

She tried the knob. The door wasn't locked. A gentle push revealed a small, unoccupied bedroom. She let out her breath.

She quickly passed from door to door, placing her trust in bravado, for she felt keenly that she'd run out of time for stealth. She investigated over a dozen small chambers, finding each one not only empty, but lacking any evidence that two young gentlewomen had been present. That was, unless young misses newly arrived from the country possessed far more lace and silk undergarments than Madelina would have guessed.

Her search returned her to the lower hall with enough mounting frustration that she half hoped to be caught. Not only had she failed to locate the girls, she'd failed to find a room suited to holding them. A fight, at least, would end her tension. She tamped down a wave of recklessness that roiled through her. She'd come to The Black Aspen for a better reason than to pick a fight.

Her gaze went to the far end of the hall and the front of the building. Come evening, bored men would gamble away their time and fortunes, enjoy the dubious attentions of women paid to be biddable, and drink until they likely couldn't see straight.

Could that lecturing voice be aimed at the young women? Madelina inched nearer the front of the building. She could crack open the door at the end of the hall and take a quick glance. The odds that anyone would notice her were slight.

The woman's voice stopped. A rustle of movement sounded. The patter of too many pairs of feet to easily count neared the hall in which she stood.

Madelina ducked into the nearest office. She pressed her ear to the door. Footsteps and feminine chatter filled the hall.

"Kitty," a woman called above the din, voice familiar from moments before. "Come into my office. I require a word."

Madelina's heart hit the inside of her chest with a hard thud. She hadn't elected to hide in Mclintock's masculine space. Her luck had run out.

She darted across the room, yanked open the adjoining door, and slipped into the bedchamber. Her hand shook as she slid the door closed as quietly as possible. Pulse hammering, she pressed an ear to the cool wood. The office's outer door opened and closed.

"Yes, Miss White?" a new female voice asked.

"I didn't say you could sit, Kitty," the lecturing voice, apparently Miss White, snapped.

"I'm sorry, miss," Kitty replied with a rustle of fabric.

"A disturbing rumor has reached my ears," Miss White said.

"A rumor, miss?" Kitty asked, voice small.

"It seems you're thinking of leaving us." Miss White's voice carried a hard edge.

"Yes, miss, to be a seamstress."

"And you feel that is acceptable? That you can simply quit The Black Aspen?"

"M-mister Mclintock said any of us can leave whenever we like," Kitty stammered. "He said he'll pay for us to learn a new skill. I don't want to do this any longer. Some of the men are.... They're very unkind. I want to be a seamstress."

Mister Mclintock had told this girl, Kitty, that she could leave and he would help? Madelina frowned, trying to reconcile that generosity with the villainous image she'd built in her mind. On the other side of the door, silence extended. Madelina realized that she held her breath and let it out in slow increments. Fabric shifted.

"Let me make matters clear for you, Kitty," Miss White said, voice soft. "You do not work for Mister Mclintock. Mister Mclintock runs a gambling hell. He sells liquor and records wagers. I paid off your debts to your former madam. I brought you here because you're exactly the sort of fluff those rich fools dream about. You are a whore, Kitty, and you work for me."

"But Mister Mclintock sai—"

The smack of flesh meeting flesh penetrated the wood of the door. Kitty cried out. Madelina winced on her behalf.

"I don't care what Mister Mclintock said," Miss White continued. "I don't care if Lord Capeter takes a crop to you, or Mister Ranthen pinches you black and blue. You aren't done working here until I say you are done working here. I will have my investment repaid, with interest."

"But Mister Mcli—"

"Furthermore," Miss White continued, "you will say nothing of this conversation to Mister Mclintock."

"But Miste—"

A second slap rang out.

"Do you enjoy being struck, Kitty?" Miss White murmured in cloying tones. "I have more clients like Capeter and Ranthen who I'd be happy to send your way."

"N-no, Miss White."

"No? Then keep this in mind." Miss White spoke in a slippery, smooth voice. "If you don't like being struck, you definitely won't like your fate should you cross me. Do I make myself clear?"

"Y-yes, Miss White."

"Good. Go put some powder on your face. You're all red. I want you looking your best by evening."

"Yes, Miss White." Footsteps shuffled to the hall door.

"You and I have been friends up until now, Kitty. Don't let that change. You won't enjoy being my enemy."

"Yes, Miss White," Kitty whispered, barely audible.

"Go."

The hall door opened and closed. A feminine chuckle sounded. The incongruous emotion baffled Madelina so, it took her a moment to realize the laughter drew near.

Madelina jumped away, flattened her back to the wall behind the door, and drew her scarf to cover all but her eyes. She tightened her grip on the pistol. The door opened.

A curvaceous figure topped with flowing auburn locks strode into the room. Even from behind, Madelina recognized the woman who'd interrupted her set with Mister Mclintock. The woman who, with a single gesture, had summoned him from Madelina's side. Miss White, his mistress and, apparently, business associate.

Before Miss White could turn to close the door, Madelina stepped around it to shove the barrel of the pistol into the woman's back. A startled cry left Miss White's throat.

Madelina kicked the door closed. "Be still or I'll shoot you."

"Who are you?" Miss White craned her neck in an effort to see Madelina's face.

"Who I am means nothing," Madelina growled, voice as low and rough as she could manage. "Where are the girls Mclintock bought last night?"

Tension left Miss White's frame. "Why, you must be Little Hook," she said, voice light. "Jasper told me about you. He thinks you wanted the girls for Madam Dequenne, but I think you rather fancy yourself a hero."

Little Hook? Had Mr. Mclintock dubbed her that? "Where are the girls?" Madelina repeated, jamming the barrel harder against Miss White's back.

"You're far too late, Little Hook." Amusement sparkled in Miss White's tone. "They're already safely back with their family. But I am grateful to you. It's not often I get to prove Jasper wrong."

"Safe with their family?" Madelina repeated, incredulous. The idea that Jasper could be a champion of innocent young women thrilled her almost enough to offset the memory of Miss White framed in the ballroom doorway, beckoning to him. "Why should I believe that?"

Miss White shrugged narrow shoulders. "I care not what you believe. Jasper Mclintock doesn't deal in abducted virgins. All of the women in The Black Aspen are here of their own free will."

"That's not how it sounded a moment ago in your office," Madelina snapped, talking to purchase time to settle her rapidly churning thoughts. Could Mclintock have purchased the girls to save them? Was liberating rather than enslaving the young women the reason he'd hurried from the ball?

"Eavesdropping?" Miss White tsked. "What a reprehensible young man you are, Little Hook."

If Miss White told the truth, that would explain why Madelina couldn't locate the young women, and why Mister Mclintock had sounded so sure she'd come to steal them from him for the Madam. Regardless, now that her presence was known, it was high time Madelina left The Black Aspen.

"We're going to the wardrobe, and you're going to take two belts from those robes," Madelina ordered, pistol barrel pressed firmly between Miss White's shoulder blades. "Then we're going to the bed."

"Why, Little Hook, this day just became far more interesting," Miss White purred.

"To the wardrobe," Madelina reiterated. She marched Miss White across the room. "Get two belts."

Miss White did as she was bade. Madelina pushed her to the bed. There, she took the silk cords and bound Miss White's hands behind her back. Keeping the shorter woman facing away from her, she tied Miss White to a bedpost.

Miss White craned her neck to look over her shoulder at

Madelina, a wide smile curving her lips. "Now that you have me where you want me, what are you going to do with me?"

Keeping the pistol pointed at Miss White, Madelina moved to the head of the bed. She tugged free a silk pillow cover and came back. "I'm going to gag you." She shoved the silk into Miss White's mouth, hard enough that it would take her some time to spit it out. Above the gag, hazel eyes flashed with anger.

Gun level, Madelina backed away to Mister Mclintock's room. When she reached the door, her searching hand quickly found the knob. Miss White glared impotent furry as Madelina edged the door open and slipped through.

She darted across the room and into the hall, startling several women. Screams followed as she ran out the back of The Black Aspen and spilled into the alley. Aware that the women's bleating would alert the men at the other end of the alley, Madelina broke into a run. Assuming the men would give chase, she didn't look back, hitting the borough's warren of narrow allies and streets like a hare pursued by hounds.

When her breath grew ragged and several glances revealed no pursuit, she ducked down an empty street and slowed to a walk. A moment later, she turned into an alley. Making sure not to stand beneath any windows, she quickly uncocked and unloaded the pistol, then tossed it into a midden heap.

She started away, pace set to evade scrutiny. Confusion accompanied her to her father's house. Had Mclintock truly purchased the girls only to return them home? Had Lord Lefthook known the man's intention? Was that why he'd so readily gone after the other young women?

Should she keep seeking the two young women, or were they already saved? Madelina didn't know who they were and had no means of corroborating Miss White's story.

Her only hope of sorting truth from lies would be to spy on Mclintock. Madelina wanted to know everything she could about the man. Everything.

CHAPTER 6

JASPER JOGGED UP THE FRONT STEPS OF HIS MOTHER'S TOWNHOUSE, a place full of happy memories of his childhood and parents, but today that happiness didn't envelope him. Today, he'd set himself the task of finally asking his mother for information about Madam Dequenne, a recourse he'd long avoided. He didn't relish tormenting her with painful memories best left in the past.

As always, the door swung open before he reached it. The duke had employed only the best staff and, to Jasper's keen relief, many stayed on after his father's death. The staff, at least, esteemed and accepted his mother.

"Good day, Jacobs," Jasper offered as he entered. He stripped off gloves and hat. "Is my mother home?"

"Miss Right is in the yellow parlor, sir."

"Thank you." Jasper handed over his outerwear. He lowered his voice, though the yellow parlor stood on the far side of the home. "Has she had many callers this week?"

"Only Missus Smith and Missus Carter."

Jasper frowned. "Thank you." He headed down the silk-clad hall.

Two visitors, when once there had been twenty. When the duke was alive....

Jasper halted that line of thought. Upon his father's death, everyone suddenly recalled that the duke had never married Jaspar's mother.

Before his death, the *ton* had been enamored with the romance of the tale. A young woman abducted. A future duke her savior, constrained by society and his family never to wed her. Yet, the duke had defied them all, residing with her, giving Jasper the name he could never give Jasper's mother.

In the glow of the Duke of Aspen's love and the shelter of his influence, all but the stodgiest had been happy to overlook the fact that Jasper's mother had been stolen from her family's care and locked in a brothel. Cheerfully, they'd glossed over the fact that Jasper's grandfather had purchased her as a birthday present for his son.

Now, it mattered not that Jasper's mother had never been with another. That she'd loved his father fully and faithfully through all his years and that the duke had never made a secret of her. With Jasper's father gone and the ducal title passed to Matthew, so too had fled the tolerance of the *ton*. The blade of betrayal sank deep when it became apparent how few true friends Jasper had. He would have spared his mother that pain.

He mustered a smile as he entered the yellow parlor, his favorite, as well. Sunlight streamed between lacy white curtains, further brightening the buttery wall cladding, elegantly offset by white trim and wainscoting. His mother, straight backed and lovely, hardly showing her years, perched on the edge of a lemon-colored sofa. Though out of deep mourning and possessed of a warm visage constantly at odds with her sever attire, his mother insisted on wearing black. She never let a day pass without memory of the duke.

Nor did Jasper wish her to, for so many of those memories were happy. Instead, he wished he didn't know how the *ton* whispered that, as his mother could not truly be called a widow, she had no right to black. Her gowns were another feather in their cap of ill content.

Certainly, he would pass on none of their words to his mother, who'd met his gaze the moment he stepped through the door. Obviously, her vigilant staff had already informed her of his presence.

"Mother." He crossed the room to place a kiss on her cheek.

"Dearest, it's so lovely to see you. I've sent for tea."

Jasper took the chair beside her. "Thank you."

"Your timing is impeccable. Only this morning, Cook made a batch of those apple tarts of which you're so fond."

"Did she? Perhaps I smelled them all the way across London and that's why I've come."

"If so, I shall order them made every day." His mother smiled.

Though he knew she didn't mean to criticize, a pang of guilt assailed him. He hadn't been home enough of late. "I'm sorry, Mother. I've neglected you."

"Nonsense. I know you're dedicated to your work. Your father was the same way. Heaps of ledgers, letters, and accounts everywhere. Always working."

Her observation was the opening he needed. Still, Jasper had to force the words out. "Actually, my work is why I've come."

Two maids bustled into the room with trays. Not tea yet, but an array of plates and napkins, silverware and trivets. They began setting them out on the low table before the sofa.

"Your work brings you here?" his mother dutifully asked.

Jasper cleared his throat and darted a look at the two young women.

"Regardless," his mother went on, sunny expression unwavering, though she dipped her head in acknowledgement, "I'm very happy you've come, and on a day with such delightful weather for the season."

"Weather wise, London has been particularly bearable of late," he agreed, relieved she'd taken his cue.

They continued to chat amiably about the weather until the two young women departed. His mother stood and crossed the room to quietly close the door. She returned to her seat and smoothed her skirt, expression expectant.

"You're sure they won't listen at the door?" Jasper asked. "This isn't a conversation you will wish repeated."

"I have complete faith in my staff," his mother said. "They know that when the door is closed, they must remain away until I ring. You forget, I once had many visitors. You cannot imagine the secrets that have filled this room." She looked about, her expression almost wistful. "When your father lived, even ladies I hardly knew would come to me for advice. For some reason, their impression that I am tarnished made them willing to confide in me."

Jasper leaned forward, his concerns overshadowed by worry for his mother. "We have the country estate. You could retire there, away from the hypocritical mores of London. You could form new friendships."

Sorrow touched her smile. "For a week, perhaps two. Then word of my shame would follow me, and I would be more ostracized than ever, and without you."

"Anyone who doesn't seek your company is doing themselves a deep disservice."

She assessed him with calm eyes. "That's kind of you to say, dear, but, I'm sure, is hardly the point of your visit. What must you ask that has you so unraveled? Do you need a donation for Second Hope?"

Jasper cleared his throat. "Not in the monetary sense," he temporized.

"Oh? In what sense, then?" she asked, hands folded and still in her lap.

He cleared his throat again. "I must inquire about the past. About your abduction." He offered an apologetic look. "I wouldn't ask were it not necessary, but I must put a stop to them. I don't wish a single girl more to go through what you did."

She pursed her lips, a frown tugging at them.

"I'm sorry, Mother. I don't mean to reawaken old pains."

His mother shook her gray-streaked curls. "It's not that, dear. I am at peace with the past. Yes, I was terrified when they took me, and hurt by how my family and friends shunned me afterwards, but nothing truly terrible happened. I was lucky. Your father came to me that first night and he took me away from there." She drew in a breath. "The fact of the matter is, though a gentleman's daughter, I lived in much lower circles than your father. If Madam Dequenne had not kidnapped me, I would never have met him. I wouldn't have had years of love and happiness, or you. How can I truly regret what happened?"

"Surely you could have been happy with someone else," Jasper said, voice rough with the knowledge of how the endless snubs and snipes must batter her. "And without what society deems such shame." And another child would have been born. One who wasn't a bastard. Who would have had a carefree, untarnished life.

His mother shook her head. "I could never have loved another as I did your father. I knew that from the day we met. A love such as we had is worth any pain."

"Is it?" His whole life, he'd longed to ask, but he'd never before had the courage. "Even now that he's left you to live under the shadow of scorn? Even though he bowed to grandfather's wishes and didn't wed you?" Even though her union with his father resulted in a child who would never be accepted into society?

His mother's expression softened. "We were very young when we met. Fifteen. Your grandfather forced him to wed Lady Aspen within the year. Could you have stood up to your grandfather at fifteen?" She shook her head. "I told your father to marry her. They would never have let us wed, and the dukedom required an heir. Once Matthew was born, your grandfather relented and left us in peace." Her look turned sorrowful. "I know, right now, that you enjoy your mistresses, Jasper, but I do hope that someday you can find love."

He already had. For all his protests, he knew precisely the feeling his mother described. That moment when the world stood still. When there could be no breath, no life, without Lady Madelina.

Not that it mattered one whit how he felt. He stood only to gain by wedding a lady. In marrying him, if he could ever prevail upon her to, Lady Madelina could lose everything. Society's favor. The respect due her rank. Perhaps even her dowry and her family's love, though Jasper dared to think better of Greydrake.

"You said you have questions about the abduction," his mother prompted. Her tone held apology.

Jasper realized she took his silence as rebuke for prying into his relationships, or lack thereof. Normally, it would be. Or, rather, he would have deflected the topic with easy banter. Today, his mother couldn't know that he lost all focus, all attention, the moment he allowed his mind to dwell on Lady Madelina's beauty. On that dusky voice revealing her unconventional opinions. The sheer elegance of her form as she danced.

"Jasper?" his mother pressed.

He shook his head, seeking focus. "Ah, yes, why I've come." He pulled his purpose to him. "I have been seeking the identity of Madam Dequenne, but there are no clues to be found. I thought, perhaps, you might have some."

"Madam Dequenne?" His mother's tone held surprise. "She still lives?"

Jasper nodded. "She does, and she is the force behind these abductions. She must be stopped."

His mother's expression took on a bemused cast. "She seemed so old, but then, I was only fifteen. I warrant, anyone over nineteen appeared old to me." She frowned, lines forming on her brow. "I saw her but once, and I don't even know where they held me. When we left there, your father took me away in a carriage. I was far too distraught to pay attention to buildings or streets."

Jasper's shoulders drooped. He caused his mother to revisit a painful topic, to no avail.

"But I know someone who will know."

His gaze snapped up to meet hers. "You do?"

"I do." Worry overtook her features. "She is not like me," his mother said in a low voice. "Hers is a true secret."

"Who?" Elation coursed through him.

His mother shook her head. "I can't reveal that. I gave my word."

Disappointment slammed Jasper's hope. He opened his mouth to voice his discontent, but his mother spoke first.

"I will make an inquiry on your behalf, to arrange for you to speak with her," his mother said. "You must understand, she is a pinnacle of society, but she was once taken by Madam Dequenne, as well. Only, no one saved her. Not soon enough. She was there for months, but she escaped, and created a lie. I can give you no more detail than that, but suffice it to say, her story must never get out. Even her husband does not know."

Jasper stared at his mother, stunned.

"She helped me, in that short time I was there," his mother continued. "I will attempt to persuade her to speak with you. If I'd any thought that vile woman still lived, I would already have asked her to help you."

"Thank you, Mother."

"I can make no promise, dear. I can only ask."

He nodded.

His mother drew in a deep breath, along with her composure. It was clear that the memories of her abduction were difficult for her to revisit and it pained Jasper to have asked her to. She reached out and tugged the bell pull, summoning tea. A smile turned up her lips. "Now, tell me of this young lady with whom you danced. The one the gossip columns say you ran out on. What manners did I teach you?"

A day ago, Jasper would have bet his entire fortune that, as a man of six and twenty, no one, not even his mother, could make him blush. Therefore, the heat that rushed up his neck must be considered a result of a too-tight cravat. And, indeed, his cravat did take on a sudden binding feel. He tugged at it. "There's nothing to tell."

His mother raised an eyebrow. "Well, were there something to tell, some affection on your part, I'd recommend making amends immediately. A grand gesture of sorts. No lady likes to be abandoned in the middle of a set. Especially not for a man's mistress."

Yes, his cravat was definitely too tight. Fortunately, footsteps and the rattle of trays sounded in the hall. Jasper ignored his mother's knowing expression and looked to the door, which soon opened to reveal her maids. Only a small reprieve but, for now at least, Jasper was saved.

CHAPTER 7

MADELINA SHIFTED IN HER CARRIAGE SEAT, TUGGED AT HER gloves, and studiously ignored Aunt Aubrey's censorious look. Aunt Aubrey did not approve of fidgeting.

"How amazing," her aunt drawled.

Madelina willed the words to stay in her mouth but failed. "What is?"

"That adjusting your gloves for the twenty-third time will make us reach the museum sooner."

Madelina scowled. "You know I loathe them. You should have made me wear them growing up so I would be accustomed to them by now, as all the other young ladies appear to be."

"Or perhaps all the other young ladies simply have more discipline than you."

Madelina looked her aunt in the eyes and adjusted her gloves a twenty-fourth time.

Aunt Aubrey's expression turned stony.

Madelina sighed and focused her attention out the window. Her mood reflected her lack of success. For days, she'd spent every moment of free time following Mister Mclintock, but the one time he had gone somewhere other than his residence or The Black

Aspen, she'd learned only that his mother's servants were entirely immune to bribes. The only thing of interest Madelina had discovered was that someone else followed Mister Mclintock, as well. A man who then reported back to The Black Aspen. Madelina didn't dare follow the watcher inside, but if Mister Mclintock was out, the man must be reporting to Miss White. Having her lover followed so closely was an odd thing for a mistress to do.

On top of Madelina's inability to discover any useful information, her aunt's informant had visited the warehouse and found nothing. No one there knew of Madam Dequenne. Not even the auctioneer, who turned out to be an unwilling pawn. The most interesting details their inquiries revealed was that Madam Dequenne never used the same building twice, extorted use of the spaces, and didn't conduct her business in person. She was a ghost, if a ghost could have young women abducted and their lives ruined.

Today, though, Madelina's bribery of Mister Mclintock's staff had born fruit. Mister Mclintock had ordered his carriage brought round to take him to the museum. While he may enjoy the finest collection of arts and antiquities anywhere in England, it seemed equally likely to Madelina that he intended to meet someone. After all, aside from a brief visit to his mother, he seemed dedicated to his work. Madelina had only followed him a week, but the outing deviated from his usual behavior enough to excite her anticipation.

She tugged at her gloves. How she preferred loitering about, dressed as a young man. The ridiculous curls, the feather-and ribbon-festooned hat, the layers of skirts and petticoats...they were so attention garnering. Both physically and socially restrictive, although skirts hid her knifes better than did trousers.

"I don't see how I'll be able to spy on him dressed like this and with you in tow," Madelina grumbled.

"You don't need stealth, girl." Aunt Aubrey tapped her cane on the carriage floor. "You go sneaking about the museum and he might not see you, but the rest of the world will, and mighty suspicious you'll seem. You've been introduced. Simply walk up to this Mister Mclintock. See who he's there with. He may even offer their name.

There's more than one way to learn about a man. Don't make it complicated."

Madelina grimaced. There may be more than one way to learn about a man, but there were no ways to explain to her aunt that she couldn't simply approach Mister Mclintock. Not after the way he'd abandoned her in the middle of her first set at her first ball. Made her an object of sidelong looks and fan-concealed titters. Landed her name in the scandal sheets.

How dare he do all that after looking at her as if she were the only woman in the room? Did he turn that heated gaze on Miss White when they were alone in one of their adjoining bedrooms?

Madelina drew in a long, slow breath, trying to banish the memory of those adjoining rooms. She didn't know which unsettled her more, Mister Mclintock's deeply masculine space, so uncluttered and alluringly scented, or Miss White's collection of lacy, frilly, and disturbingly sheer garments, strewn about her room as if ripped from her form. The carriage slowed. Madelina looked out the window to watch their approach.

"That's his carriage," she said, a thrill shooting through her. "See? That's the symbol of The Black Aspen." Past his carriage, she took in the imposing façade of the home of Sir Hans Sloane's collection, complete with gravel drive and massive front steps. She hadn't realized the scale of the building. "How will we find him in there?"

"Simple. I shall watch the grand stair. You shall make a hasty search of the exhibits. If he gets past you, at least I can see who he's with."

The carriage rolled to a halt. A footman opened the door to hand down her aunt, then turned back for Madelina. As they walked slowly to and up the steps, pace necessitated by her aunt's limp, Madelina scanned for Mister Mclintock's other shadow, the man who spied on him for Miss White. By the time they entered the overstuffed structure and headed for the first gallery, Madelina still hadn't seen him. She realized he couldn't enter because he would stick out in the same way her aunt had warned that she would if she tried to visit the museum dressed as a lad.

It galled Madelina that Aunt Aubrey was right.

Slippers tapping lightly on the marble floor, she glided away from her aunt, trying to appear as if she intently studied the various works on display, when really she endeavored to look at everything but.

Maintaining her scrutiny of each passing gentleman didn't prove easy. The entrance hall drew the gaze ever upward, onward. The broad staircase beckoned. Ladies and gentlemen gadded about, talking, pointing, and staring. Madelina tried to ignore how many stared at each other, and her, instead of the exhibits.

Still, something drew her onward, away from the newer exhibits from the South Seas. Away from stunning Greek statuary and the secrets of faraway Egypt. Mister Mclintock could be there to see the wonders collected in the museum...or to meet someone. Were she holding a private conversation, she'd leave the newer pieces and the crowds they drew.

She drifted to an uninhabited seeming portion of the building, the quiet calling to her. Soon, she found herself wandering a room that, though perfectly clean, held the lingering smell of dust. Books met her seeking gaze, cracked pages adorned by pressed specimens of plant life. Detailed drawings and careful, tightly clustered words spoke dispassionately of each one.

She hurried her pace as she passed into a second, similar room, then a third. Doubt began to press her. Perhaps he'd come to the museum to take in the vaunted South Sea exhibit, not for a secret rendezvous. If so, she'd passed up locating him. She could only hope her aunt would spot Mister Mclintock and any companion he might have met as they departed. Not that what he said or did could possibly be important to Madelina if he'd merely come to observe the art. Even if he accompanied a woman.

She entered the next room and stopped. A tall, lean form stood at the center, bent low to take in a large volume on display. He straightened and pivoted in one smooth motion. Amber eyes met hers. Light seemed to spark deep within. His expression shifted from surprise to pleasure. He approached with long strides.

Madelina swallowed against the dryness in her throat. He looked at her like a great African cat stalking its prey. She vacillated between the need to retreat and the desire to remain.

"Lady Madelina." He swept off his hat as he bowed. "I cannot imagine a more pleasant surprise."

Every lesson, every well-turned phrase her tutors had instilled in her fled. "Thank you," she murmured.

A smile curved his lips as he donned his hat.

Her mind pressed her to utter a return pleasantry to a compliment she ought to have demurred.

"You take an interest in Sir Hans Sloane's collection on flora?" Mister Mclintock asked, gesture encompassing the room, though his gaze never left hers.

"These? No. I should rather have transcribed copies that I may actually read and learn from." The words came forth unbidden. She almost closed her eyes in exasperation. In her head, she could hear her aunt's voice admonishing, "Do not answer questions. Ask them. Learn. Draw out."

"You choose an odd path, then," Mister Mclintock observed. "Are you lost?"

She shook her head. "I sought quiet."

He nodded. "I often seek quiet, as well." He pulled a timepiece from his waistcoat pocket. A look of annoyance skimmed across his features as he studied the clock face. "And should be honored to do so sometime, with you. Today, however, I'm here to meet someone and, I regret to say, I must speak with her alone."

A jolt of disappointment went through Madelina, followed hard by anger. Before she could rein in her tongue, she blurted, "Her? Your business partner?"

Mister Mclintock winced. "I'd hoped your civility meant we need not address my...unconscionable behavior at the ball."

Her hands clenched. "My civility was born of shock at the ease with which you address me. I should think you'd be too ashamed to."

He looked down for a moment before those amber eyes again lifted to hers. "You will never know how sorry I am for cutting short our evening."

The wistful remorse in his tone soothed her enough for reason to reassert itself. She did not want to keep him by her side, but rather, now that she'd found him, to follow. She couldn't employ her aunt's plan of walking up to him and whomever he met and seeking introduction. Not after he'd informed her that he required privacy. Instead, she must listen in. It would be best if he felt she'd left that wing of the museum, if not the entirety of it. It took little effort to summon the effrontery and anger required to convince him of that. "Indeed, I will not know how sorry you are. Please, do not let me intrude on your rendezvous." She swung away.

"Wait."

A large hand engulfed hers. Shocked, Madelina went still. The heat of his skin radiated through his glove. He gave a tug, not hard, but enough to turn her back. He raised her hand and, cupping her fist, used his other hand to smooth open her fingers.

"You're angry," he murmured, an odd note in his voice.

She shook her head, not at his question, but at his tone. It bespoke of...hope. What hope could he find buried in her coiled fist? He traced his fingers down her palm. The sensation sped through her, making her dizzy.

"Does your silence mean you aren't angry?" He turned her hand over and brought it to his lips.

Madelina's eyes went wide. He placed a kiss on the back of her gloved hand. Time ticked by to the giddy rhythm of her heartbeat.

"I am angry," she breathed, and pulled her hand free. Unwelcome cold immediately replaced the warmth of his clasp. No means existed by which to turn from the intensity of his gaze. "You made me feel as if you fancied me, and then you left in the middle of the set"—she barely bit back the words, 'to attend a despicable auction,' but didn't restrain—"at the behest of your mistress."

"She is my mistress no longer."

Madelina frowned. "Since when?"

"Since I saw you."

Jasper Mclintock was mad. There could be no other explanation for his words, his intensity.

"I don't believe you," she whispered. "This is some fancy of yours. Some game. You do not even know me."

"But I should like to. Permit me to call on you."

"What?" Madelina gasped.

"Call on you," he reiterated. "Come to your home. Have tea and conversation made awkward by your hovering chaperone. Bring you flowers. Take you for a ride in the park."

"You mean court me." When had the museum become so warm?

"I do." He grimaced. "Or am I fooling myself to think you would welcome such attention from someone like *me*?"

She heard the emphasis he placed on the final word. She nearly laughed. Of course, he feared she might shun him because he'd been born out of wedlock. How duplicitous that would make her!

Yet, the attention of a gentleman would be a distraction. She'd come to London to put her skills to good use. To join Lord Lefthook in stamping out evil. She may not be able to rid the world of her now-dead father, but she meant to rid it of other villainy. How could she carry on as a vigilante with a man courting her, let alone, once wed?

Mister Mclintock pressed his lips into a hard line. Hurt darkened the glow in those amber eyes. Glancing away, he sucked in a deep breath.

She couldn't permit him to believe she held the circumstances of his birth against him. That she thought his illegitimacy made him somehow less than other men. And she couldn't deny that, now that she suspected he'd left the ball to save young women rather than enslave them, his attention flattered her.

If only she could tell him what Miss White had said to the girl, Kitty. Gauge his reaction. But Madelina could think of no explanation for how she could possibly have overheard.

He shrugged. Expression bitter, he started to turn away.

Madelina caught his arm, felt the tension in the muscle under her fingers. "I hadn't planned to accept that sort of attention from any man so soon, but I should be pleased to make an exception for you."

His head snapped up. Though he didn't turn to face her, even in profile, his smile was apparent.

"Well, then," he said, tone bland. "If you're willing to make an exception for me, maybe I shall call."

"Maybe?" she asked in mock indignation, though a thrill of worry went through her.

He turned his smile full on her. Her hand convulsed on his arm. Happy, he was even more handsome.

"Yes, maybe," he reiterated.

A bell began to toll as she gazed into the depth of his eyes. Another bell joined in, and another. Around the boroughs of London, churches rang out the hour.

Mister Mclintock blinked. His gaze dropped. She followed that look to see he'd pulled out his timepiece again.

A frown played across his lips. "Business beckons."

"Oh." Madelina realized her hand still rested on his arm. She yanked it away. "I should return to my aunt."

He nodded. "I would offer to escort you, but I'm meeting someone here."

As had happened when he'd left the dance, his attention shifting from her opened a void. One that hadn't existed before they met but which now seemed dreadful and deep. "Of course."

He caught her hand and bowed over it. "I shall call tomorrow."

She mustered a smile, taking refuge in banter. "And maybe I will receive you."

His lips quirked in a fresh smile, but he released her. Madelina watched him walk away. The moment he moved from sight, she bent to one of the glass-encased ledgers, feigning great interest, and waited.

A veiled woman flittered past, a similarly cloaked companion trailing a few steps behind. Madelina permitted only a single quick glance, not wanting the women to feel observed. They crossed the room, continuing to the next as Mister Mclintock had.

The first of the two women must be who Mister Mclintock meant to meet. Her clothing exuded wealth and her bearing, superiority. A twinge of jealousy, along with the desire to gather information, welled in Madelina. She longed to follow, but the second woman kept looking back. Her veil might conceal her features but didn't hide how diligently she worked to keep her mistress from being followed.

Madelina waited until both passed from sight into the next room. Steps slow, she strolled to another case, nearer the path they'd taken. Then another, until she reached the end of the room. She pretended interest in yet another moldering manuscript while listening hard. No voices could be heard. From what she'd seen of the building's exterior, the next room would be the last in that wing. Had she any hope of entering it unseen, of getting near enough to Mister Mclintock to listen?

Adopting an unfocused, daydreamy expression, Madelina strode around the corner. Immediately, the second of the two women appeared before her. Past her, at the far side of the room, Mister Mclintock stood with the expensively dressed lady, their heads near and their backs to Madelina.

"Where are you going?" the veiled woman asked, voice pitched low.

Madelina blinked rapidly as if surprised to find she wasn't alone. "To look in the cases?" she asked, deliberately making her words a timid question.

"This room is closed."

Madelina frowned, radiating confusion to buy time. Would protesting gain her anything?

The other woman stepped closer, crowding Madelina back to the room's entrance. "I said, this room is closed."

With a toss of her curls, Madelina permitted the other woman to usher her away, aware she'd no hope of listening to Mister Mclintock's conversation. She'd gain nothing by staying, save the embarrassment of him thinking she'd followed him out of some sort of jealousy.

Aggravation filled her as she retraced her steps to her aunt. For all her effort, she hadn't learned anything new. Not about Mister Mclintock or the illegal trade of girls.

"Aubrey Saint Lawrence." The stark fear ringing through those gasped words didn't prevent Madelina from recognizing Miss White's voice, coming from the next room.

Madelina stilled. What was Miss White doing here? Was she on her way to meet Mister Mclintock, after all, despite his earnest promises, or had she come to follow him, her spy unable to enter the museum for her?

"Clementine," her aunt said, voice cold.

Madelina's aunt and Miss White knew one another?

"Wh—what are you doing here?" Miss White's voice trembled.

"I haven't come to exact revenge for the ball you put in my hip, if that's what you fear."

Madelina pressed a hand to her mouth. Miss White was the one who'd ended Aunt Aubrey's mysterious work for the crown?

A nervous laugh sounded.

Madelina edged farther down the hall. Sighting a larger-than-life statue of a half man, half aquatic life form set to one side of the room's doorway, she slipped into the shadow it cast against the wall.

"You know she made me shoot you," Miss White's tone wheedled.

"Aye. You were nothing but Madam Dequenne's instrument," Aunt Aubrey said. "Though you made your choices, girl."

Her aunt knew Madam Dequenne? As did Miss White? Why hadn't Aunt Aubrey said anything when Madelina reported what she'd learned at the auction?

"Yes, well, I've made different choices now."

"So I've been told."

"Is that a cane?" Miss White asked, her voice regaining some of its usual surety.

"It is." Aunt Aubrey's cane thumped the floor. "They never could dig that ball out of my hip."

Concealed between marble and wall, Madelina swallowed, her head spinning. Silence drew out. She resisted the urge to peek around the corner. Her aunt would see her. Even if Aunt Aubrey faced away from Madelina, Aunt Aubrey would sense her the moment she stuck her head into the room.

"You look old, Aubrey," Miss White said, all traces of meekness and fear gone.

"I am old, girl, as I hope you live to be."

"Is that a threat?" Miss White demanded.

"It was a well wish.

"You never wish anyone well."

A new silence met Miss White's statement.

"I have no notion why I'm squandering time speaking with a useless old woman," Miss White declared.

Fabric swished. Footsteps sounded, drawing near. Madelina flattened her back against the wall. Miss White strode free of the room. Her head turned from side to side as if she sought something. Madelina, not daring to move, watched her stride down the hall.

Long after Miss White's departure, Madelina remained hidden behind the statue. She waited until she heard her aunt thump her way deeper into the room. Until Madelina's limbs stiffened from remaining still.

Why hadn't Aunt Aubrey told her that she knew Madam Dequenne and Miss White? Her aunt retained connections, especially in the city. Was it coincidence that, on the first night Madelina followed Lord Lefthook, she'd stumbled on that auction?

Madelina shook her head. She wasn't certain the answer mattered so long as good prevailed. Still, she'd feel a lot better if she knew the game her aunt played.

CHAPTER 8

Jasper had never felt so tightly coiled in his life. His carriage rumbled to Greydrake's townhouse; notably, not the ancestral residence of the Westlock line, where Madelina resided. Jasper wondered if her choice to live in the family home meant she'd had a better relationship with her father or if the years she'd been away had simply prevented the depth of dislike expressed by most who knew the late marquess. For his part, though loyal to his family, William Greydrake made no secret of how he loathed any and all things related to the previous Marquess of Westlock.

Would he also make no secret of his feelings about Jasper?

Jasper clenched his fists. Greydrake was a fair-minded man. Honest. Honorable.

He was also a member of the peerage and his sister, a lady.

Not as great a lady, Jasper suspected, as the one he'd met at the museum. His mother's acquaintance, though veiled, had exuded wealth. So much so that Jasper doubted they'd met before, even when he'd been welcome in higher circles. Even had they, she'd kept her voice pitched too low to easily recognize.

Not that he cared one whit who she was. He only cared about the information she had, which was twofold. First, she claimed that

Madam Dequenne was not one person. Rather, the name was used more as a title. Each woman who held it hand selected and trained her replacement. That was why her reign of abductions never slowed or ended, no matter the passage of years.

Perhaps more importantly, Jasper had learned the location to which Dequenne's men took newly abducted women for inspection by the madam—her sorting house. Or, at least, where she had once taken them. His mother's acquaintance had no notion whether the location remained the same. Even so, the next time a distressed chaperone searched the coach stops for a missing ward, Jasper knew where to check. If he was lucky, he would finally catch the madam herself. He planned to deliver her to the watch in chains.

Ending Madam Dequenne's evil should be enough to hold his focus. Instead, he could think only of courting Madelina. He hadn't even taken time to tell Clementine how the meeting with his mother's contact had gone.

Not that he'd had the opportunity. He'd left her a note before heading to the museum, informing her that he had a lead, but he hadn't seen her since. Usually, they would have discussed their next move at length...in her bed. He realized that much of the reason he hadn't yet broached the matter with her stemmed from the desire to avoid such an encounter. How would he tell Clementine, a woman he'd once loved enough to offer for, that he wished to end their relationship?

Not that he expected her to hold his commitment to Madelina against him. After all, Clementine was the one who broke off their engagement when his father died. He rubbed his chest in remembered pain. No matter how he tried to pretend her defection hadn't hurt, that he hadn't held true affection for her, he couldn't make truth of that lie. More than anyone else's change in attitude, Clementine breaking off their engagement when he lost the influence of his father hurt.

Not that she'd used that reason. No, she'd let him save face, said she realized she didn't wish to be tied to any man. That their business arrangement mattered too much to undermine with the silly institution of marriage. If not for that business relationship, he would have cut ties with her then, but he hadn't, and she'd worked hard to make her decision up to him. Again, usually in bed, but in the realm of business, too.

His carriage rolled to a stop, jolting him back into the moment. He took a deep breath as he heard his footman drop to the ground. The carriage door opened and Jasper stepped out, then jogged up Greydrake's front steps.

The door swung open and a butler bowed. "May I help you, sir?" he asked, perfectly deferential.

Jasper had never approached Greydrake in his townhome before, but any decent butler would be well aware who he was. The man's polite demeanor reassured him. "Is Lord Westlock at home?" he asked, extending his card.

The butler received it with another bow. "I shall inquire, sir, if you'd care to wait."

Jasper stepped into a well-appointed entrance hall and the butler closed the door before striding away. Jasper clasped his hands tightly behind his back, refusing to pace. He didn't dare strip off his outerwear, fearful the presumption would go unrewarded.

Greydrake's butler reappeared in moments. "If I may take your hat and coat, sir, Lord Westlock will receive you in his study."

"Thank you." Jasper tried not to let his relief show as he stripped off gloves, greatcoat, and hat. He offered them to the butler, who in turn handed them to a footman who'd materialized while Jasper disrobed.

"This way, sir."

Jasper followed the butler down a wide corridor until it met another. Feminine chatter drifted from the right hallway, along with the voice of what he guessed to be a young lad. Though he couldn't make out of what they spoke, he recognized the women as Lanora and Miss Birkchester. He strained his ears as the butler started down the left corridor but couldn't hear Madelina's voice.

Halfway down the corridor, the butler halted, knocked once on the door before them, then pushed it open. "Mister Mclintock, my lord."

Greydrake looked up from the ledger before him and rose as Jasper entered the room. He started around the desk, gaze focused over Jasper's shoulder. "Thank you," he said, dismissing the butler before addressing Jasper. "Brandy, Mclintock?"

Jasper eyed the decanter to which the marquess strode. As much as he wanted fortification, he shook his head, worried the offer was a test.

Greydrake shrugged and poured a finger of amber liquid into a cut crystal tumbler. He took a generous sip, then returned to his desk, halting before it and setting the glass on the lacquered wood. "How can I help you? Did my man not send over my promised donation?"

"He did, and I thank you for it." Jasper cleared his throat. He should have accepted the brandy. "I'm here on a different errand."

"Oh?" The marquess cocked an eyebrow.

Inexplicably, Jasper felt certain the other man knew his reason for coming. "Yes. Of a more personal nature."

"I see. Lanora owes Miss Birkchester yet another five pounds."

Jasper frowned. "I beg your pardon?"

Greydrake shrugged. "You're here to ask permission to court my sister, correct?"

Was the marquess's amusement aimed at Jasper? He tried not to bristle. "I am."

The other man nodded. "As Miss Birkchester predicted. I can't for the life of me understand why my wife continues to accept her wagers. Miss Birkchester is always correct about these matters."

"Is she?" Jasper asked, working not to let annoyance into his tone. So, the marquess, marchioness, and their hangers on found amusement in how obviously smitten the Duke of Aspen's bastard son was with Lady Madelina.

Greydrake stepped forward and slapped Jasper on the arm. "Don't take it like that, man. Here, let me pour you that drink." He swiped his tumbler from the desk, then moved to the sideboard to splash more brandy into his glass and a second.

"If you know why I've come, do you have an answer for me?" Jasper asked.

Greydrake turned back, holding both tumblers. "That depends on how you answer this question: What will you do if I refuse permission?"

Disappointment carved a pit in Jasper's gut. Greydrake had been one of the few who hadn't treated Jasper with indifference or disdain after the duke's death. That he, too, had only feigned friendship to curry favor with Jasper's influential father cut deep.

Still, he was Madelina's brother. It wouldn't do for Jasper to let his bitterness show. He struggled to select the right words. "If that were the case, my lord, I would point out that I came here as a courtesy and that it is the lady's place to decide if she wishes to receive my attentions."

"She's nineteen. She cannot wed without my permission."

"Two years is not long to wait," Jasper said stiffly.

"Well, then, you have my permission." Greydrake proffered a glass.

Jasper stared at him. "I do?"

"Of course. I've no doubt you'd be a good husband." One glass still extended, the marquess took a sip of the other. "I simply wanted to test your resolve. Madelina doesn't need someone who would give up at the first obstacle."

"Then you don't object to...to my heritage?" Jasper grimaced as the word left his mouth.

"How could I? You're descended from a very respectable line."

"But I'm a bastard."

"Does that make you any less the duke's son? Any less a man?" Greydrake nodded to the glass he still extended. "It would be rude to make me drink both, and Lanora wouldn't approve."

Jasper accepted the brandy. Tension drained from his frame. He felt as if he'd survived ten rounds with Gentleman Jack.

Greydrake raised his glass in salute, then drained the content.

Jasper followed suit. "Thank you."

"For my permission?" the marquess asked as he set his empty tumbler on the side table.

"For not condemning me for my birth." Jasper struggled to keep emotion from jumbling his words.

"Do you really believe I, of all people, would judge a man based on the actions of his father?" Greydrake asked softly.

"I suppose not." Jasper crossed to place his glass beside the marquess's. He glanced at the mantle clock. For all the strain of the situation, he hadn't been with the marquess long. The hour remained appropriate for calling. Exhaustion slipped from him. "If you'll excuse me?"

"You're going to go see her now, aren't you?" Amusement rekindled in Greydrake's expression.

"I am."

The marquess nodded. "Good luck. I have a feeling this was the easy part."

Despite a similar premonition, Jasper grinned as he bowed his way from the room. A footman waited without, but Jasper didn't need to ask the way. He turned and strode down the corridor. In no time at all, he climbed back into his carriage, giving directions to the driver before closing the door.

Traffic proved daunting, especially as they neared the exceedingly fashionable neighborhood in which the Westlock London home stood. Jasper chaffed at every pause, each delay. Still, he kept his head inside the carriage, his gaze on the opposite wall. He would start enough rumors by being seen there. He didn't need to be observed gawking. Somehow, he didn't think Lady Madelina enjoyed appearing in the scandal sheets.

When they arrived, with supreme self-control, Jasper waited for his man to open the door before he exited his carriage. He then walked up the steps rather than taking them three at a time, reached the stoop and knocked.

Time ticked by. Jasper worked not to fidget, aware of passersby, both on foot and in carriages, staring. He longed to knock again, to pound on the door and demand to know if Madelina sat within. On the ride over, the very real chance that she could be out making calls of her own hadn't occurred to him.

The door swung inward to reveal a young man in butler's livery. He gestured Jasper inside.

Jasper obeyed, relieved to be off the street and one step nearer Madelina. He tugged a card from his coat pocket and proffered it. "Is Lady Madelina at home?"

The butler, who'd been watching Jasper's mouth with disconcerting intensity, dipped his head and took the card. "I will ask, sir," he said, voice overloud. He dropped his gaze to Jasper's mouth again, stared for a moment, then dipped his head and hurried away.

Jasper rubbed at his jaw, unnerved by the man's scrutiny. He looked about for a reflective surface, but the only touch of brightness in the darkly paneled entrance hall was gilt frames. Within those frames, stony-eyed men gazed down at Jasper in condemnation. The tap of footsteps announced the butler's return, saving Jasper from any more time spent under the scrutiny of Madelina's forefathers.

"Your outerwear, sir," the man shouted.

Jasper complied, unsure of the butler's aggressive tone. The man's expression appeared hospitable enough. He gave every appearance of being deferential as he accepted Jasper's coat and lay it carefully over his arm.

"This way," the man said in that same loud voice. Again, he studied Jasper for a long moment before turning away.

Jasper followed, frowning. "Did I spill something on myself?" he asked.

The butler gave no indication of having heard.

"Is there's a mirror about?" Jasper tried, only to be similarly ignored. Did the man condemn Jasper for being bold enough to court Lady Madelina? Was the butler's aloofness indicative of his personal opinion, or a reflection of how the lady of the house felt about Jasper's visit? He fervently hoped not the latter.

The butler stopped and turned to Jasper. "Here you are, sir," he all but yelled.

The man's expression, as he gestured to an open parlor door, remained neutral. Perfectly devoid of judgement. Jasper frowned. Maybe.... "Thank you," he mouthed, giving no sound to the words.

"My pleasure, sir," the butler boomed back. "Will that be all?"

Bemused, Jasper nodded. What had inspired her ladyship to hire a deaf butler? Did the man check the door frequently, or was a second staff member required to alert the butler when someone knocked? Jasper watched the man head back down the hall, then turned into the parlor.

Hideous. The only word that suited the décor. Dark, nearly black, paneling lined the lower halves of the walls. Above, they were clad in a red silk so deep as to resemble dried blood. Gold brocade abounded, and black marble clad the fireplace across from Jasper. A feeble flame flickering within the grate, as if loathe to give too much light to so grim a room. On the edge of awareness, Jasper noted a woman seated on the sofa to his right.

Before the fireplace stood Madelina Greydrake. White-blonde curls framed her perfect oval face. Clear gray eyes watched him over a slender nose and bow-like lips. Her lithe frame, clad in cream, stood as a ray of light in the otherwise oppressive room.

"My lady," Jasper greeted as he stepped into the parlor. He offered a low bow.

"Mister Mclintock," she acknowledged, her tone devoid of the warmth he felt certain he'd stirred to life at the museum. "I don't believe you've met my aunt, Miss Saint Lawrence."

Jasper followed Madelina's gesture to his right. A never married chaperone was an unconventional choice, but Jasper could immediately see that Miss Saint Lawrence was a rather formidable woman. In build and features she resembled her niece, but Miss Saint Lawrence's gray eyes were granite hard and her nose crooked at the end, raptor-like. She sat forward on the overdone gold sofa, both hands resting on the top of a cane. A bird of prey—the cane's handle —glared from between her fingers.

Jasper offered another bow. "Miss Saint Lawrence. It's a pleasure to make your acquaintance."

She studied him for a long moment, expression unreadable. Jasper resisted the urge to tug his suit coat straight. Finally, Miss Saint Lawrence pressed her palms down on her cane and levered to her feet.

"I feel like a book," she said and limped nearer Jasper, where he stood just inside the door.

Was that why they'd hired a deaf man, Jasper wondered, because Miss Saint Lawrence held sympathy for those society might deem less than perfect?

"You're leaving us alone?" Madelina asked.

Did he detect a note of worry in her voice? Did she not trust him? He took in the pink that colored her neck, threatening her cheeks. Perhaps the lady did not trust herself?

Miss Saint Lawrence didn't halt her progress. "I'll return, and in the meantime, I'll leave the door open. I don't care to listen to you interrogate the lad."

Jasper turned back to Madelina.

A frown pulled at her lips as she watched her aunt depart.

Interrogate him, would she?

Madelina's frown disappeared as she turned to him. "Did you enjoy the museum?"

"I always do but, as you know, I was not there for pleasure."

"Yes, business, you said."

He nodded, ill at ease with her choice of topic. Nor had she invited him to sit or offered refreshments. Obviously, he stood on trial. If only he knew the reason.

"Two veiled women passed me as I departed the wing. Not something you witness often. Your *business* meeting?"

Jasper didn't miss her emphasis. Did jealousy lay at the root of her lack of enthusiasm for his presence? He could only read that as encouraging. "Precisely."

"So, you were not meeting one of them for...for the pleasure of her company?"

"If I were meeting a woman at the museum for pleasure, it would be to walk the exhibits with her, but that is not what I was about."

He took in the disbelief on her face and knew he must add more. "She had information for me."

"She seemed very wealthy."

"I cannot reveal her identity."

"Then tell me what information she had for you."

He shook his head. "It is not a topic for ladies."

"I've no doubt she was a lady."

Jasper pushed a hand through his hair, trying to figure out what he could tell Madelina to convince her that he'd done nothing untoward.

"If, and I do mean *if*," Madelina said, words crisp, "I permit you to court me, I can only assume your goal is an honorably wedded state, not some sort of dalliance."

He opened his mouth to reassure her, but she continued before he could.

"And if we ever entered into such a wedded state, do you mean for me to understand that you will meet mysterious women at museums and not provide me with details of your interactions with them?"

That stymied him. If he married a gently bred woman like Madelina, what would she think of The Black Aspen? Would she understand that he and Clementine gave a safe place to women who enjoyed their profession, and assisted those to leave who'd come to it unwillingly?

"If we were to wed," he couldn't keep sorrow from his voice, for he doubted they would, "it would be with the understanding that I will not, cannot, alter my business."

"And that business includes Miss White, the mistress you tell me you've given up?"

Jasper grimaced. "Yes. We manage my business together, and my charity. Miss White is invaluable to me." He met Madelina's gaze squarely, his own pleading. How could he make her see that from the moment he set eyes on her, there was no one, could be no one, but her? "Would you really ask me to break our business ties, as well? Miss White helps me do good in this world."

Madelina glared at him, her eyes nearly level with his. "I saw Miss

White at the museum. I find it beyond me to accept her presence as a coincidence. She obviously intended to meet you."

Ahh. He would be equally incensed if she'd sworn off seeing a man and then met with him moments later. But why she thought she'd seen Clementine, he didn't know. "You saw the veiled women and assumed one to be Miss White." He shook his head. "Neither was. The one lady was the person with whom I required a discreet meeting. The other, her companion."

Madelina shook her head. A light, honeysuckle scent reached his nostrils. "I passed them," she said. "Then I saw Miss White."

Of all the rotten luck. Had Clementine indeed been looking for him? He'd left a note telling her where he'd gone, but he hadn't seen her at the museum. She hadn't been at the Aspen when he returned, either. "Perhaps she sought me on a matter of business." He shrugged. "If so, she did not find me and must have resolved the issue, for she hasn't mentioned going to the museum."

"So, you have seen her since telling me she is no longer your mistress."

"I have not, but I will, and I must," he snapped. "Can you not extend me a fraction of trust? Look into my eyes and see the truth when I say I want only you. If not for our business ties, Miss White and I would have parted ways long ago. I do not love her, but I do need her. I cannot see anything more to do about that than to tell you so."

Madelina shook her head. "I'm not certain Miss White is who you believe her to be."

"How do you mean?"

Pink crept up her long, slender neck again. "I've had you followed. Some reports of how Miss White treats the...the young women of your employ are disturbing." Madelina clamped plush lips closed, gaze dropping to the garish red and gold carpet.

Pleasure shot through Jasper. "You had me followed?" For all her anger, her coolness, her constant questioning of his sincerity, she'd had him followed. Nothing could better declare her interest. "So you could arrange to meet me? You are the one who was not at the museum by coincidence, Lady Madelina."

Red flooded her cheeks. Her expression suffused with chagrin.

Jasper chuckled. "Your poor man, loitering in the streets so he could report my movements to you. One of the buildings near my residence rents the upper floor rooms. I believe they have a vacancy. You could secure it, so your staff can spy on me in comfort."

"We shall bear that in mind," Miss Saint Lawrence said, behind him.

He refused to give in to the impulse to swivel to face her, though her presence took him by surprise. How could someone who walked with a cane reach the doorway unheard?

He pivoted slowly to address them both. "I think, before you judge Miss White or me too harshly, you should see what it is we do. I should like to call round and take you to inspect our charity." He dipped his head to Madelina. "Your brother has contributed considerable funds to our endeavor."

Madelina bit her lower lip, expression conflicted. His hand twitched with the desire to cup her chin, to smooth his thumb along her lip. Worry was not what that lush mouth was made for.

"We accept that offer, Mister Mclintock," Miss Saint Lawrence said. "We shall send word as to an afternoon that suits us. Don't worry, we know where to find you."

Jasper heard the dismissal in Miss Saint Lawrence's tone. Striding closer, he caught Madelina's hand and bowed over it. He didn't miss the slight tremble, or the heat still flushing her face. He could only hope both were good signs for his cause.

Releasing her, he turned to bow to Miss Saint Lawrence. "I shall eagerly await your summons."

"Shall you?" she asked, expression inscrutable. "Well then, to spare you anxiety, know that they will not come tomorrow, nor the following day. Madelina and I have plans."

Jasper longed to know what plans would prevent them from joining him, and if he could join them, but Miss Saint Lawrence's tone forbade questions. He turned back to Madelina, hoping she might speak, but her lips remained clamped. Feeling thoroughly dismissed, Jasper offered a final bow and departed the room. On his way past Miss Saint Lawrence, he couldn't help but notice she didn't hold a book. He wondered if she'd ever moved more than a step beyond the doorway.

CHAPTER 9

SEATED ATOP THE MAIL COACH AS IT BOUNCED ALONG THROUGH the dark night, Madelina adopted a wide-eyed, gawking expression to give the impression that everything she saw seemed amazing and new. In a way, it did. In the past, she'd always taken a private carriage to London, not ridden in on the mail coach.

Nor had she ever ridden in an exterior seat before, but she and Aunt Aubrey had decided her disguise warranted the placement. Madelina wished to appear nothing more than a poor country miss, summoned as a kindness by her wealthier city relations. Besides which, her perch outside ensured she could see and be seen.

The exterior seat also made it impossible to sleep, though Madelina wasn't supposed to succumb to the need. She and Aunt Aubrey had journeyed quite a way from London before selecting a coach for Madelina to return on. Because of how quickly the girls were snatched upon arrival, Aunt Aubrey suspected they were being selected long before they reached the busy heart of London. That pointed to accomplices at one or more of the stops outside of town. If possible, Madelina meant to spot the blackguards.

Whether her aunt was correct about when the girls were selected for abduction or not, Madelina's plan hinged on being one of those girls. She would ride in on the mail coach and be taken by the madam's men. This would permit her to dismantle the vile woman's operation from the inside.

Then she would go to Jasper and confess what she'd done. Perhaps even apologize for attacking him in his carriage. With irrefutable proof of her skills and value, she would inform him that her work would continue whether he courted her or not, but her hand would only be given if he accepted her chosen role as a champion of the innocent.

And he would agree...wouldn't he? He worked to save women. She did, as well. What match could be more perfect? Maybe he would even cut ties with Miss White. Why would he need her help once he had Madelina's?

The coach slowed and Madelina jerked upright. Mind on her daydreams, she'd nearly drifted off. She took in the rising glow on the horizon and realized they'd found the dawn.

The coach rumbled into an innyard. Stiff, Madelina hoped for a chance to walk about. She observed several other passengers shivering in the cool morning and could only be pleased she'd donned multiple layers of clothing. Under the bulk of her rough-spun country dress, she wore her black garb, complete with knives and pistols. Another reason to feign lowly circumstance, as the muslin of the upper class would never have hidden the guns.

People swarmed the coach as it rolled to a halt, greeting, selling, proffering mail. Trying to mute the sharpness of her gaze, Madelina gawked at them. A young man came to stand below her perch.

"Traveling alone, miss?" he asked.

"Y-yes," Madelina stammered, as if embarrassed to speak with him.

"Do you need help with your cases, miss?"

"N-no." She shook her head. "I'm going on to London."

"Well then, you've a long way still to travel. You should stretch your legs." He held out a hand, a pleasant smile on his face.

Madelina didn't let his smile distract her from the greed in his eyes. She placed her hand in his and let him help her down, then yanked her hand away. "Thank you."

"A few bobs would be a greater thanks than your words," he said, smile becoming ingratiating.

"I've nothing to spare," she muttered and hurried away. She sought the safety of several women walking the yard together, as any miss traveling alone might.

In the guise of taking in the scenery, Madelina kept track of the young man. He and another handed several people from the carriage. They also lifted down a few trunks but didn't carry them into the inn. Instead, they loitered near the coach.

Madelina made a slow circuit of the yard, not wishing to catch up to the other women. She'd no idea if they'd be welcoming, but she couldn't risk distraction by social niceties, or to make friends who might actually look out for her once they reached London. The two young men continued to linger. The coachman entered the inn.

The men drew together, speaking rapidly, though they were too distant for Madelina to hear. She raised a hand to shield her gaze, making a show of studying the eastern horizon. In truth, she meant only to shadow her eyes beneath her hand so she could watch the men askance.

They each pulled something from their pockets, then walked about the coach. With quick gestures, they marked several spots on the outside, some near seats, some not. Apparently, what they'd pulled from their coats was chalk. The one who'd helped her down made a mark under the footboard where she sat. Madelina angled away from them, still under the façade of taking in the newly risen sun. Sure enough, out of the corner of her eye, she saw the man look her way.

Both men stowed their chalk and sauntered to the inn. Their bantering, jovial tones as they passed near her rankled. One laughed and slapped the other on the shoulder. Madelina fought not to hoist her skirt to get at a pistol.

She completed her circuit of the yard and returned to the coach, making sure to pass by the other marks before she climbed back up to her seat. Aside from the one referencing her seat, they all looked the same. But then, she was the only young woman traveling alone.

The coach set out again and Madelina worked to rein in her seething anger. If she read the men's actions correctly, she'd been selected for abduction. A small part of her whispered that she should be afraid, another that she ought to be pleased, but those parts held no weight in the face of her fury.

Several more hours passed before the coach reached the outskirts of London—not nearly enough time for her ire to cool. As they rolled through increasingly choked streets, Madelina worked to adopt a sleepy expression, as if her journey fatigued her so, she could hardly remain awake. People scurried about on the rough cobble streets. Merchants hawked their wares. A cart rolled past, piled high with horse manure. As they neared their stop, the scent of meat pies overwhelmed other odors, announcing as clearly as church bells that the hour neared noon.

As had happened at the inn, people swarmed the coach when it halted. Madelina spotted a group of young men approaching and quickly looked away. One appeared before the footboard. He scanned the chalk marks there and looked up.

"Good afternoon, miss." He smiled and extended a hand. "I'm to get your cases down. Could you show me which ones?"

She took the young man's hand and let him help her down, then turned back to the coach and pointed to the small bag she and her aunt had packed with suitably countrified garments. The barrel of a pistol jabbed into her side. She made to swivel to face the young man, but he clamped her arm in a tight grip.

"Now, miss, that's a pistol pressed into your ribs," he said in a low voice, mouth near her ear. "I don't want to have to use it, but if you make a sound or do anything but what I tell you, I'll put a ball right in your side, and you'll die."

Madelina let her face go slack with surprise. In truth, she was shocked. At the brazenness. At the way people bustled about them, no one paying them any mind.

"Awe, little sis, you took too much sun," the man said in a loud voice. "Here, Mum sent a shawl. Put this over your bonnet and wrap up. Keep your face out of the light."

He released her arm and shoved a wad of cloth at her, pistol still pressed firmly to her side. The moment she took the shawl, he grabbed her arm again.

"Wrap it around your head and shoulders," he hissed. "If anyone recognizes you, I'll shoot you first, and then them."

Madelina doubted he would actually shoot her in the middle of the busy square, but she felt certain his tactic scared most young women into compliance. Dutifully, she wrapped the worn cloth about her, aware it would be difficult for anyone to recognize her once she was done.

"Come on," he said, and yanked her arm, heading for the street opposite the inn.

The bustle of the square quickly faded behind them. The man led her along winding, narrow streets. After a short time, another young man spilled from an alleyway in front of them and cast her abductor a grin. Madelina recognized him as another from the group at the coach stop. Soon after, they turned onto a different lane, where a third man from the stop joined them. Peering ahead, Madelina concentrated on the maps she'd memorized, working to keep track of where they went.

"Where are you taking me?" she hissed.

"Stay quiet or I'll put a ball in your side," the man growled, squeezing her arm tighter. Apparently, he didn't know any other threats.

They followed the other men into an alley so tight, they had to walk single file. At the end, the first man pulled free a large key and opened a door. The acrid smell of smoke fueled by pitch wafted out. The man entered and stepped down, and Madelina realized they were taking her into a cellar.

"I'm not going down there," she squeaked, as if terrified.

The pistol barrel jabbed her ribs. "You'll go where I say."

They marched down a crumbling, torchlit staircase. The opposing stone walls wept moisture, leaving the air a fetid mixture of mildew and smoke. Madelina could just make out a second set of steps, these wooden, leading upward at the end of the corridor.

The man in the lead halted halfway down, outside the only door in the hall. He applied a different key, and Madelina felt relief as she caught a glimpse of the shaped metal. Nothing special distinguished the key. That meant there was nothing unique about the lock. The key turned with almost no sound. Despite the damp, the lock was kept in good working order.

The man with the key stepped back and Madelina's abductor pushed her into the unlit space on the other side of the door. Sobs met her, and someone wailed. Madelina caught a glimpse of three huddled forms in the middle of a low ceilinged, stone room before the door slammed closed behind her, throwing the cell into darkness. The key turned in the lock.

Madelina returned to the door and pressed her ear against it. Without, three sets of footfalls moved off. Apparently, her abductors saw no reason to guard the girls. She turned back to the room and, voice pitched low, said, "Hello? Who is there?"

More sobs answered.

Madelina peered into the murk. The only light that filtered in came around the edges of the close-fitting door. "Have you been held here long?" she tried. "Where did they take you from?"

"They took me from in front of The Swan," a tear laden voice said. "I-I don't know how long ago. It feels like weeks. They've fed me over a dozen times."

How long did they keep girls, Madelina wondered. Did they wait to ensure no one sought them? Most young women escaping an impoverished, labor filled life in the country would be missed by no one.

"And you've been here the longest?" Madelina whispered.

"No, I have," a different voice replied.

"Once, I heard them say they only call the madam once they have enough girls," a third speaker offered.

"Wh-who is the madam?" the first girl queried.

"I don't think I want to meet her," another whispered, too low for Madelina to sort out which spoke.

Madelina did, but she hadn't counted on not meeting her immediately. How many girls were enough to bring Madam Dequenne?

Madelina better organized the dirty shawl, now glad the man who'd taken her insisted she wrap her face. Although it didn't appear as if they would be permitted any light, she wanted to be sure none of the other women would be able to identify her.

"And other than bringing food and more girls, they leave you alone?" Madelina asked.

"So far," said the girl who'd been there the longest.

"What time of day is it?" one of the other two asked. "Is anyone looking for us?"

This spurred a great many questions. Madelina tried to answer as if she were an innocent country miss. Eventually, food arrived, the open door offering a brief, blinding glimpse of one of the men she'd already seen. As soon as the door closed, Madelina went to it to listen and, once again, the man walked away, leaving them unguarded. After they ate, Madelina indulged in a nap, having been awake all night. When she woke, she knew she was losing track of time and wished she'd thought to secret a timepiece somewhere about her, not that she'd be able to read it in the dark.

Finally, after what she guessed to be two days, she began to worry about what her aunt might be thinking. Madelina had to work not to pace the cell, to instead stay focused on the door and the sounds without. The door never seemed to be guarded, the men apparently confident that a scant handful of country misses couldn't hope to get through the stout wood. Should she wait until all fell silent and free the girls? Doing so would squander her chance to catch Madam Dequenne, but remaining in the cell wore on Madelina.

Footfalls sounded in the corridor. Madelina stepped back, checking that the dirty shawl covered her face. The door opened and a weeping girl was shoved inside. The sobbing girl stumbled across the room in the dark. Madelina stepped aside, letting her reach the others. She hurried to the door, senses alert.

Men walked past. One called for water. They moved off, but dull sounds reached her from somewhere else in the building. Ignoring the girl's tears and chatter, she kept her ear to the door.

After a time, footsteps returned. Madelina stepped away as the door swung open and two men entered. She tensed, hand sliding down her leg, ready to pull a pistol from under her skirt. The men each set down two buckets and left. A third, the one who'd abducted Madelina, entered with a stack of dingy looking towels topped with shavings from a block of soap. He set the stack on the floor.

"Get cleaned up pretty like. The madam is coming to see you," he said and went back out, closing the door.

"The madam," one of the girls whispered as elation shot through Madelina.

Someone began to cry.

Taking that as her cue, Madelina dropped the makeshift shawl to the floor and started to unlace her gown. She'd had enough of her role as a frightened country miss. Now, let them deal with Little Hook.

While the others whispered and stumbled through the dark to the buckets, she shucked off her dress, letting it pool at her feet. She adjusted her knives and pistols for easy use, then knelt to rummage in her discarded dress. She'd left the house with her bosom strapped down under her second disguise but stuffed her bodice with her hat and mask. Tying the mask about her face, she set to ensuring her hair was well enough pinned. Satisfied, she shoved the hat down on her head and moved to the door, hands outstretched to avoid running into anyone.

"What are you doing?" one of the girls asked.

"Washing up," replied another.

"I mean her, by the door. It sounded like she undressed."

"She did not," Madelina said in her best young-man voice. "I did."

A startled squeak sounded, punctuated by another sob.

"Who are you? Who's there?" the first girl cried.

"Little Hook, at your service, ladies."

"L-little Hook?" the sobbing girl repeated. "Not Lefthook?"

"If only Lord Lefthook would save us," the third girl said.

"I will save you," Madelina snapped, rolling open her lock picks and laying them within easy reach in the dark.

"How can we trust you?" the first girl asked. "How did you get in here?"

"I disguised myself as a girl so they would take me," Madelina answered and selected two tools by feel. She slid a hand up the rough wood of the door until she located the lock. "I'll have this door open in no time."

"Then what will we do?"

"You will stay safe in this cell while I deal with the madam and those men."

"But what if you can't? Shouldn't we run while we can?"

Madelina shook her head, though they couldn't see her. "You don't want to be out on the streets alone. I will take you to people you can trust." She'd already decided the girls must go to Second Hope. Not only was Jasper's charity organized to help them, he should hear their tale. He could put the information to good use. "They will help you."

"Shouldn't we tell the watch?" one of the girls asked.

"I'm not telling anyone," another said. "If anyone finds out about this, I'll never get a husband."

"But we were never alone," another pointed out.

"You may not have been," said the one who'd been there the longest, "but I was. I'm not telling a soul."

Madelina tried to ignore their chatter as she worked the mechanism inside the lock. She reached for a third pick, the first two already deployed. She slid it into place, then turned. With a click, the lock slid open.

Madelina quickly stowed her tools and pushed to her feet. One hand on a pistol hilt, she pressed her back against the wall beside the door and cracked it open. No alarm was raised. As her eyes adjusted to the flickering torchlight without, she saw no one. She opened the door wider and shifted to peer in the other direction. The corridor appeared empty.

"How did you do that?" the bravest of the girls asked.

"I picked the lock," Madelina replied, voice low and as deep as she could manage. "I'll check the back staircase. Stay here."

She slipped from the room. Drawing a pistol, she silently traversed the short hall then climbed the stone steps. At the top, she put her ear to the door.

Two men spoke without, voices quiet. Madelina frowned. Where there were two, there could be more. She looked down at the lock. It wasn't engaged, but she could lock it, and wedge a pick inside so the key wouldn't work from without. That way, whoever loitered out there couldn't get in.

But if she did that, it would take her time to open the door, as well, should they suddenly need to leave that way. She bit her lip, trying to select the best course. Leaving the lock undisturbed, she turned and climbed back down the steps to find four heads sticking through the doorway of their cell. She hurried back before they were foolish enough to call out.

"Isn't that the way we came in?" the brave one asked.

"Is it locked?" another added.

The other two stared at Madelina with wide eyes.

"It's not locked, but there are at least two of them out there," Madelina said in a low voice. "I'll check the other staircase. If needs be, I can fight past the two out there."

"We'll stay here," the brave one offered. She cast a look at the others. "And stay quiet."

Madelina nodded. She headed past them to the wooden steps. These, she took with great care, fearful they would creak. As she neared the top, she heard a woman speak and a man's answer. It took her only a moment to recognize the woman's dulcet tones. Even as hatred for Miss White burned away Madelina's surprise, her mind could form but one question...did Jasper know his mistress was party to abductions?

"...five, you say?" Miss White asked as Madelina pressed her ear to the door. "And all of them pretty? Pretty like that cow you dragged in last month, or pretty by my standards? Consider your answer with care, Smith, because I'm losing patience with you and your men."

"Uh, pretty, Madam Dequenne," the man stammered.

Madelina jerked as if shot and swallowed down a gasp. Madam Dequenne? Miss White wasn't simply involved. She *was* Madam Dequenne?

"Real pretty," Smith continued. "Tall, the one, and two are plump in a real nice way. They'll fetch a good price, madam, I promise. At least one looks like a gentleman's daughter, madam."

"I'll have to inspect them," Miss White said. "And they better have most of their teeth. Without teeth, they're hardly fit to sell to Madam Ester, and you've seen her slags."

"Yes, madam."

How could Miss White be Madam Dequenne? Hadn't Madelina overheard her and Aunt Aubrey speaking of how Miss White once worked for Madam Dequenne? Could Madelina have misunderstood?

"Bring them up one at a time," Miss White said. "And for Heaven's sake, tie them up and blindfold them. It was a shame to put down that redhead after she saw my face. She would have sold for ten times what the others did."

"Yes, Madam."

Footsteps approached the door. Madelina knew she should retreat. Tell the girls what to do. Perhaps give the brave one a weapon. Anything but charge headlong from the stairwell.

Her rage a living thing trying to claw its way free, she hefted a pistol and tugged her mask to ensure the slip of black fabric remained firmly in place. She drew in a quick breath and flung open the door.

The man who'd brought her in gaped at her against the backdrop of a luxuriously appointed room. "What the devi—"

Madelina reversed her hold on the pistol and smashed the butt into his face. Her foot collided with his midsection. He doubled over. She slammed a knee into his chin. Shoving him to the floor, she spun the pistol in her hand and aimed at Miss White.

"Guards," Miss White yelled. "Guards, to me."

"Be quiet or I'll shoot," Madelina growled. Too late. Shouts and footsteps sounded from somewhere deeper in the building.

Miss White's gaze narrowed. "I'll give you one chance to drop that gun, Little Hook."

Madelina grinned. "And I'll give you one chance to explain why I shouldn't shoot you." She cocked the pistol.

CHAPTER 10

Jasper had avoided Clementine for several days, rehearsing what he must say to her, but he needed to discuss the information he'd learned from his mother's informant so they could formulate a course of action. He planned for that discussion to take place in his office, in a professional manner. The time had come to make it clear to Clementine that their involvement must now be limited to business. They were no longer lovers.

Yes, he'd told her that after she broke off their engagement, but this time he meant it. Besides, since ending their engagement, she'd not shown the slightest hint of jealousy when he took other women to his bed. Pursuing marriage was different, true, but she'd no right to be angry with him. Once, he'd offered her all he was. He wasn't the one who'd ended it.

He strode through the club, nodding to those few poor sods who found themselves in a gambling hell in the middle of the day. He didn't see Clementine on the floor, so he made his way into the back corridor and knocked on her office door. No answer came. Jasper grimaced, glancing at her bedchamber door. Clementine usually had only one thing on her mind when she lingered in bed until midday.

Steeling his resolve, he moved down the hallway to her bedroom door. Each of them had one at the Aspen. They often worked late nights or entertained, both one another and others.

Jasper would have to turn his chamber at the Aspen into another storage room, or a sitting room for Clementine. Not only wouldn't he be inviting anyone to share his bed, he intended to be home every evening, once he convinced Madelina to accept his suit.

He knocked on Clementine's door. No reply came. He knocked again. After a long moment, he cracked open the door, knowing it wouldn't be locked, and stuck his head in. The room stood empty. The remnants of a fire flickered in the grate.

Frowning, he returned to the door leading into Clementine's office. He opened it, as well, to be sure. Again, only furnishings met his seeking gaze. He crossed to his office, then the little parlor, his chamber. Clementine was nowhere to be found.

Annoyance and relief warred within him. He'd resolved to have what he suspected would be a difficult conversation, one he knew must come. After days of avoiding Clementine, he'd readied to speak with her, and now couldn't. Frustration surged foremost, yet the sense of reprieve at Clementine's absence couldn't be denied.

He strode back to his office. Rapid footfall sounded in the hall behind him, too heavy a tread to be Clementine. Jasper turned to find one of the men who watched the coaching inns for him hurrying up the hall.

"Mister Mclintock." The man bowed. "Sir, there's a couple outside the Bull and Mouth asking after their niece. They say her cases arrived on the coach, but she's nowhere to be found. I thought I best come tell you, sir."

Elation surged through Jasper at the long-awaited news. After his mother's informant told him the only place he could count on finding Madam Dequenne was her sorting house, where newly abducted women were taken, he'd set a discrete watch on the place and on as many of the coaching inns as he could. His mother's source said the two tasks the madam never delegated were the inspection and allocation of each new acquisition.

"Has anyone reported in from the sorting house?" Jasper asked. Would she go immediately now that a girl had been taken?

As if in answer, another of his men rushed in. Sighting Jasper, he hurried down the hall. "Sir, a carriage arrived at the building you told us to watch and someone went in. She had her hood up, but I could tell by the walk it was a woman."

He would finally catch her. "Have my horse made ready," he ordered. "Gather up anyone who's about and find them mounts." How long would Madam Dequenne spend deciding the girl's fate? "Ready everyone you can, but speed is more important than numbers." Jasper frowned. "And bring some rope if we've any handy."

"Yes, sir." The men bowed and then jogged back down the hall.

Jasper went to his office and loaded a pistol. He hoped not to need it, but there was no way to know how many men and what sort accompanied Madam Dequenne. He grabbed his coat, forwent his hat, and headed for the Aspen's back door.

Jasper led his men, half a dozen in total, down increasingly narrow streets. He had to sacrifice time for safety, his mount's hooves unsteady on the broken cobbles. Gritting his teeth at the delay, he finally turned onto the lane he sought. Madam Dequenne's sorting house was located halfway down. As he drew near, Jasper spotted a door standing wide.

That gaping maw filling him with sudden unease. Jasper leapt from his saddle and quickly secured his mount to a rusty hitching post. Gesturing his men to follow, he rushed inside to find a short hall. In moments, it spilled him out into a lushly decorated room. By the glow of candlelight, three men lay prone on a large axminster carpet. Across from Jasper, a masked young man slammed the hilt of a knife into a fourth man's jaw. The man's head snapped back, his eyes rolled skyward, and he crumpled beside an elegant mahogany desk. There was no one else in the room.

"Little Hook, what are you doing here?" Jasper cried. Were the men on the floor the madam's? They didn't look like the watch. Where was Madam Dequenne?

"Mclintock." Little Hook's mouth pulled into a nearly feral grimace. "I should have known you would come to save her."

Jasper lunged forward. If he couldn't have Madam Dequenne, he would get answers from the masked youth. The watch wouldn't arrive to save Little Hook this time.

The lithe young man dodged back. Jasper dove for him again. Little Hook ducked under his arms, in the direction of a second door. Jasper's men surged into the room. Beyond the doorway Little Hook maneuvered toward, Jasper caught sight of a staircase leading down.

"Sir?" one of his men cried.

"I can handle the boy. Get down the steps," Jasper ordered, skirting left to cut Little Hook off. "Bring back anyone you find." Had the madam gone that way? Did Little Hook seek to follow her, or to prevent Jasper from doing so?

His men clattered down the staircase.

The worry on Little Hook's face made Jasper wonder what his men would find. The youth dove at him.

At the last minute, Little Hook changed trajectory to angle around Jasper rather than barrel into him. Jasper brought an elbow down on the boy's back. He'd been waiting for the move.

Little Hook twisted, turning what should have flattened him into a glancing blow. His fist snaked out. Jasper tried to swivel out of the way but took a hard punch to the side.

They both jumped back, arms spread wide. Little Hook still held a knife, but kept his hold reversed, using the hilt to augment his fists rather than trying to draw blood with the blade. Recalling the uncocked pistol of their first encounter, Jasper wondered at the compunction.

They circled. Little Hook feinted. Jasper's whole body longed to take the bait, to lunge in, but he held back. A moment later, he tried a similar gambit. Little Hook didn't flinch.

The candles in the chamber revealed much more than the far-off torches had on the night of their first encounter. Studying the man across from him, Jasper didn't think Little Hook was even old enough to shave. How had such a young man become involved in the world of Madam Dequenne?

A scream, high and feminine, sounded from the staircase. Little Hook lunged for the doorway. Jasper grabbed him by the collar and hauled him back, trying to get an arm around his neck.

Little Hook ducked low. His body twisted, bunched. Jasper flew through the air.

He landed hard. Air rushed from his lungs. Little Hook's form was a dark blur through the film of pain-induced moisture that welled in Jasper's eyes. He kicked out as the boy made another dive for the steps.

Little Hook landed with a startled yelp. Jasper rolled. He flung his body atop the boy, pinning him. Jasper shook his head to try to clear the ringing there. The ply of the carpet was thick, but he'd hit the floor hard. The boy thrashed beneath him like a beached salmon.

"Be still," Jasper growled.

Little hook stopped struggling. Through the shock of capitulation, it took Jasper a moment to realize the tip of a knife dug into his side.

"Get off me or I'll decorate the room with your blood," the boy growled.

Jasper blinked. The boy smelled like mildew and smoke and ever so faintly of...honeysuckles. Jasper stared intently at the masked visage, taking in a pair of clear gray eyes.

"I said off," Little Hook growled.

Pain exploded in Jasper's side. He rolled off, away from the blade. His hand came up to clutch his side. Hot blood met his palm.

Little Hook sprang to his feet. Knife held before him, blade first now, he backed to the door that led to the street. "This isn't over between us, Mclintock. You can't protect her forever." Little Hook turned and fled.

Jasper stared after him, mind numb. He braced his free hand against the wall and pushed to his feet. Footsteps sounded somewhere below, and women's voices. Belatedly, Jasper recalled he had a gun. He pulled free his pistol and aimed it at the doorway, one hand still clutching his side.

It couldn't be. There was absolutely no way…. He'd pressed that slender form to the floor. Felt it writhe under him.

Jasper gave his head another shake, and nearly toppled as a wave of dizziness assailed him. His skull throbbed. Had he just had the stuffing beaten out of him by a girl? Could Madelina be so bold, so brazen, so fierce a fighter? He looked about the room at the unconscious men. They must be Madam Dequenne's, but what had Little Hook—Madelina—been doing here?

One of his men stuck his head out the staircase door. He spotted Jasper, his expression transforming from worry to relief until his gaze fixed on the hand Jasper clutched to his side.

"We found four young women, sir," his man said, coming out of the stairwell. He made a gesture and the rest of Jasper's men came up. "And these two."

Jasper's men urged two other men forward at gunpoint. His men gestured their captives to a corner, then stood before them, pistols unwavering, as four young women crept through the staircase door. Two were in tears and two merely pale.

"Where is Little Hook?" one of the girls whose cheeks weren't streaked with tears asked.

"Little Hook?" Jasper repeated dully. "He escaped."

"Escaped?" The girl frowned. "I wanted to thank him. He got us out of that cell. I hope he's not hurt." Her gaze dropped to Jasper's side. "Are you quite well, sir? You're bleeding."

"It's nothing." At least, nothing he had time for. "Little Hook freed you from the cell?" Jasper pressed, his pounding head sluggish. Of course, Madelina had freed them, but how had she found them? How had the sister of a marquess learned to fight the way she did? "Who are those two?" he asked his man.

"They were down in the hall, trying to remove these young women against their will."

Jasper nodded. "Tie them up, and this lot." He gestured at the men on the floor. "We'll call in the watch, but while we wait for them,

I have some questions for those two." He wished more of the men were conscious. Perhaps being bound would wake them.

"Yes, sir," his man said, then gestured to two companions. "Get rope, and, you, go for the watch."

Jasper turned back to the woman who'd spoken. "What do you mean, Little Hook freed you? Did he come to the door and let you out?"

All four shook their heads. "They thought Little Hook was a woman when they locked him in our room, but then he took off his dress and he was really a man, and he picked the lock, and said he would save us."

"They thought he was a woman?" Madelina had permitted them to abduct her? Impossible. No sane woman would do such a thing. "Did he look like a woman?"

The man who'd left returned, arms full of rope, and Jasper's men began tying up Madam Dequenne's people. He pressed his hand harder against his side. He needed to stay upright and conscious long enough to question the captives.

The girl shrugged. "They must have thought so, but I didn't see him. The room they put us in didn't have any light."

"I saw him as he left," one of the other girls said. She wiped at her cheeks. "When he opened the door. There's a torch in the hall. He was so handsome."

"He was wearing a mask," a third one said.

"He was still handsome."

Jasper closed his eyes. The room spun slowly about him, thanks to Little Hook flipping him head over arse and landing him on the floor, not to mention stabbing him.

"Sir, what will happen to us?" the first girl asked, her voice soft. "We were never alone with any men. I swear."

"We'll see you returned to your families," Jasper said, opening his eyes. That was usually Clementine's department, but his men knew the routine well enough. "Unless you need somewhere else to go?" His men could take them to Second Hope.

"I'd like to go to my family," one said.

"I don't have anywhere to go," another offered in a small voice.

Again, Jasper looked to his people. "Take care of it," he said. The spinning in his head seemed to amplify by the moment.

"Yes, sir." Despite his agreement, Jasper's man didn't move. "Are you sure you're well, sir?"

"Well enough." The hand Jasper pressed to his side felt hot and sticky. He needed to sit down. Free hand on the wall, he made his way to the chair placed behind the wide, delicately carved desk. A nice piece. Expensive. Jasper slumped into the chair. His blood would ruin the light blue brocade. "Bring me someone to question."

"Yes, sir." His man nodded but didn't move. "If I may, sir, I'd like to send for a doctor."

Jasper nodded, though it somehow seemed rather an effort. "Make sure these young women are away from here before anyone else arrives, even the watch. We didn't go through all this trouble to see their reputations ruined."

"Yes, sir."

His man's face wore a look of concern. The young women peered at Jasper with worried expressions, as well. He grimaced and sat straighter in the chair. He would be perfectly well. The wound wasn't deep, and his head would stop spinning in time. He felt much improved now that he was seated.

Physically, at least. His gut roiled with deep, simmering anger that they'd failed to capture Madam Dequenne. They may never have so good a chance again.

"All right." Jasper nodded at one of the men who'd come up the steps at gunpoint. "Bring him forward."

As Jasper questioned the ruffian, getting nowhere, two of his men took the girls away and another went to fetch Doctor Carter, a doctor on Amber Street known for his discretion, and a man whose mother was one of the few who did not shun Jasper's mother.

Jasper was forced to explain what had occurred to the watch while standing in the middle of the room, shirtless, with his arms stretched out at shoulder height, so Carter could bandage his side. Despite the pain and what felt to him like a lot of lost blood, the wound proved shallow, though long. Madelina had deliberately sliced Jasper's side rather than ram the blade in.

He didn't know if he should take that as affection, but at least it proved she didn't want to kill him. After the anger in her voice when she accused him of coming to save Madame Dequenne, and the ferocity with which she'd fought, he'd wondered.

Jasper kept the version of events he supplied the watch truncated, to avoid questions about how he'd known where to find Madam Dequenne, and the fate of the abducted women. He also swore, in all honesty, that he'd no idea who the young women were. He then remained while the watch questioned Madam Dequenne's men. The watch's methods, though far less civilized than Jasper's, yielded a similar lack of results.

The sun hung low on the horizon by the time Jasper strode back into his chamber at the Aspen. He stripped off coat, waist-coat, and shirt, and inspected the heap of ripped, blood-stained garments. Likely a loss, especially the thickly embroidered waist-coat, but perhaps he'd give them to one of the girls to attempt a restoration. One of them had plans of becoming a seamstress. Kitty, he seemed to recall, though she hadn't made recent mention of the idea.

In the mirror, Jasper studied the white wrapping of bandages, a stark contrast to his black trousers, taking in the line of blood that had soaked through. He glanced at the garments again. Maybe the coat, at least, could be saved, dark as the fabric was. Yes, he'd give it to Kitty. Perhaps, if he paid her for her work, she'd rediscover the desire to learn a trade.

If he could, he would turn all the women Clementine oversaw to less subservient trades. Every time one left for Second Hope, another young woman came in off the streets of London to take her place. Some of them never left. Clementine often reassured him that some women were born to her trade; enjoyed what they did.

The door to his chamber clicked open and Clementine strode in. Closing the door, she glided across the thick carpet to stand between him and the mirror.

"They told me that vicious Little Hook knifed you," she said, her voice honeyed with concern.

"It's little more than a scratch." Jasper endeavored for a casual tone, but tension twisted through him. For as many times as Clementine had seen him in a state of undress, it now seemed inappropriate.

"The men said they summoned Doctor Carter to examine you?"

"Yes." Jasper glanced at his wardrobe. He should don a clean shirt, at least.

A warm, long nailed finger traced a line across his chest. Jasper went still, his mind blank of any notion how to let her know her attention was no longer welcome. She sauntered in a slow circled about him, finger gliding across his upper arm, along his back. There, she halted and slid both arms around him, her palms splayed across his chest as she met his gaze in the mirror.

"Well, if the doctor is done with you, I know a way to put all the unpleasantness of the day from your thoughts," she murmured into his ear.

Jasper reached up and pulled her hands away. He shook his head. "I can't."

"Surely, that's not a deep wound," she said, sliding her hands back around him. "Don't worry, I'll do all the work. It's the least you deserve for being so brave."

Jasper removed her hands again. He turned to look down at her. "Rather, I won't, Clementine."

Her brow furrowed. "What do you mean, 'won't'?"

Jasper caught her fingers in his. "You will always be one of my dearest friends, but I've met someone. I want to pursue a life with her. It wouldn't be right to keep company with you while I court her."

A frown marred Clementine's beauty. "And after you're done courting her?"

"Hopefully, she will agree to be my wife, and I shall devote myself to her."

Clementine chuckled, a brittle edge to the sound. "You'll soon grow weary of that."

He shook his head. "I don't believe I will."

She snatched her hands from his. "You will, but don't expect me to be waiting for you when you do, Jasper Mclintock. I am no man's second choice."

"No man's second choice," he repeated, confused by the anger in her voice. "But, you were my first choice. You broke off our engagement, not me." He couldn't keep layers of anger and hurt from his voice as he added, "You didn't want me once I no longer held a duke's favor."

Her eyes widened. "Is that what you think?"

"Why else would you throw me over not a month after he died?"

She pursed her full lips. "Why indeed?"

He frowned, the room still spinning slightly, feeling as if he'd missed something. "Then why?"

"You never asked before."

"I'm asking now."

Clementine shrugged. "I'd recently come into something in the nature of a fortune. I took it into my head that I couldn't trust you with it."

"How could you think that?" She'd left him, crushed his heart, because she thought he would take her money?

"You had recently lost your allowance from your father. How was I to know he'd bequeathed you everything that wasn't entailed? That he'd left you even richer than your brother?"

She'd cast aside his heart over money? "And once you realized I am still wealthy?" he asked, voice tight.

She shrugged. "I could see I'd already lost you and that it would take time to win you back. What do you think I've been trying to do for the last two years?"

Jasper looked away, swallowing down pain. Years. It had all happened years ago. Why did her rejection still hurt? "Yes, well, even if you made a mistake then, you cannot expect me not to love another."

"Love?" she scoffed. "Lust, more likely. As I said, once you bed the girl, you'll weary of her." She reached up to cup his chin. "You're mine, Jasper Mclintock. Even when I broke your heart, you came back to me. Someone else claiming it won't keep you away."

He pulled his face away. "You had to know that, eventually, I would wish to wed and have a family."

She studied him for a long moment. A slow sigh left her lips. Anger drained from her. "Yes, of course, I knew." She smiled. "It's just a surprise. You're only six and twenty. I thought we'd have more fun first. Really, this is wonderful news, and I am happy for you."

Tension left Jasper. He didn't believe Clementine had given up, but at least the worst was over. "Thank you." He grimaced, suddenly struck by how ludicrous his words about a family and children were. Did Madelina even wish for those things? She was Little Hook. "It's not a set thing, of course. The lady must agree."

"The lady?" Clementine raised her eyebrows. "Ah, Greydrake's sister. I should have known that even the prospect of a sizable donation wouldn't spur you to dance in a room full of people who look down on you."

Jasper bristled.

"She is a lovely thing, but so young." Clementine pouted. "Not even twenty, I should think. Do you believe the marquess will grant his permission?"

"He already has."

"My, my. You have been busy. Asking permission to court diamonds of the *ton*. Getting knifed by Little Hook." Clementine patted him lightly on the cheek. "You rest up now." She offered a wide smile. "I'm sure I can find someone else to entertain me this evening."

Jasper caught her hand before she could turn. He brought her fingers to his lips. "Thank you for understanding."

"You know your happiness is very important to me, Jasper." She tugged her hand free and sauntered from the room, each sway of her hips an obvious reminder of what he could no longer have.

Jasper didn't mind. All in all, telling Clementine about Madelina had gone much better than he'd hoped. Clementine could be a very passionate woman. He'd expected shouting, threats, and a much more concerted effort at seduction.

Then again, like as not, she'd crawl into his bed later. In fact, when he did go to sleep, he would lock the doors. Not only tonight, but every night from now on, until he moved out of the Aspen, which he'd do as soon as possible. Clementine White was a very persistent woman.

Still, he'd told her. Having that task behind him and knowing they'd saved four young women, dulled some of his frustration over Madam Dequenne evading him. Unfortunately, the more his mind cleared and the longer he thought about the situation, the more his confusion and worry grew over Madelina being Little Hook.

CHAPTER 11

MADELINA PACED BEFORE THE FIREPLACE, RECOUNTING TO HER aunt everything that had transpired since Aunt Aubrey had dropped her at the coaching stop far outside London. Overwarm, and forced to wear a long-sleeved gown due to the bruises on her arms, Madelina wished no fire blazed in the grate. In truth, they had no need of extra heat. The staff only sought light, she knew, to stave off the parlor's oppressive darkness.

"...and then, before I could take down the final man and go after her, who should come in but Mister Mclintock." Rage roiled through Madelina. How dare he pretend to care about the plights faced by women? Take donations for his so-called charity? Make Madelina think he harbored feelings for her?

"Mister Mclintock's arrival would have posed no problem if you'd shot her," Aunt Aubrey snapped from her place on a sofa.

Madelina halted, back to her aunt. Her fists clenched, nails biting into her palms. "I couldn't."

"Why not?" Aunt Aubrey's words were clipped. "She is, according to you, Madam Dequenne. The woman is evil. You only needed to pull the trigger to make the world a better place."

"W-we needed information from her. To unravel her organization."

"Killing her would have unraveled it aplenty."

Madelina squeezed her lids shut, glad her aunt couldn't see her face. She remembered her bravado, the certainty that facing a cocked pistol would reduce Miss White to a teary confession of all aspects of her organization. Madelina pictured the fear in the other woman's eyes. Heard the sound of men running to the room. Saw them burst through the doorway. Worst of all, she read the moment of vicious joy when Miss White realized Madelina couldn't shoot to kill.

"I shot one of her men," she offered, opening her eyes. He'd pointed a pistol at her as he came through the door. She'd shot him in the leg. "And I cut Mclintock."

"What does that matter?" Aunt Aubrey asked. "Mclintock? Some hired ruffian? They aren't the force behind the abductions."

Perhaps if Miss White held a gun. Maybe even if she'd thrown something. But Madelina simply couldn't stand before a person and shoot them down. She was no executioner.

And now Miss White knew as much.

"Do you even know if the girls are safe?" Aunt Aubrey asked. "I assume you left them there when you fled."

A new heat suffused Madelina's face. "No, I don't know." The words came out a whisper. She should have asked for names. Found out who the other girls were. At least, then, she'd be able to hunt down their relations. Instead, she'd deliberately kept to herself, to better perpetuate her ruse as Little Hook.

"I see."

Behind her, Madelina heard Aunt Aubrey push to her feet.

"I'm disappointed in you, Madelina. Eleven years I've trained you, brought in men and women from my past life to educate you. You could have made us all proud yesterday."

"Why?" Madelina blurted out the question she'd longed to ask for so many years but had never mustered the courage to ask. Daunted by her aunt's constant judgement, her lack of warmth, Madelina had always expected to be sent away if she disappointed Aunt Aubrey, and questions aggravated her. "Why did you train me?"

"To kill your father. You know that, girl."

"But when he died, we kept training."

"Because there's so much potential in you. Because I had reason to believe you have inside you the means to be a great defender of the weak, at least as good at Lord Lefthook. Not to simply take revenge on one man, but on anyone like him." Aunt Aubrey shook her head in a slow, ponderous movement. "But now, I know you couldn't have killed your father. You couldn't have avenged your mother...my sister. You don't have it inside you, what it takes to do what must be done. I think we should return to the country for a time. London is too much for you."

"But I did see how they mark the carriages," Madelina offered. "How those young men pick out the women and mark where they're sitting with some sort of code. We could have them arrested."

"I don't believe you can have someone arrested for smudging chalk on a carriage."

"Or have men of our own watch for them and stop them, or get to the girls first, since now they'll know who the targets are," Madelina said in a rush.

"It's possible. I'll give it some thought. It doesn't solve the true problem, though." Her aunt thumped from the room.

Madelina hung her head. She scrubbed her hands over her face, then crossed to slump onto one of the sofas, away from the fireplace. Fleetingly, she wondered if some of her aunt's disappointment sprang from the fact that it was Miss White who had, long ago, put a pistol ball in Aunt Aubrey's hip.

Madelina distinctly recalled her aunt saying that Miss White had worked for Madam Dequenne, but now it seemed Miss White was Madam Dequenne. How was that possible? Madelina couldn't ask. To do so would be to admit she'd eavesdropped.

Could the position be a title, almost like being a duke? Or perhaps more like a town crier, since Madelina doubted the post was hereditary. She had too many questions. Did she dare try to get the answers, now that Miss White knew her for the coward she was?

A knock sounded on the doorframe. Madelina looked up.

"Mister Mclintock to see you, my lady," Wilks yelled into the room.

Mclintock? Fury rekindled inside her. "Show him in, please, Wilks."

Wilks couldn't have read her tone, but he must have noted her narrowed gaze and the anger that suffused her features. He hesitated in the doorway. "Are you sure, my lady? Shall I send for your aunt?"

"I am sure, and there's no need to send for Aunt Aubrey. Mister Mclintock will not remain long."

The butler nodded. Expression worried, he departed. Madelina clenched her hands and waited the short time it took for footsteps to return down the hall. She surged to her feet as the two men appeared in the doorway. Mister Mclintock, too, must have read her expression, for he stopped one step into the room.

Madelina leaned to the side so Wilks could see her face around the tall gentleman. "That will be all, Wilks. Thank you."

He offered a hesitant nod and left.

She turned her ire on Mister Mclintock, trying to ignore his strong, even features, his golden curls, his long-fingered hands. She'd felt their strength on her person.

He rocked back on his heels. "What have I done now?"

Should she tell him? Her aunt had said they would leave London. What difference would it make? "You and Miss White abduct young women. All your talk of charitable efforts is a lie."

If he'd appeared taken aback by her anger, his expression became doubly so. "I beg your pardon?"

"It is not *my* pardon you should beg."

He took a long stride into the room, confusion giving way to irritation. "We do not abduct young women. We're trying to save them, to put an end to such atrocity. Furthermore—"

She rushed up to him, unwilling to endure the pain of his lies. "Really? Then why did I overhear Miss White threaten a girl at your club, Miss Kitty, for trying to get away from her life there?" Even as she spoke, Madelina recalled Miss White had also forbade Miss Kitty from telling Mister Mclintock of their conversation, but passion spurred her on. There could be no stemming her words. "Why did Miss White shoot my aunt? Why—"

"Miss Kitty? Shoot yo—"

"I am not finished," Madelina yelled. "Why was she there yesterday, giving orders about selling those girls and inspecting their teeth? And why did you come rushing in to save her when I nearly had her?" And why, why hadn't she been able to squeeze the trigger and shoot that vile woman?

Triumph lit Mister Mclintock's features. "So, you admit, you are Little Hook."

"I am, so you can save your lies, Mclintock."

"My lies? You've been running about London dressed as a lad and you accuse me of lies?"

"You bought girls at that auction." Madelina ticked the points off on her fingers, a body of evidence she'd been wrong to ignore. "You own a gambling hell. You employ lightskirts. And you kept me from chasing Miss White yesterday. What did you do with the women she held? Tell me where they are."

He caught one of her hands in a strong grip. She pulled her other back to slap him, but he captured that one, too. He studied her face.

"I bought those young women at the auction to free them, just as I freed the ones we found in the cellar yesterday." Question filled his amber eyes. "Is that why you dress as Little Hook? To save women? They said you were trying to help them escape."

"Of course, I was." She yanked, but he didn't seem to notice her attempt to free her hands. "Just as you were there to ensure they did not."

"I, too, came to save them." He shook his head. "Why will you not believe me?"

"Because Miss White is Madam Dequenne." Madelina couldn't stop the words. Not with betrayal and guilt swirling like a poisoned draught in her gut. How had she let that woman get away? Madelina pulled against his grip again, harder.

Mister Mclintock pinned her palms to his chest. The scents of cedar and cloves slipped about her. "That is impossible. You must be mistaken. You've seen Clementine what, once? From across a ballroom?"

So, his mistress hadn't mentioned Little Hook's visit to The Black Aspen. "I'm not mistaken, and if she is Madam Dequenne, then you are a villain, too." Her voice caught oddly on the accusation. She swallowed.

"I am not a villain." He lowered his voice. "How can I prove it to you?"

She read his intention in the heat of his gaze. He held her hands against his chest, but she could turn, pull away. Instead, she tipped her face up to receive his kiss.

His lips questioned, but hers did not. Anger, confusion, and a desire so deep it sparked fear, all drove her kiss. His mouth stilled.

Shame shot through her. He'd meant something sweet, reassuring. She'd practically attacked him with her mouth.

He released her hands and wrapped his arms about her. Although she stood nearly as tall as him, he swept her from her feet, crushed her to him. Kissed her with a passion to rival her own.

When he finally released her lips, her head tipped back. His mouth blazed a trail down her neck. The room seemed to spin. The red walls. The dark trim. The open door.

Madelina's head snapped up. She unwound hands she didn't know she'd buried in his curls. "Mister Mclintock." Her voice came out low and rough. "We have to stop."

His lips found hers again. A delicious weakness spread through her. She struggled to remember why she ever wanted him to stop.

This wasn't real. He didn't love her. He lied. He bought and sold women. She got her hands between them and shoved. Hard.

He lifted his head. His amber eyes glowed from within, like tinted lanterns brought back from the east. "Madelina?"

The entreaty in his voice, the longing, tugged at her. Her breath quickened. She shook her head. "Release me."

He blinked, then looked down. Expression bemused, he set her feet on the floor. "I apologize. I...got carried away."

She took a step back, out of the circle of his arms.

"Do not think I meant to take advantage of you," he said. "I do not. I wish to marry you."

The room tipped. Her hand shot out but found nothing to support her.

His gripped her shoulders, braced her. A smile tugged his lips. "Even though you stabbed me."

Stabbed him? Yes, she had. Because... "I cannot marry you. How can you think I would?"

His arms fell to his sides. The light left his eyes. "Because I'm a bastard?" he asked, voice harsh.

"Because you are working with Miss White, and because I know, I am completely certain, that she buys and sells young women. She is Madam Dequenne."

"That is ridiculous," he snapped.

"Is it?"

His gaze narrowed. "Is this some sort of jealousy? I told you, I work with Clementine. Moreover, she has been my friend and confidant for years. I swear to you, she is no longer my lover, will never be my lover ever again, but I cannot betray years of friendship."

"Jealousy?" A high, screeching note Madelina didn't recognize rang through her voice. "I am not jealous. I am disgusted."

He stared at her, expression stunned. "I disgust you?"

She thrust her shoulders back. "You do, and you will continue to do so for so long as you associate with that woman."

He shook his head. "I'd heard rumors your father was unbalanced. Now I see it runs in the family."

Rage shot through her at the comparison. "How dare you equate me to that man?"

"How dare you malign Miss White?" He raked a hand through his hair, anger clear in his face. "I think we've both said enough. If you'll excuse me, Lady Madelina." He offered a sharp bow and retreated.

Immobile, she watched as he strode from the room, shoulders rigid, head high. He didn't halt. He didn't look back.

If Mister Mclintock was so vile, why did each step that echoed down the hall feel as if it fell on her chest? Squeezing, crushing, until she could hardly breath. She raised a hand to her throat, half expecting to find something restricting the flow of air.

"Your beau did not look pleased as he departed," Aunt Aubrey said, thumping her way into the room.

"He is not my beau," Madelina whispered. Nor would he ever be.

Her aunt proffered a letter. "This came for you while you were having your row."

Madelina took the folded paper with numb fingers. Attention fixed on the doorway as if she could conjure Mister Mclintock back, she cracked the seal and unfolded the page.

"You'll have to look at it if you want to know what it says," Aunt Aubrey said.

It took effort to drag her gaze from the empty doorway to the page.

I know what was revealed the night your mother died. Leave London or the world shall learn your secret.

Madelina stared at those two lines. Only she'd been there, and her parents and...the woman whose presence began her parents' argument. Whose gasp made Madelina's mother look away and given her father the opportunity for murder.

"What secret?" Aunt Aubrey's voice was sharp.

Madelina looked up from the page to find her aunt leaning close, scanning those words. Dread snaked through her. Aunt Aubrey did not take well to secrets.

Eyes like granite met Madelina's. "What secret?"

"I...I never told you what my father said before her pushed her."

"You said they argued about the woman he had with him. His mistress. The one who gasped."

Madelina offered a shaky nod. "But she didn't gasp because Mother said she had lovers."

Her aunt's gaze flicked to the page, then back up. "Why, then?"

"Because my father admitted he and Mother were never truly married." Madelina swallowed, her throat so dry, her words came out broken. "He said...he said William's mother was still alive when he and my mother wed, so it wasn't a real marriage. She wasn't a marchioness and I...I'm not a lady. I'm a bastard." Just like Mister Mclintock.

Aunt Aubrey's gaze burrowed into Madelina, but Madelina refused to look away. It was Madelina's secret. No harm had come from not sharing it. Her aunt did not need to know everything. Aunt Aubrey kept plenty of secrets from her, after all, like who'd shot her all those years ago.

"He didn't even have the decency to legally wed my sister?" Aunt Aubrey hissed. Her visage twisted with such malice that, for the first time, Madelina felt relief that her father was dead.

She shuddered to think what her aunt would do to him could she but lay her hands on him. Undoubtedly, he would have deserved whatever horrors her aunt invented. No, a purely selfish fear roiled within Madelina. She didn't want the nightmares that would come from knowing just how cruel her aunt could be.

Aunt Aubrey pulled the page from Madelina's hand. She scrutinized both front and back, then turned and fed it to the fire. "Who was there that night?"

"I told you, I never saw her," Madelina said.

"Yes, and I would believe you, if I didn't know you keep things from me."

"I don't keep things from you." At least, not many. To that list, Madelina would add the kiss she'd shared with Mister Mclintock. No good could come of mentioning that, and there was no reason to. No fear existed that it would ever happen again.

"Did you think I would look on you differently, girl?"

Biting her lip, Madelina studied the garish carpet. "I was ashamed. My birth is a sin. And, if I'm not truly a lady, not the rightful daughter of the marquess, who am I? I get no inheritance. I have no name. I am nothing."

A hand gripped her arm. "You are my sister's child. That is all that matters to me."

Pain made a hard knot in Madelina's throat. She should have told her aunt. Who could she count on, if not Aunt Aubrey? Only William and, if he knew the truth, perhaps not even him, though she didn't care to believe that. "I'm sorry I didn't tell you," she whispered.

"I understand, girl." Her aunt's hand dropped back to the raptor topping her cane. "It wouldn't have mattered. I could love you no less and hate him no more."

"Are we leaving London, then?" Earlier, Madelina had railed against the idea. Now, she welcomed the respite. Her aunt was correct. Madelina wasn't ready yet. She was a disaster as Little Hook. Yes, she could fight well, but she felt less and less confident about who she should fight, except for Miss White...and she'd let Miss White escape her.

If they left London, maybe the memory of Mister Mclintock's touch would fade, for she'd never know peace if it did not.

"Leave London?"

The derision in Aunt Aubrey's voice brought Madelina's head up.

"Under duress?" Aunt Aubrey continued. "Because of a threat? Blackmail? Never."

"But earlier you sai—"

"That was before you received that letter." Her aunt wore a nearly gleeful expression. "If someone wishes for you to go that badly, the only thing for it is to stay. I thought you were being ineffectual, but you've obviously ruffled some feathers. We've shaken the tree. Now we must discover what sort of bird flies out."

"But who could have sent the letter?" Madelina gestured to the fireplace, where their only clue, such as it had been, swirled in the warm eddies, a dusting of ash. "Only the woman who gasped that night could possibly know the truth of my birth."

"And you saw nothing of her? Heard nothing, other than a gasp?"

Madelina shook her head. No matter how many times that

horrible night replayed in her mind, she could dredge up nothing about the woman who'd been with her father. Madelina simply had not seen her.

Aunt Aubrey braced both hands on her cane, her lined face folded in thought. "The note comes now because of your work as Little Hook. Someone else must know your secrets. Both of them."

"No one knows I am Little Hook." Except Jasper Mclintock...who was sure to confide in Miss White. Madelina swallowed down bile. That explained who might know she was Little Hook, but who would know of her heritage? If the woman who'd gasped had told anyone.... "Who would she tell, that woman?"

"She would tell Madam Dequenne," Aunt Aubrey said with surety.

"Then? It was nearly a dozen years ago. Miss White can't have more than thirty years. She couldn't have been a well-established madam back then." And Madelina had heard Aunt Aubrey refer to Miss White as the madam's creature. Not the madam, but one of her girls.

"There is always a Madam Dequenne."

Understanding flashed sharp in Madelina's mind. "So, the name is hereditary. Miss White is not the first Madam Dequenne."

Indecision flickered in her aunt's features, there, then gone.

Only years of knowing that face permitted Madelina to read it. "What are you not telling me?" When her aunt didn't answer, Madelina squared her shoulders. "I told you my secret."

Aunt Aubrey pursed her lips.

Madelina waited.

A moment passed before her aunt offered, "Once, I thought Clementine was the means by which I would, singlehandedly, unravel and destroy Madam Dequenne."

"Singlehandedly?"

Her aunt grimaced. "I thought I was ready. Well trained enough. Inexperienced, but smart enough. I wanted to impress my superiors so they would send me on more glamorous assignments, out of London. Out of England."

"What happened?" Madelina whispered, unnerved by the way her aunt's youthful surety mirrored her own.

"I gained Clementine's trust. Turned her. The madam had taken her as a babe from one of her women. She had a concoction she made them drink, you see, that kept them from quickening with child, but one of the girls managed to stay pregnant and then hide the babe for a time. I don't know what Dequenne did to the girl, but she kept Clementine and raised her to the trade. Clementine knew everything about the business and about Dequenne." Her aunt fell silent.

Fascinated, Madelina pressed, "What went wrong?"

Aunt Aubrey thumped the tip of her cane hard against the floor. "Clementine backed out. She told Dequenne everything and then, to prove her loyalty, she shot me. She must have been about fourteen at the time."

Pieces fell together in Madelina's mind. "You think it was one of Madam Dequenne's girls with my father that night."

"She trades in the best."

"And that girl, whoever she was, told Madam Dequenne, who passed the knowledge on to Miss White."

Aunt Aubrey thumped her cane again. "Aye, but what I cannot make out is how Miss White would know you are Little Hook, except as a guess, suspecting because you are related to me."

Madelina swallowed. She had a very good idea how, but she simply could not admit that she'd permitted Mister Mclintock to see through her disguise.

Her aunt studied her for a long moment. Madelina met her gaze with calm, but her insides writhed. To overcome her shame, she nearly admitted that she'd given the knowledge of her undoing to Mister Mclintock, but she held it in. Maybe she could still fix this. Make everything come out right. Then she would never need to fully explain her ineptitude.

"Go ready for dinner, girl," Aunt Aubrey said, then limped her way from the room.

Madelina sagged in relief. She stared about the parlor, trying to force shaky limbs to move. She felt as if she'd been trampled by a stampede of horses.

CHAPTER 12

Jasper burst into Clementine's office but stopped short as three pairs of eyes turned to greet him. Two of the women who worked in the Aspen sat before her desk, expressions surprised. Clementine stared at him, as well. Her eyebrows shot up. She turned back to the young women.

"Are we agreed that the two of you will work to put this incident behind you?" Clementine asked in the light, pleasant tone with which she always addressed them.

They pulled their gazes from Jasper to offer nods. "Yes, Miss White," they chorused.

"You are excused."

They jumped to their feet and hurried past Jasper, studying him askance.

Clementine rose. She crossed and closed the office door before turning assessing eyes on him. "You look a sight. Is something amiss?"

"She said no," Jasper blurted.

"She said...." Clementine's confusion shifted to surprise. "You asked her already?" She frowned, her eyes screwing into the same thoughtful look as when she did figures. She grimaced.

"What is it?" he asked.

Clementine refocused on him. "Nothing. I wrote a letter I needn't have written. You know I hate to play my hand too soon. It's unrelated." She made a swishing gesture, as if brushing away the interruption. "You truly asked her to marry you, already?"

"I did, and she refused me." After accusing Clementine of being Madam Dequenne. He studied Clementine again. Was it possible? Jasper raked a hand through his hair, knocking his hat from his head. Realizing he hadn't shucked his outerwear, he stripped off gloves and coat.

Clementine dipped low to scoop up his hat, which she tossed into the seat of a chair. "You went there already, today, and asked her?" she repeated, incredulous. "You only told me of your plan yesterday."

Misery, suspicion, and anger warred within. He shrugged. "Why would I wait?"

"You may have wanted to woo the girl a bit more, to start."

Jasper grimaced. She made a fair point. She also didn't sound like a devious, cold-hearted trader in women's flesh, but like the woman he'd once loved enough to take to wife.

"Why did she refuse you?" Pity sprang to life in Clementine's eyes. "Because of your lineage." She rested light fingers on his arm. "I'm sorry, Jasper. Even though she's young and entitled, I'd hoped she would be able to see past your birth."

"My lineage? No." He rubbed his temples. He should have better organized his words. He'd the whole carriage ride back to compose them. Only, he'd been too agitated for coherent thought.

"What is it?" she asked. "You look as if the Aspen just burned down."

He sucked in a breath. "She asked me to cut all ties with you."

Clementine's eyes went wide. She opened her mouth as though to speak, but snapped it shut.

"I refused, of course," Jasper added.

"You refused?" she breathed. "For me?"

He'd never seen her look vulnerable before. Not Clementine, whose confidence exceeded that of anyone else he knew. She seemed almost confused.

"Of course." He shook his head. "You are my confidant, my friend. My business partner. How could I cut you from my life? Being in love shouldn't make me do what is not right."

The look of wonder dropped from Clementine's face. "You still love her."

"I do." He wished he could qualify that agreement. Put it in the past tense. Yet, he could not. Although her ultimatum and her attack on Clementine angered him, his love wouldn't dim. He balled his hands. He'd rather it would.

Clementine watched him through wary eyes. She moistened her lips. "I suppose it's only reasonable for a young woman not to wish her betrothed to associate with his mistress."

"Former mistress," he corrected. "I told her as much. I wish she would believe me."

"You know, you don't really want a woman who won't believe you. What sort of life would you have?"

Jasper shrugged, aware Clementine couldn't know her comment held as true for Madelina as him. Why would she want a husband who wouldn't believe her? But how could he? He'd known Clementine for years. She worked with him to save young women.

A keen mixture of anger and despair swirled through him. He wished he didn't want Madelina. He wished he'd never seen her. His mother was wrong. Loving someone with all your being didn't bring great happiness. It brought pain. Of all people, his mother should know that.

Clementine stroked his cheek. "I don't like to see you so unsettled, dearest. Perhaps you could convince her that you and I are no longer lovers."

He twitched his shoulders, the motion sharp with frustration. "That was not the extent of her complaints."

A dull ache settled in his gut. The sensation threatened to work up his throat to cut off air. He couldn't go through life without Madelina, could he? There had to be a way to convince her that he and Clementine would never be lovers again, and that Clementine wasn't Madam Dequenne. The second ought to be simple. Obviously,

Madelina had only made the accusation out of jealousy. She must have.

"Oh dear." Clementine's brow knit. "Have I done something to offend her?" Clementine offered an exaggerated frown. "I did pull you away from your dance with her. I am sorry for that. I'd no idea I interrupted something so important."

Jasper shook his head. "No, it's not the dance, although I daresay that stung her." Could he tell Clementine of Madelina's accusation? Surely, Clementine would laugh. Maybe her amusement would pull Jasper up from the despair threatening him. Then she could help him plan how to win back Madelina.

But what if.... No. He would not believe that of Clementine. He drew in a deep breath, focused on Clementine's face and said, "She feels she cannot marry me until I accept that you are Madam Dequenne."

Clementine froze, something akin to fear dulling her gaze. "What?" she gasped.

Jasper flung up his arms. "You see? The girl is unhinged. How could I accept that as a reason to cut you? We both know the accusation was made out of misplaced jealousy."

Clementine licked her lips. "Yes. She must be very jealous."

Jasper paced away, then back, and away again. "She refused to listen to reason, or even admit she's jealous."

Auburn locks swept back and forth as Clementine shook her head. "How would she even come across such an idea?" she breathed. "Madam Dequenne is hardly a topic for genteel parlors."

Jasper stilled, his back to Clementine. Could he share Madelina's secret with a woman she despised? His side twinged. He rubbed at the tightly wound bandages. Telling seemed like a betrayal, and yet, he always told Clementine everything.

Jasper drew in a deep breath. "Lady Madelina is Little Hook." The stillness in the room alarmed him. He turned.

The hard look on Clementine's face shifted immediately to incredulousness. "Jasper, that's ridiculous. She's a slip of a girl."

"And yet, it's true."

Clementine searched his face. "You're certain about this?"

"I am."

She pointed to his side. "Then, she stabbed you."

He nodded. A thread of appreciation sliced through his misery. She'd easily held her own against him during both of their encounters. Cut him. Tossed him like a sack. What an amazing woman.

"Are you sure you want to love a madwoman, Jasper?" Clementine pursed her lips. "Or one underhanded enough to try to make you believe I am Madam Dequenne?"

He'd hoped she would find the accusation laughable, but he understood her tartness. For her years of loyalty to him, for the work she'd done to help other women, Clementine deserved better than slander.

He crossed back to capture her hands. "I can't help that I love her. If I could stop myself, I would, but I can't. Since the moment I set eyes on her, I knew I had to win her heart."

Clementine let out a sigh. "But she refused you." Her lids half closed. "She said no," her voice dropped to a familiar purr. She pulled her hands free to glide them up his arms. Long fingers slid under his waistcoat to splay across his chest, her hands warm through his shirt. "Perhaps I can find a way to put her from your mind."

He studied her full lips. Expert lips. Her skin, which he knew to be silken. Faint lines etched her brow but did nothing to detract from her lusciousness. It would be easy to slip back into the life he'd lived before Lady Krestlin's ball. Before he beheld Madelina. Easy to walk the Aspen in the evenings, making small talk. Attend events, begging funds from his old companions. Join Clementine in her bed whenever they felt like enjoying each other's company.

An aloof, guarded pair of gray eyes filled his vision. A perfect, bow shaped mouth. That beautiful contralto speaking frankly, seemingly incapable of lying.

Somehow, Madelina must truly believe Clementine to be Madam Dequenne. Madelina was not conniving. Not subtle. Showed little skill in the art of idle chatter or prevarication.

And she hadn't actually said no. Not to him. She'd objected to

Clementine. Not once had she intimated that she wouldn't care to wed him.

He realized Clementine's hands stroked his chest. He caught them again, his smile fond. "I appreciate the sentiment, but surely I'm overreacting. You were correct when you said I haven't wooed her enough."

Clementine blinked up at him. "You're going back to her?"

"I must. Like a moth to a flame, as it were."

"But she obviously despises me."

"We can change that." He squeezed her hands. "Perhaps if you met her? She would see you for who you truly are." He nodded, pleased with the idea. Once Madelina came to know Clementine, she would see why the idea of Clementine being Madam Dequenne was ridiculous. "Then, too, you'd be better able to advise me on how to court her. Obviously, I'm doing a terrible job."

Clementine yanked her hands free. "Under what unholy circumstance would Lady Madelina Greydrake socialize with me, Jasper?"

He frowned, but his expression quickly lightened once more. "At my mother's. She could invite you both for tea."

"Your mother despises me."

His happiness skipped a beat, disrupted by surprise. "Why would you think that?"

Pity returned to her expression. "Oh Jasper. For all you've suffered since your father's death, you still live in a coddled, fanciful world. Why wouldn't your mother hate me? She knows that, before I met you, I was a whore. How could a woman like your mother ever see me as anything else?"

Jasper shook his head. "No, that's not true. My mother understands. If anyone could, she does. Madam Dequenne took her."

"Yes, but your mother escaped. Your father was her first client, and he took her away from there. Gave her a beautiful life." Clementine's eyes shimmered. "No one came to save me. I worked at that life for years before you found me. No one has ever cared for me but you."

"The girls care for you. My mother most certainly does not hate you." He'd no idea Clementine felt so alone. "The women we save, they must adore you."

Clementine dabbed her eyes. She shook her head, went back around her desk, and took her seat. "You live in a wonderful world, Jasper Mclintock, despite your father's choices, despite the faithlessness of you peers."

"You're being dramatic," he said. Clementine had that tendency when she didn't get what she wished for. He was uncertain, though, what she wished for now and wasn't receiving.

"You are being naive." She began ordering her desktop. "I have work to do, and soon I'll be needed on the floor. We can talk more about your undying love later."

"I've upset you." He knew that much, even if he didn't know how.

She glanced up again, then went back to her papers. "The world upsets me, Jasper. Run along now."

Chatter filtered through the door as some of the girls walked past, undoubtedly to take their preferred places in the club. He scooped up his coat, gloves, and hat. Often, it proved best to allow Clementine time to get over her moods.

"I'll be in my office should you need me," he said.

Clementine nodded, not looking up.

Jasper offered a bow, regardless, and quit the room. He nodded to the girls walking past, most smiling cheerfully, then crossed to his office. Kitty came down the hall, alone, face angled at the floor.

"Kitty, a word?" he said, the sight of her recalling another of Madelina's accusations.

Kitty glanced up with red-rimmed eyes. "I'm sorry, Mister Mclintock, but I really mustn't tarry." She cast a quick look right.

Jasper followed her gaze to Clementine's door. Was Kitty afraid to be overheard speaking to him? The idea was ridiculous. Madelina made him imagine things. "I thought you wished to become a seamstress. I've already arranged a place for you at Second Hope."

She darted another glance at Clementine's door. "Oh no, sir. I'm very happy here, sir. I'm doing so well for myself. I shouldn't wish to begin again yet. Maybe when I'm older and I've lost my looks. I want to save more first, sir."

Jasper nodded. "Yes, well, if that's what you wish. Come see me the moment you change your mind."

"I will, sir. Thank you, sir." She hurried off down the hall after the other girls.

Jasper pushed open his office door, strode in and closed it behind him. Kitty had seemed so eager to leave, so full of enthusiasm. He would have checked on her sooner if not for his preoccupation with Madelina. Still, it hadn't been that long since she'd come to him, asking to go. When had Kitty changed her mind?

Her red-rimmed eyes came to mind. Her fearful glances at Clementine's door. Surely, the product of a misunderstanding. Clementine could be assertive, overbearing, but her heart was good. Of that, Jasper felt certain.

Or did he?

CHAPTER 13

MADELINA PRESSED HER EYE TO THE CRACK, TAKING IN THE
tableau of her parents at the top of the staircase. As she'd watched
them do countless times, they began their argument. Each angry
gesture, each word, indelibly engraved on Madelina's mind.

"I'll bed who I will, when I wish, just as you do, and there's not a
thing you can do about it, old man," her mother spat, voice dripping
venom.

Her father laughed. "I'll have you know, William's mother still
lived when I wed you. I can cast you aside whenever I choose. You,
my dear, are no marchioness. No lady. You're a bigamist and a whore,
and your precious Madelina is a bastard."

Then the gasp, the push...the scream.

Her mother's scream mingled with her own. Her father turned.
His eyes narrowed. He charged at her bedroom, her death in his eyes.

Madelina scurried back. She fled into her bathing chamber and
yanked open the door to the servants' stairs. Blacker than night, that
rectangular maw gaped before her. She would never be able to
descend quickly enough in the darkness. She would fall. Die like her
mother.

She whirled, searching, frantic. Sighting the tub, she dropped to the floor and slipped between the cold iron and the wall. She pressed clenched fists to her mouth to hold in her sobs.

Her father burst into the bathing room. He saw the open door to the servants' stairs. But unlike that first time, unlike every other time, he stopped. He didn't charge down the steps, giving her time to flee back into the hall, to find William. Instead, he turned, so slowly, until his gaze found her.

"I see you, you little bastard," he snarled. He lunged for her.

Madelina's eyes flew open. Her breath came in ragged gasps. She pressed a hand to her pounding heart.

Tears seeped from the corners of her eyes. She'd been a fool to return to this house. She should have listened to her brother and rented a different place. She would never fight free of the memories here. Never walk down that staircase under her father's menacing gaze.

She should add doing so to her list of failures. The only thing she'd succeeded at in coming to London was the one thing she hadn't been trying to do, the thing everyone thought she'd come to do. She'd attracted a man.

She didn't want a man. Her decision to follow in Lord Left-hook's footsteps had never seemed like a sacrifice because she'd always assumed she would end up alone like her aunt. How, after all, could she begin a relationship—forge a life—when her standing in society was a lie? She couldn't start by confessing her lack of proper linage to a gentleman but waiting to do so would squander time and trust. No man would be pleased to discover the woman he courted and the connections he sought weren't what he'd bargained for.

Except Mister Mclintock. He wouldn't care that Madelina had been born out of wedlock. He'd empathize.

Or would he? Did his interest in her stem from a need to regain his footing among the peerage? To wed a lady? Had he hoped that, since she was newly returned to London, he could capture her heart before she found out he was a social pariah?

She shook her head, sitting up. That couldn't be his plan. She had

William, and Lanora, and Miss Birkchester. Anyone would expect them to inform Madelina of Jasper's lineage.

She stood, crossed to the window, and tugged aside the curtains. Light filled the horizon in streaks of color, but the ball of the sun still hung out of sight.

If Miss Birkchester proved correct and the Earth was flat with the sun circling around it, the sun must also warm the bottom side. Did anything grow there, soaking up that warmth? Would they ever dig deep enough to poke through and find out?

Madelina went to her basin and poured out cold water to begin her morning ablutions. The hour was much too early, she knew, but she couldn't return to sleep now. Instead, she washed, dressed herself, and attempted her hair.

Her brother hadn't warned her of Mister Mclintock's lack of legitimacy. William must know. Did that mean he didn't care, or that he didn't think she and Mister Mclintock were in danger of forming a connection? Even if William believed the latter, he regarded Mister Mclintock well. William had specifically called the man his friend.

Her arms aching as she struggled with her hair, Madelina bit her lip. She considered her brother a good judge of character, but had she any basis for that belief? Simply because he disliked their father? Only a dedicated sycophant or someone of extremely limited intelligence could view the late marquess as anything but one step removed from the devil.

Madelina let her hands fall from her lopsided coif. She wanted William to be right. She desperately wanted Mister Mclintock to be good, but only he could have told Miss White that Madelina was Little Hook. Even if he cared for Madelina, he'd already betrayed her. Whether he believed her about Miss White or not, he'd no business telling the secrets of the woman he professed to love to his mistress. How could she long so deeply for such a man? How could she revel in the memory of his lips?

Mister Mclintock had seemed so sincere in his denial, which made him either a great fool or an expert liar. He didn't strike Madelina as either. Frustration at how reason ran in circles when it came to Mister Mclintock threatened to overtake her. She resisted the urge to bang her forehead into the wall.

Quiet footsteps sounded in the hall, followed by a light knock at her door. Madelina crossed and tugged it open. One of the maids stood without.

"My lady." The young woman dipped a curtsy. "I didn't think you'd be awake."

"Yet, I am. You are looking for me?"

The girl offered a nod. "There's a carriage without, my lady, and the driver told me he's to wait for you to go with him or to tell him to his face that you won't." She proffered a folded page. "I didn't know if I should wake you. I tapped on Miss Saint Lawrence's door, but she didn't answer. It's awful early, and you know how grouchy she is, so I came to you."

Madelina nodded, unsurprised at the girl's reluctance to wake her aunt. Aunt Aubrey had the staff well cowered. Wondering at the driver's strange request, she tugged the page from the girl's fingers, which clenched it tight. "Thank you," she said and unfolded the paper to find a strong script.

Please give me one more opportunity to prove myself to you. I cannot live without you. We must speak —J

Madelina read the lines again. Excitement bubbled through her, but she tamped it down. She should not be excited to see a man who had shared her secret with his mistress. Her hands trembled as she folded the note. "The driver said I'm to go with him?"

"Or tell him that you will not, my lady." The girl wrung her hands. "You cannot get in that carriage. Not without your aunt or...or, at least, bring me."

No, she could not. "I won't. I'll go down and tell him as much." Jasper must be in the carriage. Why else insist she come out? Before she sent him away, should she tell him she knew what he'd done? That he'd shared her secret?

"Shall I come out with you, my lady?"

"That will not be necessary," she said as she hurried to her wardrobe to pull free a cloak, gloves, and bonnet.

"But, my lady, your reputation."

"Will not suffer from standing in the street speaking to a coachman." Nor even from stepping up to the window to reprimand Mister Mclintock. Madelina tied on her bonnet. At least it covered the mess she'd made of her hair. She flung the cloak over her shoulders and turned back to the girl, gloves in hand.

The maid's cheeks flamed. "Begging your pardon, my lady, but it's not only a coachman waiting out there for you."

"You read the note." Madelina didn't feel surprised so much as annoyed. She shoved the folded page into her gown.

"It weren't sealed," the maid said, cocking her chin in the air despite her red cheeks.

"No, I suppose not." Madelina crossed to the door. She made a sweeping gesture, for the maid stood in her way. "If you'll excuse me."

"I don't think Miss Saint Lawrence would like you to go without talking with her first."

Madelina looked down at the maid, a good foot shorter. She could easily overpower the girl, but that would be very poor behavior, and likely make a ruckus. She couldn't risk waking Aunt Aubrey. The girl was right. Aunt Aubrey would wish to discuss the idea. Like as not, she wouldn't permit Madelina to go out to Mclintock's carriage but would rather insist he come in. What Madelina had to say to him, she didn't want overheard by anyone.

Madelina let her shoulders slump. "You're correct, of course. I don't know what I was thinking." She tugged out the note and proffered it. "You take this. Burn it or something." For good measure, she started to untie her bonnet.

"So, you won't go?" The maid twisted the paper in her hands.

Madelina shook her head. "It would be foolish to do so. It's hardly dawn. What honest reason could a gentleman have for appearing at such an odd hour to see me, and for not coming to the door? No, I'll stay here and wait for my aunt to wake. If the carriage must remain until I go down, let it remain."

"I think that's the right thing to do, my lady."

Madelina offered a wry smile. "I'm glad you agree. Now, would you mind readying some tea and toast? I may as well eat something while I wait."

"Not at all, my lady. I'll be back in a jiff." The girl hurried away.

Madelina watched her go before closing her bedroom door. She re-secured the ties on her bonnet and crossed to the window. At that early hour, the street below stood empty. There would be no one to see her climb out, or back in. She simply had to inform Mister Mclintock that she knew what he'd done, so he'd see why she couldn't trust him with her heart.

The climb proved more difficult in slippers and a dress than when she clad herself as Little Hook, but she made quick work of her descent. Fortunately, the kitchen windows were on the back of the townhouse. She doubted anyone would be in the front parlor. If someone was, they'd be sweeping out the fireplace, their back to the windows.

Still, it wouldn't do to get caught, so Madelina bundled her cloak close and hurried to the waiting carriage, door embossed with The Black Aspen's symbol. There wasn't a tiger or footman in sight. The driver, facing front, didn't seem to notice Madelina as she reached the door. Not wanting anyone to glance out and witness her speaking through the carriage window, she grabbed the handle and yanked.

Miss White sat inside, pistol aimed at Madelina's chest. She made to slam the door closed, but Miss White stuck out a foot and kicked. The door swung outward with enough force to pull the handle from Madelina's hand.

"Get in or I'll shoot you where you stand," Miss White ordered, voice hard.

Chagrin shot through Madelina. Her mind whirled through possibilities. She could scream. She could run.

"Run, and I'll shoot you. Scream, and I'll shoot you. Now, get in. I won't invite you again, my lady."

Madelina could see the muscles in Miss White's hand tense. Just as the night her father had chased her, Madelina read murder in the other woman's eyes. She harbored no doubt that Miss White would shoot. She climbed into the carriage.

Miss White scooted away, across the seat, as Madelina entered. "Sit in that corner and close the door."

Madelina took the indicated spot, diagonally across the carriage from Miss White. The coachman appeared. He didn't look at Madelina as he secured something across the outside of the door, then disappeared. Miss White relaxed marginally. The windows, curtains open, were not overly large. They offered some hope of escape but would not be easy to climb through. Madelina eyed the pistol still leveled on her. She'd been in such a hurry to sneak out before the maid returned, so certain that Mister Mclintock waited for her, she hadn't brought even a knife.

"What do you want with me?" she asked. The carriage rolled into motion, stirring worry in Madelina's gut.

"With you? Nothing, really," Miss White replied, her hand steady as she kept the pistol aimed at Madelina. "But I do want Jasper."

"You needn't worry. I already refused him." Madelina worked to contain a wince, for refusing him stung like a fresh wound. Using her discomfiture as an excuse, she stole a quick look out the window, marking the street, trying to work out where they headed.

Elegant fingers rippled through the air as Miss White made a dismissive gesture with her free hand. "It doesn't matter. He's in love with you, the fool. First, he stopped sharing my bed. Now, I'm losing my hold on his heart. His affection for me won't stand up to the suspicions you've planted in him. Yes, he refuted them, but they'll wiggle their way into his mind, and then he'll begin searching for proof."

So, he hadn't only told Miss White about Madelina being Little Hook, but also her accusations about Madam Dequenne. Fear joined the worry roiling within Madelina. Miss White wouldn't permit her to live, knowing the truth as she did.

A second realization drove some of the fear away. Elation shot through Madelina despite the pistol and the barred door, making her lightheaded. "He truly doesn't know you are Madam Dequenne."

"No, but he will soon." Miss White's eyes narrowed. "Now that you've planted the notion in his head."

Madelina tamped down her excitement. Jasper had still gone straight to his mistress with her words and now a very jealous, very dangerous woman sat across from her with a gun. "You must realize he'll no longer have anything to do with you, at the least."

"Oh, not only that. He'll have me locked away. Maybe even see me hung," Miss White spoke lightly.

"You don't seem very worried." The realization cut through Madelina's joy like a knife. She stole another quick look out the window.

"I'm not." Miss White shrugged, the movement graceful but the gun unwavering as it pointed at Madelina's chest. "But as you've pressed my hand, there's only one thing to do now." Her lips stretched in a slow, wide smile. "And you should know it is your doing. You've driven me to it."

She paused, seeming to savor having Madelina as her audience. Madelina steeled every muscle. She wouldn't give this woman the satisfaction of a response.

Miss White's smile only grew. She lowered the pistol to her lap but didn't release it. Leaning closer as if to impart a secret, but not close enough that Madelina dared dive across the carriage, she said, "Jasper Mclintock and I must marry."

Madelina's heart made a leap for her throat. She gaped at the other woman. "He won't."

"He will if I promise to give up my evil ways."

Something in Miss White's smile told Madelina that promise would be hollow. Would Jasper believe her? "He still won't. He'll hate you for what you've done."

"Of course, he will, at first, but once we're wed, I'll have years to win back his affection. I did it once. I can do it again."

Madelina shook her head, struggling to think through the horror of Jasper bound to this woman. "Did it once?"

Miss White's expression lit with glee. "But don't you know, we nearly married once before. He offered for me, and I accepted."

Madelina stilled. "No."

"I assure you, it's true. It broke his poor little heart when I backed out."

"I don't believe you. Why would you back out?"

Miss White waggled the gun at her. "I became Madam Dequenne. I couldn't risk having Jasper so close, or have him gain access to my finances. Even I couldn't lie my way out of that. I needed time to perfect my cover. I thought I had to choose between Jasper and being Madam Dequenne, but now that he knows the truth, there's nothing to stop me from marrying him." She paused to study Madelina, satisfaction overtaking her features.

Madelina didn't care if her face gave away her emotions. She couldn't hide how repulsive she found the idea of Miss White with Jasper.

"I suspect now you wish you'd left London," Miss White said, her voice light with amusement.

Madelina nodded, but not in agreement with the statement. Rather at the confirmation that, "You wrote the letter."

"I did."

"And you...you must know who was there that night. Who else witnessed my father murder my mother."

Miss White's eyebrows shot up. "Aren't you a clever little thing."

Much as she didn't wish to owe this woman anything, Madelina had to know. "Who? Is she still alive?"

"Not so smart after all, then," Miss White said. "It was me, and I traded the information to Madam to gain favor with her. She never had the opportunity to use that bit of blackmail, so it's only fitting that I be allowed to."

Madelina stared at her in disbelief. "You would have been what, thirteen?"

"You're too kind," Miss White said, tone flat. "Fifteen. Your father preferred his women at a malleable age. Actually, I believe he was losing interest in me. We'd already been together for some time."

Madelina squeezed her eyes closed. A deeper sickness even than Jasper's betrayal of sharing her confidences with Miss White settled on her, bringing bile to her throat. This woman, this trader in human flesh, had born witness to her mother's death. To Madelina's worst moment.

"I don't suppose it matters, but it was a shame to see such a beautiful, courageous woman die."

Madelina opened her eyes to take in the wistful look on Miss White's face.

Miss White felt something akin to regret over Madelina's mother's death? Anger stirred in her, clearing her thoughts, bracing her. Miss White had no right to feel anything for her mother. No right to any memories of her.

Vicious with anger, Madelina snapped, "So, you were a pawn in Madam Dequenne's game. You probably had delusions of marrying my father, just as you now have delusions that you'll wed Jasper."

Miss White's gaze flashed with anger. The pistol snapped back up, aimed at Madelina's chest. "I was a pawn, true enough," Miss White spat, "but you are wrong. No woman would willingly wed your father, may he rot in hell, and I will marry Jasper." She let out a harsh laugh and lowered the pistol back to her lap, finger still on the trigger. "I will have whatever I want. I am Madam Dequenne now."

The carriage began to bounce and jostle. They'd left the finer parts of London for uneven streets and missing cobbles. Madelina cursed inwardly, trying to guess how far they'd come and in what direction. She'd become distracted from watching out the window. She shouldn't have let herself be drawn into conversation.

Miss White chuckled, regaining her humor. "No one ever came close to the truth. Not in all the years the Crown, or Jasper, or that thorn in my side, Lefthook, have tried to end Madam Dequenne's reign. There is no Madam Dequenne. It's a façade. It's a mantle, passed down like a title, only better, because the chance of birth doesn't decide who wears it. Only the best is chosen."

The maliciousness returned to Miss White's smile. "In fact, shooting your aunt was my final test. She'd come too near my predecessor. Aubrey offered me an education, a life in a shop, to turn over the madam. I almost accepted, but Madam Dequenne offered me the world." She made a sweeping gesture with the gun.

"Where are you taking me to kill me?" Madelina asked, done providing amusement for Miss White.

"So dramatic." Miss White sighed. "Then, you are somewhat young."

"You deny you plan to kill me?"

"No, but I deny that I plan to do it soon. I need three weeks. Actually, a touch more."

Madelina frowned. "Three weeks?"

"For the banns to be read, dear." Miss White's tone held false patience, as if she spoke to a young child. "I might be able to get away with killing you now and simply telling Jasper I'll keep you until we're wed, but I might need to bring you out a few times to be seen. He will, of course, be rather suspicious of me."

Madelina stared at her, horrified anew. This wasn't simply a kidnapping, or even an execution. She would be held for ransom, and the price was Jasper. "I'd rather die than see him wed to you."

"How fortunate that I'm in a position to make certain of both."

CHAPTER 14

Jasper looked from the spread of papers on his desk to the closed door of his office. Thuds sounded down the hallway, the rhythm mingled with footfalls. He'd heard that combination of pounds and shuffles somewhere before but his mind, sluggish from lack of sleep, refused to tell him where. He'd already lost the effect of the coffee he'd had with breakfast an hour ago.

His office door slammed open. Miss Saint Lawrence stood framed by the dark wood of the hall. Behind her, several of the girls stopped and gaped. Jasper blinked, half certain his exhausted mind played him a trick, but Miss Saint Lawrence's livid countenance didn't disappear.

"Where is Madelina, Mclintock?" Miss Saint Lawrence demanded, her features hard lines of anger.

"What do you mean, where is she?"

Madelina's aunt thumped into the room, the raptor head on her cane glowering as formidably as she did. She slapped a piece of paper down on his desk. "Explain this."

He dropped his gaze to read.

Please give me one more opportunity to prove myself to you. I cannot live without you. We must speak —J

"I didn't write this," he said, his mind whirling. Had Madelina run off with another man? He started a list of everyone who could claim the initial J for their first or family name. "Who else courted her?" Jasper would find the cad and stick a sword in him.

"Only you, Mclintock, and the note came delivered in your carriage." Miss Saint Lawrence tapped the page where it rested on his desktop. "Prove you didn't write it."

He slid the ledger he'd been attempting to work on across the desk. "If I'd run off with her, I would hardly be here, working."

"You would be if you have her secreted somewhere nearby." She bent low, hawk nose hovering just above the page. After a moment, she straightened with a grunt. "You didn't write it."

"I told you as much." Head whirling, he ran down a new list, those who might commandeer his carriage. It was a very short list. "How long has she been gone?"

"Since sunup." Miss Saint Lawrence studied him through keen, narrowed eyes. "Your carriage came with the note. She climbed out her bedroom window and, presumably, got in. The driver told our staff that he wouldn't leave without her, or until she tendered her refusal in person."

Jasper shook his head again. "She wouldn't have let anyone force her to go."

"Maybe, maybe not. She didn't take any of her weapons, fool girl."

Jasper's eyes flew wide. "You know?"

"Know? I saw to her training, boy."

"You encouraged, nay, enabled, her to race into harm's way?" Anger welled in his chest.

Miss Saint Lawrence eyed him coldly. "She's never in real danger. I have someone keeping an eye on her." Her gaze raked over him. "But I never thought she'd sneak out at the crack of dawn over some fool boy. She was trained better than this. You're the one who's put her in danger."

Jasper drew in a breath, swallowing a sharp retort. Now wasn't the time for an argument with Madelina's strange and overbearing aunt. "Have you gone to the marquess yet? We must launch a search. Greydrake has considerable resources."

"That won't be necessary," Clementine said from the open doorway. "Aubrey," she added, with a nod to Miss Saint Lawrence.

"Clementine." Miss Saint Lawrence replied, her eyes still narrowed on Jasper.

"You know one another?" Jasper asked, startled.

Clementine strode into the room and around the desk. She stood beside Jasper, resting a hand on his shoulder. The gesture obliquely annoyed him. Clementine was definitely on his short list of those who might order his carriage made ready. "Aubrey and I are very old friends. I gave her that limp, back when I was a girl."

Jasper snapped his head around to look up at Clementine. "You what?" His breath quickened. The room seemed to throb in time with his pulse.

"Oh dear," Clementine murmured. "You're starting to understand." She moved behind him and began massaging his shoulders. "Don't worry, darling, all will be well."

Jasper shrugged off her hands and stood to face her. "It's true, then." Madelina had been correct, and he'd refused to believe her, had failed the first test of trust. Bile scalded the back of his throat.

Clementine proffered a beatific smile. "Yes, dearest," she soothed, "but I'm willing to give it all up for you. Madam Dequenne will end with me. Your goal is at hand. You've worked so hard, raised so much support and funding. You deserve this."

He shook his head. "You're a monster."

"You do insult to monsters," Miss Saint Lawrence said, her knuckles white around her cane as she glowered at Clementine, her granite-gray eyes like a bird locked onto its prey.

Jasper stared at Clementine, trying to see her as she really was. Their life together sped through his mind. Every confession. Every night spent together in bed, laughing, talking. Hopes shared. Dreams whispered. He'd been lying beside a monster. Caressing a monster.

"Jasper, dear, please sit back down," Clementine said. "You don't look well." She reached to smooth his hair, but he backed away. "Come now," she cajoled. "You know me. Anything I did or have done, was only for us. To survive. To build a life."

"There is no life built on this," Jasper said.

"What is it you want, Clementine?" Miss Saint Lawrence cut in. "What is your price for the girl?"

"You've taken Madelina." That truth lanced pain through Jasper, even as he realized he shouldn't be surprised. "Where is she?"

"She's safe." Smiling, Clementine sat on the edge of the desk and smoothed her skirt. "There's nothing you can give me, Aubrey. Except silence." Clementine's tone held a hard edge Jasper had never heard, or, he thought, never wanted to hear before. "There will be no involving the marquess."

"If you've harmed Madelina...." Jasper breathed.

"Don't think so poorly of me, dearest." Clementine's features pulled into a pout. "That isn't fair. I only borrowed the girl because you've been terribly unreasonable since meeting her, and I require something from you for which I need you on your best behavior."

Jasper crossed his arms, his heart a hard knot in his chest. If Clementine didn't hold Madelina as leverage, he'd half a mind to lift her from her seat on his desk and.... He stopped himself. He wouldn't become a monster, too. "What?"

"Marriage. I wish to be Missus Mclintock. I should never have broken off our engagement. Look what it almost cost me: losing you to some silly girl. I want a wedding. I want it done proper, with banns and a ceremony; a breakfast at your house afterwards. Your mother can come."

"My mother?" Jasper repeated. Clementine had gone mad. Or, had she always been, and he'd been too blind to see? "You think I will marry you, now?"

"Yes." She stood, clasped her hands behind her back and sauntered closer. He backed against a bookshelf as though from a rising snake. "I promise to stop my evil ways, as it were." She stepped close to him and pressed a hand to his chest. "Further, I can't free your little Madelina unless you agree."

Miss Saint Lawrence thudded her cane hard on the wood floor. "How do we know you haven't killed her already?"

A chill fear raced through Jasper at Miss Saint Lawrence's question.

Clementine patted his chest and her lips widened into a grin. "You'll have to take my word for it, of course. And if you're both very, very good, I'll let you see her the day of the wedding."

Jasper growled. "What's to stop me from killing you now?"

Clementine pouted again, a petulant, spoiled look that used to get her anything she wanted. How had he ever found her beautiful? Her lips were a slash of red, the blood-like color painted on as thick as the lies she'd worn for years.

"Come now, you're not a killer," she said. "And it's me. You know me." She reached to stroke his chin, but he turned his head away. "You're upset."

"I won't marry you."

"Because I did what I had to? Not all of us can be born to wealth. I had to build my fortunes."

"Because you are Madam Dequenne. You've ruined the lives of how many young women? Shattered those who love them. Stolen their futures." He shook his head. "And stolen from me. How many thousands of pounds have you taken from myself and my friends, funds I promised to use to help the very girls you took?"

She shrugged. "I never meant to steal from you, darling. The others, though...." She smiled, malevolence clear in her eyes. "That was part of the fun. They think they're so much better." She eyed Miss Saint Lawrence up and down. "You have no idea how much relieving the wealthy of their undeserved money delights me."

Jasper's mind raced through the years of scheming. Each lie unfolded before him, leading to another, and another, as far back as he'd known her. She'd stolen the girls, sold them to him, then pushed him to campaign for more funds as she plucked more innocent girls from their families right under his nose. If he'd listened to Madelina, if he'd seen the evidence in front of his face.... He glared at Clementine.

"I need an answer, Jasper," Clementine said. "If my man doesn't receive word from me soon, I daresay harm might befall that little lass who has temporarily ensnared you. Promise you'll marry me, and she lives. It's not hard."

"Mclintock?" Miss Saint Lawrence growled. "Time is wasting."

Jasper met Clementine's gaze. "You're the devil," he said.

A smile spread across her face. "You don't mean that, and I'll make you a wonderful wife, dearest. I won't bother you with petty concerns. We shall continue to run the club together, and it will be like it always was."

Jasper grit his teeth. She had him in a corner, but if he must agree, perhaps some good could come of it. "The girls all go."

"They like it here," Clementine said. "They're our clientele's biggest draw. You can't send them away."

He shook his head. "You said I get two things for wedding you, Madelina's life and no more Madam Dequenne. The girls go."

Miss Saint Lawrence rapped her cane again. "Madelina is waiting."

"Stay out of this Aubrey, or I'll put a ball in your other hip," Clementine snapped. She turned back to Jasper. "Surely," she purred, "the girls can decide their own fate. Isn't that what you always wanted?"

"It's what I thought I was getting, but I know better now."

Clementine pursed her painted lips into a fresh pout. "We can work on that detail later, love."

"We can work on it now."

She rolled her eyes. "Fine, the girls can go to your Second Hope or the street or wherever they choose."

"And I get access to all your finances."

Clementine's eyes narrowed. "Why?"

"You know why." He had no delusions she truly meant to give up being Madam Dequenne. The only way to ensure good behavior would be to monitor her funds.

"That, we can definitely work out later."

Jasper glared at her.

"Dearest, we'll need an attorney, and my books. Honestly, we cannot hope to accomplish it before my man puts an end to your little Madelina."

"Mclintock," Miss Saint Lawrence growled.

Pain lanced through him at the thought of harm coming to Madelina, but Jasper continued to eye Clementine coldly. "How can I trust you?"

"Consider your stipulations my wedding present to you." Clementine's smile returned. "Spend some time thinking about what you'll get me." She moved back around the desk. "Now, if you'll both excuse me, I have to get word to my friends that a certain *lady* gets to live a little longer...word they must receive at regular intervals. While I'm away, dearest, arrange to have the banns read. For now, that's the only time you'll see me, in church each Sunday for the banns." She batted her lashes. "This time apart will make our wedding night that much more special."

She swiveled to face Madelina's aunt. "Aubrey, I don't expect to see you again. Ever." In a whirl of auburn locks, Clementine turned and sauntered to the door. "And I better not learn you're searching for her, or that you've run to her brother to put the weight of his fortune into the hunt," she added. "You won't like what happens to your precious Madelina if you do." Clementine strode from the room.

Jasper sagged against the bookcase. Nausea roiled in his gut. He glanced at Miss Saint Lawrence.

Her gray eyes, clear like Madelina's, simmered with hatred. "Should you follow her?"

Jasper shook his head. "She'll have someone watching me. She must think she's won."

"You will marry her, if it means saving Madelina." Her words were more a command than a question.

"If it means saving Madelina, I will." Jasper slumped into his chair at the desk. "Getting her back unharmed is all that matters." Even if it meant a lifetime of misery at Clementine's side.

"Good." Miss Saint Lawrence turned.

"Where are you going?" Jasper asked, sitting straighter.

"My business is my own, boy."

He surged to his feet. "You must take care. If Clementine catches you interfering, she'll kill Madelina. I've no doubt of it."

"She won't." Miss Saint Lawrence headed for the door.

Jasper came around the desk. "Wait," he hissed, moving to stand between her and the door. "If you're going to search for her, at least let me help you."

Iron gray eyebrows lifted. "You?"

"Me."

"What can you hope to do and, if Clementine will have you followed, how do you expect not to be caught?"

Jasper gestured her back into the room. Expression churlish, Madelina's aunt complied, sinking into one of the chairs before his desk. In turn, he went to both doors and peered out, then closed them firmly. Jasper pulled the second chair near hers rather than going back around his desk.

He leaned close and, voice nearly too low to hear, whispered, "I have men I can trust not to go to Clementine, and ideas of where she may have taken Madelina, where I can search on my own. I've also had dealings with Lord Lefthook. I have a way to get in contact with him. A place to go where we meet. I can enlist his aid. If Clementine is Madam Dequenne, she's spent years trying to track him down and cannot, so going to him should be safe."

"Lord Lefthook, is it?"

Belatedly, it occurred to Jasper that, as Little Hook, Madelina might work with the man. Aubrey Saint Lawrence might already have a way to let Lord Lefthook know of Madelina's kidnapping. "Or will you tell him?"

"You may have the honor."

That told him nothing of Madelina's relationship to Lefthook. "Does Madelina already know him? Do you?"

Miss Saint Lawrence studied him a long moment, cold assessing gray eyes oddly similar in cast to Clementine's. Another woman who would do whatever necessary to get what she wanted. Fortunately, Jasper rather thought he and Miss Saint Lawrence wanted the same things.

"You really think you love the girl, don't you?"

"I know I do," Jasper replied.

"Like you knew you loved Clementine?"

He winced. "I admit, I thought I loved Clementine, once." He met Miss Saint Lawrence's gaze squarely. "Do you suppose Madelina intends to say she loves me and then throw me over? Is everything she's led me to believe about her a lie?"

"Girl's never been as good at lying as I'd hoped."

"Well, then, I love her."

Miss Saint Lawrence nodded. She levered up from the chair. Without another word, she started to limp from the room.

"Wait," Jasper called again. He hurried to her side. "Shall we agree to meet, in case one of us learns something?"

Eyes like granite peered at him from a lined face. "No."

"What do you mean, no?"

"I don't know you, boy, and I do not trust what I don't know."

"But, wouldn't we accomplish more if we—"

"No," Miss Saint Lawrence repeated. "You do your best. Make your plans. I'll make mine."

She thumped her way from the room, leaving Jasper staring incredulously after.

CHAPTER 15

Icy cold seeped from the stones into Madelina as she sat on the floor, legs pulled up to her chest. She tugged her cloak and the thin blanket they'd provided closer about her. She should gather up a thicker pile of straw. She'd little else to do.

The cell permitted her to stand or sit but didn't offer room to lay stretched out. She didn't know if they'd purchased or found the apparently unused gaol, but her cell exuded an ancient feel, like a dungeon of old.

Walls, ceiling, and floor were hewn from bedrock. No seams existed. No cracks. Nothing to pry loose to escape, or even to use as a weapon. Only a dusting of straw and stray pebbles met her searching hands. A stout door, a single three-inch slab of oak with hinges on the outside, barred her freedom. There wasn't even a lock to pick. Instead, bolts were driven home at the bottom, middle and top of the door.

The base of the door stood a few inches off the floor. High enough to slide food and water in and out. Madelina ate the food, trying to keep her strength. She drank the water only when they brought more, worried they would deprive her.

The few inches under the door were also enough for Madelina to stick her arm through up to the shoulder. If she lay on her back, legs braced halfway up the wall, she could reach through and undo the bottom bolt, for whatever good that did her. The door also boasted a window, smaller than Madelina's head and latticed with iron bars. Without, a torch flickered. They replaced the spent torch when they brought food. Otherwise, there was no light.

She liked to think they brought food once a day but couldn't be certain. As others had before her, evidenced by the walls, she used a pebble to scratch out a mark each time food and water arrived. Marks that would disappear once the torch gutted out. The long, dark hours gave her plenty of time to relive her final moments of freedom and wonder what more she could have done.

The coach had turned into a narrow alley, off an only slightly wider street. The carriage had come to an abrupt halt. The nearness of the buildings she could see through the windows suggested a less prosperous borough, as did the general disrepair of the structures. Both details bore out the story of the increasingly unkept streets they'd ridden over, but she hadn't seen any landmarks she recognized.

Before Madelina had time to grapple for Miss White's gun, the woman had passed the pistol out the window beside which she sat and accepted a strip of black cloth in return. She'd turned back to Madelina with a smile. Then the door beside Madelina had wrenched open. Seven burly men stood without, all pointing guns at her.

Miss White had proffered the cloth. "Blindfold yourself."

Madelina took the cloth but made no move to obey. "Why?"

"Because I've been waiting to see you tied up since the day you broke into my bedchamber."

Madelina surveyed the men. Seven to one. All large. All armed.

"They've been ordered to shoot at the least provocation," Miss White advised. "Even if they hit me, and some of them would be happy for the chance, they have orders to see you dead."

Madelina had tied the blindfold about her head. Someone pulled her from the carriage. They tested her knot and secured her hands. She'd been led through a doorway, able to feel the world closing in about her, through a building, and down stone steps. They'd shoved her into the cell and closed the door. Then the bolts slid home.

It hadn't taken her long to free her hands. She still had rope and blindfold, and fond dreams of using both on Miss White's neck. Only, Miss White never came. Just the food, delivered by two ruffians at a time, in rotation, without need to open the door. They'd fed her three times now. She assumed that meant she'd been missing for three days.

Light filtered around the edges of Madelina's eyelids. She blinked them open. How long had she dozed? She hadn't finished the series of stretches and calisthenics she completed after each feeding, to keep her body strong enough to escape. It seemed too soon for more food, but time had little meaning in the cell.

"Madelina, dear," Miss White's voice called. "Do come to the window. I want to show you my dress."

Her dress? The woman was mad. Madelina stretched her cramped limbs but didn't obey.

A confection of pastel fluff, color indeterminant in the yellow torchlight, appeared at the opening under the door. Miss White's face, shadowed, filled the little window, though she remained a hand's width away. "Come now. Don't you want to see what I'm wearing to my wedding?"

Madelina closed her eyes against the pain of Jasper's capitulations, surprised by how much his betrayal hurt. He would marry Miss White, the woman he refused to believe was Madam Dequenne. The woman he'd run to with Madelina's secret.

What did Jasper think now? If Miss White had delivered her ultimatum, he must know she'd taken Madelina. With that evidence before him, how could he fail to realize she was Madam Dequenne?

"Come now," Miss White cajoled. "I want your honest opinion." She squinted into the darkness of the cell.

Madelina slid silently across the floor, a vindictive smile curling her lips. She shot to her feet in a smooth motion. Her face filled the window.

Miss White let out a squeak and jumped back.

Darkness swarmed at the edges of Madelina's vision. She braced her hands on the stout oak door to keep from swaying but didn't allow her smirk to falter.

"That was mean," Miss White snapped, false kindness gone from her voice.

Madelina kept her eyes cold as she took in Miss White's gown, a pale, lovely confection suitable for a miss just coming out. Seeing those lush curves straining against such virginal attire disgusted her, and she knew her face betrayed her feelings. When would she learn to control her impulses?

"I see you do like my dress," Miss White said with a smirk of her own. "I knew you'd appreciate it. I want Jasper to have a perfect, blushing bride. What all men dream of. A demure, delicate flower of a girl who, come her wedding night, is a hellion in bed."

"Hellion is accurate," Madelina said.

Miss White let out a sigh. "Not that I'll be able to maintain delicate and demure for long. Women like you are so very boring. I guess that's why you had to dress up like a man and run about in the streets. Not that you were good at it."

The bars were close together, but if Miss White pressed her face to them, Madelina might be able to strangle her. That long white neck would be easy to encircle. Easy to snap.

Miss White stood out of reach, though, her expression touched with anticipation. Even though it might draw the other woman near, Madelina refused to engage with Miss White's attempt to roil her.

Finally, Miss White let out a sigh. "Fine, don't play with me. I would have thought you desperate for something to do by now, but maybe not much goes on in that pretty little head of yours. Jasper would have bored of you within hours." Pivoting, Miss White began to pace. "I didn't come simply to show you my dress, although the look on your face was delightful. For some reason, my sweet Jasper doesn't trust me. He's asking for proof you live." Miss White grimaced. "We agreed on a note. If it were only Jasper, I would write it myself, but he'll undoubtedly show it to your aunt, and she'll recognize a forgery."

Miss White halted before the door again, still out of reach. "Now, don't tell me you won't write anything for me."

Madelina pretended to yawn.

Miss White rolled her eyes. "The men will bring you writing supplies. Paper and charcoal. I don't trust you with an inkwell and pen. They're ordered not to feed you again until you give them a note." She turned up her lips in a sunny smile. "Think on it, dear. I imagine you want to keep your strength up so you can try to kill me. You can't do that without eating, and it's just one little note to ease Jasper and Aubrey's minds." Miss White made an airy gesture. "Now, I must go. I need to take off this dress. I don't want to risk spoiling it before Jasper has the chance to tear it off me."

She turned on her heels and sauntered away. The muslin gown swished against the sway of her hips. Madelina counted her retreating footfalls on stone; tried counting the number of treads on the stairs, though she'd no idea if the information could help her. A door opened and closed above. A room stood at the top. In it, based on the rhythm and pitch of the unintelligible hum she could often make out, her guards played games of chance. Likely, at least five of them, if not more.

Paper and charcoal? She stepped away from the door, lips pursed. She could think of little to accomplish with paper and charcoal. Now, a candle....

She forced her body through her regiment, pausing at every sound, waiting for her guards. Sooner than she hoped, footsteps thudded without. Something slid under the door. Paper.

Madelina ignored the offering and jumped to the window. "Wait."

The two men stopped. Her heart nearly did as well, until they turned.

"What?" one muttered.

"I can't see to write," she said, tone meek. "How can I write a note in the dark?"

The two men exchanged an uneasy look. Likely, they'd been told not to converse with her. None had before.

"Torch is lit," the one finally said.

Madelina tried to adopt an unthreatening expression. "That light doesn't make it in here. I can eat in the dark, but write?" She hoped that letters were a mystery to them, which would make her argument more convincing.

The one who hadn't spoken grabbed the other's shoulder. He pulled and they both turned away and put their heads together. She couldn't make out their whispers.

Finally, the second man shrugged. They headed up the steps. She clenched her teeth to keep from calling them back.

She bent to retrieve the paper they'd slid under the door, unsure if their silence meant victory or defeat. Something rolled away, back out of her cell. The charcoal, no doubt. Well, at least they would see she hadn't lied. She could see little.

Footsteps sounded. Hope caught her breath. She forced her limbs still. It wouldn't do to rush to the window. Instead, she called, "I didn't see the charcoal. I think it rolled out."

A grunt sounded in reply. The charcoal rolled back in, followed by flickering light. The shortest candle stub she'd ever seen slid under the door, the flame nearly guttering out.

"Write quick. You won't get another," her guard said. Two sets of footsteps tromped away.

She grabbed the short length of rope and lit its end before the candle could gutter out. Leaving the rope crackling on the floor, she took up the blindfold and shoved it into her little bowl of water. Next, she lay down and reached under the door to unlock the bottom bolt.

That accomplished, she grabbed her blanket and piled it loosely under the edge of the door. She slid the rope up against the rough fabric, grabbed a piece of paper, twisted it into a taper, then lit it. This, she carefully placed on the blanket, then repeated the process. She kept going until all five pages were alight, the first two already ash against the threadbare cotton.

Madelina backed away from her growing blaze. She retrieved the wet blindfold and wrapped it over her mouth and nose. Flames licked upward. The wood of the door began to darken. Already, the heat felt overbearing. Smoke plumes rose to the ceiling. She threw handfuls of straw onto the blaze.

Footsteps pounded down the staircase. Men shouted. Madelina picked up the little earthenware water bowl and dumped the rest of the water over her hair and face. She put the bowl down and stomped on it, then snatched up the largest shard to use as a weapon.

Water sloshed under the door. The blanket disappeared, yanked outward. She heard boots stomping. More water sloshed in, swamping her straw and cloak. The flames on the door sputtered out. Her hope died with them.

Without, men cursed. Feet raced. More water washed under the door. Still more poured through the little window.

"I think it's out," one of them said.

"Who gave her a damn candle?"

"She said she needed it to write."

"Let her write in the dark."

"The madam said we need that note from her or it's our hides."

They argued as they tromped back down the hall and up the steps. Madelina dropped her pottery shard and tugged the wet blindfold from her face. She could only hope her guards would be too afraid of Miss White's wrath to report what she'd done. She'd no doubt Miss White would place her in chains at the least provocation.

Madelina went to the door and kicked, but the wood didn't budge. Her fire had scorched the wood but not weakened it. She looked down and grimaced. Even by what little light filtered in, she could see she'd made her living conditions significantly less bearable. Her blanket was gone. Wet, burnt straw coated the floor of the little cell. Her cloak was sopping. She let out a sigh, rolled her cloak, and used it to push the mess under the door. At least the cleanup gave her something to do while she plotted another way to win her freedom.

CHAPTER 16

For the fourth time in as many nights, Jasper scaled the church in London's poorest borough. He didn't know what else to do. He'd spoken with all the contacts he trusted not to alert Clementine. He'd personally searched everywhere he could think to search.

The day before, when he'd arrived to hear the banns read, he'd run after Clementine when she left the church and begged her to let Madelina free. Then threatened, then promised.

Nothing moved her. She'd merely repeated that, should any harm befall her, Madelina would die, and reiterated her promise to let him see Madelina on the day of the wedding.

Jasper needed Lefthook. The trouble was, he had never found Lefthook. In the past, Jasper went to their meeting place and, if Lefthook was about and felt Jasper hadn't been followed, Lefthook found him.

The slightly crumbling church had been added to many times and boasted a variety of roofs, each of which could be used to gain a higher purchase. Jasper waited on a newer, flat section built off the side of the original nave and bisected by the deeper shadow cast by the spire against the nearly full moon. He paced the edge of the roof, coat drawn close against the chill autumn wind, hoping to be seen. The moon slid across the sky in a slow arch. The shadow of the spire slid across the rooftop. Doubt began to fill him.

"Looking for someone, Mclintock?" a low voice called from the deep shadow of the spire.

Jasper squinted but could see nothing in the inky blackness. "Lefthook?"

"It's hardly likely to be anyone else."

Jasper let out a relieved sigh. "You aren't easy to find."

"Should I be?"

Normally, their banter pleased him, but knowing Madelina was locked away somewhere robbed him of humor. "I need your help. Desperately."

"Oh? Another auction? I've heard nothing."

Jasper followed the voice but didn't step into the deeper shadow. If Lefthook was a gentleman, as Jasper suspected, he might be someone Jasper had met. Hence, the reason Lefthook kept to the darkness cast by the spire. He wouldn't want Jasper to come too close.

"A girl's been kidnapped. Lady Madelina Greydrake." Silence met that declaration. Jasper hurried on, "I know you don't usually concern yourself with the nobility, or even the gentry, but you must help. I'm at my wit's end. She must be found."

"Why do you think the young woman is missing?"

Did Jasper imagine the strain in Lefthook's voice? Jasper lowered his own. Secluded as the rooftop felt, he couldn't risk anyone over-hearing. "Because her aunt came to me and said she's missing, and Madam Dequenne issued a ransom for her."

This met with another silence. Jasper resisted the urge to enter the shadows, to find the man, and shake acquiescence from him. Every moment Madelina spent in Clementine's clutches was a moment too long. "Please, I've looked everywhere. Sought information from everyone I can trust. Either no one knows where she is, or they're all too afraid of Madam Dequenne to tell me."

"Have you told her brother?"

"Madam Dequenne specifically forbade informing the marquess, on pain of harming Lady Madelina."

Something moved in the shadow of the spire. "Come. Follow me. We can't talk here." More movement, and a grating squeak. "Come. Don't fall in."

Barely discernable, a lighter square appeared on the rooftop, then disappeared and reappeared as something came between Jasper and the light. He moved to it, then stopped at the edge and tapped with his foot. He almost toppled into a hole.

"I said, don't fall in," Lefthook called from somewhere below.

Jasper bent down. After a moment, his eyes adjusted well enough to see ladder rungs. Somewhere far below, light filtered through. He went around to the other side of the trap door and started down.

"Close the door behind you," Lefthook said, below him. "There's a latch. Lock it."

Jasper climbed down several rungs, then reached out and levered the door closed. He patted about until he found the latch and secured it before climbing down. A few moments later, he stepped off the ladder.

"This way."

Lefthook, little more than a shadow, led him along a dim hallway. Light seeped in through cracks in the floor. They took another ladder, then a narrow staircase. The room at the bottom of the staircase held a single lit candle. Lefthook passed it and moved to the wall, where he pulled aside a tattered curtain to reveal a stout wooden door. He took an object from his coat. A moment later, a lock clicked and the door opened. Jasper followed him through.

"A moment," Lefthook murmured. For the first time, he didn't alter his voice.

Though the words were muted, they sparked a hint of familiarity. Still, Jasper couldn't grasp from where.

Lefthook reapplied his tools to the lock and soon it clicked again. He led the way from the room down a long hall but stopped halfway.

Another curtain revealed another door. This one opened to a stair-well leading downward, light visible at the bottom. Soon, they stood in a catacomb that ran the length of the church, carved of stone and lined with candle-punctuated sarcophagi. Lefthook took up a lantern and lit it from one of the candles at the base of the steps, then led the way between the rows of dead.

At the far end, he stopped and turned back. Jasper followed his gaze. Just enough light filled the crypt to ensure they would see anyone who entered, and they were likely too far from the stairwell to be overheard. He could appreciate why Lefthook chose so grim a place.

"You said Madam Dequenne forbade you from informing the Marquess of Westlock that his sister has been kidnapped?" Lefthook asked as he set the lantern on one of the sarcophagi.

Jasper nodded.

"Then we already have a problem." Lefthook reached up and pulled off his mask and hat.

"Greydrake." Jasper rocked back on his heels, eyes wide. How.... Why.... If.... "Then, you know—that is, Little Hook and you—" Jasper squeezed his eyes shut, trying to think. "Was everyone in the Grey-drake family mad?"

"That depends on how you define madness," Greydrake said, tone mild.

"I didn't mean to voice that question," Jasper admitted, only real-izing he'd spoken aloud as Greydrake responded. "You knew what Madelina was doing?" Outrage stirred in him. "Do not tell me you encouraged her."

Greydrake held up a hand, palm outward to ward off Jasper's ire, hat and mask dangling from the other. "I did no such thing. She doesn't know that I know, or that I'm Lefthook."

"She just happened to follow your example, without realizing?" Jasper found that rather difficult to swallow.

"Aubrey Saint Lawrence pushed her."

"And you let her?" Jasper asked with growing anger. "Madelina could have been hurt, or worse."

"Has she been? Why do you believe she's been taken by Madame Dequenne? How would you even know?" Greydrake shook his head, expression clouded with disbelief. "How long has she been missing? Her aunt has said nothing to me."

"Four days, and Miss Saint Lawrence wouldn't have. The madam —that is, Clementine—said not to go to you on pain of Madelina's death." And now Jasper had done just that. He suppressed a groan. Madelina's training hadn't put her in danger, he had. First by letting Clementine know he loved her, and now by going to Greydrake.

"Do you mean to tell me that your colleague, Miss Clementine White, is Madam Dequenne?" Greydrake's question lashed out with sudden cold. "Explain yourself, Mclintock."

Mimicking Greydrake's earlier gesture, Jasper held out staying hands. "I didn't know. On my honor. I didn't know until after Clementine took her." But if he'd listened to Madelina, believed her, he would have. Jasper scrubbed at the tension in his forehead. Voice almost a whisper, he repeated, "I didn't know." He cleared his throat and added, "She's been Madam Dequenne this entire time. Or, nearly so. I'm not certain. Apparently, the title is passed down. She once worked for Madam Dequenne, but now she is Madam Dequenne."

"Pass the title down?" Greydrake repeated, some of the anger draining from him. "So that's how she's been menacing London for over fifty years."

Jasper nodded. "And we, at least I, have been looking for an old woman." He grimaced. "Clementine encouraged that idea. She often told me that, when she was young, Madam Dequenne was already old."

Greydrake studied him, expression inscrutable. "I believe you," he finally said. "But why didn't Miss Saint Lawrence come to me immediately?"

Jasper grimaced. "She seemed keen to have me tell you."

"She is fond of her games."

"At the expense of Madelina's life?"

Greydrake's expression grew contemplative. "Look, Mclintock, I don't have all night. I have to search for Madelina, but if you're going to be caught up in all this, if you're going to marry my sister, there are some things which you must understand."

Jasper nodded, caught by a mixture of anticipation and dread.

"First, I know all about Miss Saint Lawrence and the so-called training she and her former associates have given Madelina. For a time, I pretended I didn't, but that time ended when my father died. I know what Madelina's been up to and I've kept an eye on her, and Miss Saint Lawrence is aware of that."

"So-called training?" Jasper interrupted. "I ask, again, why? Why would either of you push such ideas on a young woman? Especially one about whom you care?"

"Miss Saint Lawrence's motives were simple. She trained Madelina to kill our father."

Jasper gaped at him. "I-I thought he died of a sickness."

"He did, and that's when Miss Saint Lawrence asked to send my sister back to me. She would have cast Madelina from her, my sister's usefulness at an end."

Jasper paced away, through the rows of the dead, and back again. "Miss Saint Lawrence wanted to send Madelina away? Because your father died." Confusion shifted through Jasper. "She hated your father. Didn't she love Madelina?"

Greydrake's mouth pressed into a firm line. "I'm not certain that woman is capable of love. I'm sure her lack of emotion recommended her in her youthful profession, but she didn't likely make much of a mother."

"Yet, you sent Madelina to her."

"I was only seventeen when I convinced my father to send Madelina away, and I'd no idea, then, that Miss Saint Lawrence took her from school." Greydrake's voice cracked with anger.

Jasper took a step back. He'd never seen the marquess express such high emotion. "I beg your pardon. I didn't mean to accuse you."

Greydrake sucked in a slow breath. "Let me start at the beginning of Madelina's tale, and let me be brief."

Jasper resisted the urge to pull out his watch and check the time. How much of the night remained for Greydrake to search for

Madelina? Yet, this might be Jasper's one chance to hear the truth. "Tell me."

Greydrake nodded. "When Madeline was seven, our father killed her mother. Pushed her down the stairs, and Madelina bore witness."

Jasper couldn't prevent a gasp, but he clamped his mouth closed over any further interruption.

"Worse, our father knew. He came after Madelina. He would have killed her."

Greydrake passed a hand over his eyes and suddenly, even though the man spoke of events that took place a dozen years ago, Jasper read the strain of that telling.

"I hid her," Greydrake continued. "When my father regained some semblance of calm, I talked him into sending Madelina away. I told him a girl of seven would forget. That she already thought she'd dreamed the incident. I pointed out how suspicious it would look for both a wife and a daughter to have fatal accidents, one so hard upon the other."

Jasper offered a shaky nod of agreement.

"Miss Saint Lawrence is the older sister of Madelina's mother."

Jasper nodded again. He'd known that and yet, he hadn't put all the pieces together. "That is why she hates your father."

"And why she felt the perfect revenge would be to have him die at Madelina's hands."

"Do you.... Do you think she could have killed him?" Jasper asked.

"I don't know." Greydrake's gaze focused on one of the sarcophagi, but his attention seemed far away. "I never could bring myself to." He shrugged, bringing his attention back to Jasper. "As I said, when my father died, Miss Saint Lawrence tried to send Madelina home. By then, I'd known for some time about the training. I'd learned that my sister hadn't attended school and had sent men to discover what happened to the money and where she went. I approved of her training, but not of the way Miss Saint Lawrence intended to cast Madelina aside once my father died. I went to Miss Saint Lawrence and told her that I am Lefthook. I fostered the idea that Madelina could join me with a little more training. That she could do great good."

Jasper took in the hard planes of the marquess's face in the flickering light and phrased his next question with care. "I understand you not wanting Miss Saint Lawrence to abandon Madelina, but how can you endure your sister taking such a path? The danger...." He shook his head, confounded.

Greydrake studied Jasper for a long moment. "Do you know what it's like, Mclintock, to be at the mercy of absolute evil? To be a child and watch your mother die, and have no recourse? No way to help her?"

"No," Jasper's voice came out a near whisper. He cleared his throat. "No, you know I do not. My mother is very much alive."

"Yes, I should have Lanora call on her."

Jasper stifled a half-mad laugh.

Greydrake's gaze raked over him again, assessing. "There aren't many ways to cope with witnessing such a thing. With that...trauma." His pose remained nonchalant, but tension radiated from him. "You can despair and cry. Rather, you do despair and cry. But, at some point, you must reclaim your life. This"—his sweeping gesture encompassed his black-clad frame—"this is control. Knowing how to fight? That is safety. You can never go back and change what happened, but you can prove, every night, that you'll never have to stand by and witness such an atrocity again. You will stop it."

Jasper noted the blade-sharp edge to the marquess's voice, the strain about his eyes. The old marquess had lost two wives and his firstborn son. The revelation about Madelina's mother must encompass but a portion of a much larger tale. "I'm not certain I understand any of this, but I'm sure we must get Madelina back."

"Agreed. Enough reminiscing. Why is my sister missing?"

"Because Clementine wants me to marry her."

"She saw an obstacle in my sister?"

Jasper nodded, trying not to recall flinging that same accusation at Madelina. "And an opportunity. If I'd known that Clementine still wanted to marry me, I would have been less candid."

"She offers Madelina's life in exchange for your vow?"

"The first banns have already been read," Jasper could hardly force the words through his lips.

"So, you're willing to go through with it?"

A wave of nausea surged through him. "I'd rather die."

"It's not you she'd kill," Greydrake said quietly.

Jasper nodded. "If it saves Madelina, I'll do it." Even though it would kill him inside. "Clementine swore there will be no more abductions, no more auctions."

"Do you believe her?"

"Not for a moment. She's lied to me for years." He scrubbed a hand over his face again. "I've made my capitulation contingent on full control of her finances, although I'm not sure if that's enough. But we can worry about Clementine later. Now, I need to know that Madelina is well. We must secure her freedom."

Greydrake nodded. "I'll join the search. I assume that Aubrey Saint Lawrence is also searching for her?"

"She is. She came to me the moment she realized Madelina was gone."

"Between us and her, we'll find my sister." Greydrake clasped Jasper's shoulder. "If you learn anything, come tell me immediately. You can tell me or Lanora, or our adopted son, Dodger. No one else, and not within hearing of anyone else. Do you understand?"

"Yes, completely."

Greydrake dropped his arm. He tied the folded triangle of black silk back in place, masking the lower half of his countenance, then donned his hat. Above the mask, his features fell into shadow.

"If it comes down to it," Jasper said, "Clementine promised to show us Madelina, at a distance, just before the wedding, and to release her after. I'll tell you where the wedding is to take place, so you can get to her. I don't trust Clementine to free her."

"Nor do I."

"And...." Jasper cleared his throat. "That is, if I'm forced to go through with the ceremony, tell Madelina I'm sorry, but don't permit her to see me." His throat tightened. He hoped Greydrake understood. Jasper couldn't see Madelina once he'd wed, once she was forever beyond his reach.

"It won't come to that."

Jasper cleared his throat again. "I hope you're right."

Greydrake offered a sharp nod. Leaving the lantern, he headed back down the line of sarcophagi to the steps, then up to rejoin the night.

CHAPTER 17

Madelina didn't need her tally to keep track of days. Each time the banns were read, Miss White came to taunt her, though she stayed well back from the door. Much as Madelina wished otherwise, Miss White's taunts proved all too successful. Madelina worked to keep her body strong, but her mind ate away at itself, endlessly running in circles.

At first, she longed for the chance to confront Jasper. To demand to know why, if he loved her and was through with his mistress, he'd refused to believe Madelina and had told Miss White that she was Little Hook. Anger at Jasper simmering, Madelina found solace in the idea that Jasper and Miss White were meant to be together. That Miss White was what he deserved.

But Madelina couldn't quite believe that to be true. The more she thought on it, the more she realized how her accusation must have seemed to him. Yes, he was enamored of her, but he hadn't known her for long and likely found her behavior rather erratic, if not a touch unhinged. In contrast, he'd known Miss White for years.

Now, he obviously knew the truth about Miss White, or he wouldn't ask for letters proving Madelina lived. He'd not only asked for them but demanded them. Despite Miss White's bravado, Madelina sensed a growing, seething hatred each time the woman came to taunt her. What would that hatred be born of if not Jasper's steadfast affection?

By the time the banns were read the third and final time, Madelina came to realize that her greatest regret was the day she'd turned Jasper away. She should never have halted his kisses, never rebuked his suit. Every moment that ticked by served to convince her that she would not get another chance to be in his arms.

During those weeks, they made her write several letters. They would tell her snippets of news, something that had happened that day, so she could speak on a recent event. They also permitted her to add whatever she pleased, but she suspected they smudged out anything they didn't wish Jasper and her aunt to read. It would be easy enough to do. Her words were in charcoal.

She worked the stays from her corset. Thin as they were, she could slip them between door and wall, but each successive one snapped when she attempted to work the bolts free. She doubted she'd managed to move one even a quarter of an inch.

After the final banns were read, an abnormal amount of time passed without sight or sound, save an endless, taunting drip some-where without. Ignoring the heavy darkness, Madelina went through her stretches and calisthenics, trying to keep her mind from the real-ization that no one was about because, even then, Jasper and Miss White were marrying. Miss White didn't need Madelina any longer.

More time passed, her world dark and silent, and she went through her routine again, though she usually waited until they brought food. Still, no one came. The horrible suspicion that they'd left her there to die wiggled into her thoughts.

Heavy boots thudded on the steps, jerking her awake. She hadn't realized she'd fallen asleep, her back against the wall opposite the door. Hurriedly, she tried to count the footfalls. Many pairs. Perhaps six. Maybe more. Flickering light filled the hall without. Torches, more than the usual one.

Madelina pressed to her feet, back against the wall. Relief that she hadn't been left to die flooded alongside apprehension of what might come next. Worse, the faintest hope, though she knew it unlikely, sparked that the tromping men were allies.

The top bolt grated back, then the second. There came a grunt and the bottom one slid open. The door swung wide.

Men crowded the narrow hall. Two tromped into the room, shackles in hand, followed by a third with a torch. Without, cocked pistols pointed her way. More men holding more torches stood to either side.

"They're going to chain you," the torch wielder in her cell said. "Don't fight. We've orders to shoot you where you stand."

Madelina pressed off the wall to stand straight, blinking in the abundance of light, and held out her arms. At least seven men filled the cell and hall. All large, all armed. She'd rather find better odds, unless this was her last opportunity to fight. "Why chain me now?"

"The madam wants you," their leader said. He gestured the other two men forward.

So, Miss White wished to torment her in some other place. Madelina anticipated another chance for escape, perhaps with better odds. She made no protest as they clamped cold, weighty, chain-linked iron on her wrists and ankles. They strung another chain between the two, and lead to that. One of the men wrapped the lead about his meaty hand.

"Come," the leader said. He backed from the room, not turning away from her until he reached the safety of his throng of men.

The one holding her chain gave a tug. He led her into the hall, where the others backed away. After she passed, they followed. The steps took them to a basement, in the center of which stood a table littered with cards. All around the walls, pallets cluttered the room. The odors of stale sweat and boiled cabbage gagged her.

"Blindfold her," the leader said.

Someone behind Madelina wrapped a cloth about her face and tied it tight. They led her through a doorway and down a hall, then up another set of steps. Fresher air met her seeking nostrils. Another hall and another door and a welcome, cool breeze. They pushed her up carriage steps and one of them put a hand on her head to ensure she ducked low enough not to strike the roof.

They pressed her into a seat, a man on each side of her. More crowded in opposite. The carriage sank with each addition. Several more clambered up to ride on top. She hoped they had a strong team. With a lurch, the carriage started forward.

"Where are we going?" she ventured.

"The madam wants you," the spokesman repeated.

Madelina suspected that's all they were told to say, and so didn't press. She concentrated instead on the sounds without. A lessening of jostling, creaking springs suggested better maintained roads in a more prosperous part of town.

Finally, the coach stopped, and the door opened. They ushered her out and down what had the smell and damp, closed feel of a space rarely touched by the sun. An alley. The man holding her chain tugged repeatedly. She had the impression they very much didn't wish to be observed.

They entered a building through what, based on the mouthwatering, gut twisting aromas of rising bread and brewing tea, must be the kitchen door. A steep, narrow set of steps took them up and through a doorway. They led her down a hall, plush carpet thick under her slippers. She hoped she left dirty, sooty tracks. Finally, they paused and then filed through a doorway.

"Good Heavens," Miss White cried. "Has she been writing with the charcoal or rolling in it?"

Madelina smiled. They hadn't told Miss White about the fire.

"You two, stay here," Miss White went on. "The rest of you, in the hall. Do not leave the hallway. I know she doesn't look like much, but she's dangerous."

"Yes, Madam," a chorus of male voices replied. Booted feet tromped out.

Lighter footsteps approached. "It's a good thing I thought to have a bath drawn and a gown brought," Miss White said.

Madelina's blindfold was yanked free. Miss White stood before her in the fluffy pastel dress with which she'd taunted Madelina. Her auburn tresses were arranged in perfect, shiny ringlets. She wore only a hint of face paint, not her usual garish coating.

Miss White stepped back, blindfold dangling in one hand. "Do you like the effect?" Smiling, she pivoted against the backdrop of a sumptuous, ivory and silk clad, windowless room. "More importantly, do you think Jasper will like it?"

Madelina eyed her. Even manacled and shackled, she could probably throttle the life from Miss White's bright eyes.

"Keep a good hold on that chain," Miss White addressed someone over Madelina's shoulder before turning back to her. "We must work on your ability to bluff, dear. I would have had you unchained if you'd appeared properly cowed."

Madelina maintained her stare.

Miss White shrugged. "Be that way. It matters little to me. What does matter is that we get you cleaned up. Or, rather, that you get yourself cleaned up. I wouldn't trust you with a maid."

The door through which they'd entered stood behind Madelina. Another interrupted the wainscoting to her right. Behind Miss White stood an oversized fireplace. If servants' doors hid in the molding, Madelina couldn't readily pick them out.

"Ah, yes, the bathing chamber," Miss White said, nodding to the second door. "Here is what shall happen. You are going to be escorted to the door and unchained. You will go inside or be shot. Within, you'll find a tub and clothing.

"In an hour, you will be let out of the bathing room and rechained," Miss White continued. "Then taken out onto a balcony with a lovely view. If you resist, you will be shot. If you attempt to escape, you will be shot." A hard smile curved her lips. "In truth, I'm hoping you give my men a reason, any reason, to kill you. I enjoy permanent solutions. It's something Aubrey taught me. Now, my dear, are we clear?"

Madelina stared at a point over Miss White's left shoulder.

"I'm afraid I'm going to insist on a reply this time, dear," Miss White said in a sweet, mild voice.

"Yes, Madam," Madelina infused all the mockery she could into that title.

Miss White frowned. Lips pressed into an unhappy knot, she turned to one of the men behind Madelina. "Call in the others."

The door opened and men tromped in. Madelina didn't try to turn. She'd no intention of resisting being put into this so-called bathing room.

Miss White moved near. Smile sweet once more, she ran the back of her hand down Madelina's cheek. "By noon today, I'll be Missus Mclintock, before all our guests and in the eyes of God." Glee bright on her face, she added, "Have a nice bath, dear," before stepping away. She pulled out a handkerchief to wipe her hand. Then, addressing the men, said, "Be ready to shoot if she tries to escape."

Miss White chuckled as Madelina was made to shuffle away across the thick carpet. When she and the man holding her chain reached the far door, he pulled free a set of keys. Grunting, he knelt to unfasten her shackles, then stood and unlocked the manacles. He jumped back with the chains, as if Madelina were a viper.

Madelina reached for the door, hoping this wasn't some strange trick. She pushed.

A fair sized, candlelit chamber met her seeking gaze. The room within must indeed be for bathing, as tile covered the floor and clad the walls, not a square interrupted by another exit. A large, filled, steaming tub stood in the center of the room. Candles, set on a chair rail, ringed the space. Their presence confirmed that Madelina's guards had never apprised Miss White of her attempted escape. Madelina stepped in and closed the door. A key slid into the lock and clicked behind her.

Aside from the tub, the room held a small dressing table and chair. Only towels and a comb rested on the tabletop. There was no mirror, but a pile of clothing draped the chair, slippers on the floor below.

Madelina washed her hands, then went through the clothing one piece at a time. She found nothing of use. Nor did the slippers offer any hope. She piled the ensemble on the dressing table and wedged the chair against the door, then went to the far corner to strip off her grimy clothes.

Possibly, she should take some action other than bathing. There might be something she could do to further her cause. Quietly break up the chair to create weapons. Stand on the dressing table and try to scratch a hole through the plaster ceiling. Something. In truth, though, she couldn't resist the allure of the warm tub of water. Not after weeks locked in that cell, coated with soot and bits of straw.

She washed her hair first, then the rest of her. The task wasn't quickly completed, but no one disturbed her. After toweling off, she combed out her wet locks, then dressed quickly. Her hair lay damp against her back, but no ribbons or hairpins were in evidence. Her lips twitched in a mirthless smile. Apparently, she was too dangerous to be given hairpins. She pulled the few she'd been wearing the day they took her from the bodice of her ruined gown, rinsed them, and tucked them away in her dress.

She eyed the chair. Could she break free any of the legs without them hearing? She crossed the room and slid the chair away from the door, then turned it over to examine the construction.

A knock sounded. "Miss, we're coming in. We're out of time."

Madelina flipped the chair over and slid it into place before the dressing table as the lock clicked back. The door opened. An array of pistols pointed at her. Beyond the men, the room appeared empty.

"Hold your arms behind you," the spokesman ordered.

Madelina stared at the pistol barrels. Eight in all. Would they ever let their guard down? Possibly, once Jasper and Miss White were married.

Pain lanced through Madelina at the thought, but she turned her back and held her arms out behind her. The man with the chains, who didn't have a pistol in evidence, came forward and manacled her hands. He knelt and shackled her ankles, then took up the lead chain.

"Follow me," he ordered.

The others formed up around them as they headed across the room, but none came too close. No one blindfolded her as they made their way through an elegantly appointed townhome. They went up another flight of steps, then down a long hall to the last door, centered at the end. The leader opened it, revealing a lovely rose and silver sitting room. He crossed to a set of tall curtains and flung them open to expose balcony doors. They led Madelina out.

After so long indoors and blindfolded, the sunlight brought stinging tears to her eyes. She blinked rapidly, fighting to clear her vision. The wind, too, needled, light though it was.

As her vision cleared, she realized the house stood at the end of a long street. Down its length, at the other end, rose a lovely church. On the steps stood two figures, Miss White and...Jasper.

He spun to face her, somehow aware she'd appeared. One arm lifting, as if he reached for her, he descended a step in her direction.

Miss White reached out and grabbed his arm. She leaned forward and spoke to him, the distance far too great for Madelina to hope to hear, or even interpret the movement of her lips.

He shook off her hand, the gesture sharp with anger. She grabbed him again, mouth near his ear as she spoke. The wind lifted Madelina's locks, floating those that had already dried about her head.

Miss White tugged harder, mouth moving. With her other arm, she made an angry gesture in Madelina's direction. The chain yanked. Madelina stumbled backward into the sitting room. A cry tore from her throat when the curtains fell into place, concealing Jasper from sight.

She jerked forward. The chain yanked backward. Madelina leapt away from the balcony and slammed the back of her head into the man's face. His nose gave a satisfying crunch, audible even over his yowl. She sprang back to the door, ducked through the curtains.

The tail of Jasper's coat, a last glimpse of his blond curls, met her desperate gaze. The church doors closed behind him.

"No," she yelled, fruitless as she knew it to be. "Jasper, don't. Don't marry her."

On the street below, heads tilted. Faces looked up. A strong pull to the chain dragged Madelina back inside.

"Shut that door," the leader barked.

A man walked around her, headed for the balcony door. She

jumped sideways to collide with him, but the chain tugged her back. They converged on her. Hands pinned her arms to her sides. Chain wrapped about her thrashing form. Together, two of them lifted her from her feet.

"Get her back to the bathing room," the leader growled. "We'll lock her in. If anything interrupts that wedding, we're all dead."

Madelina struggled, but too many hands held her. The chains were too strong. They bit into her. Bruised her. The men carried her away. She fought on, writhing against the image of Jasper and Miss White saying their vows.

CHAPTER 18

Jasper let Clementine tug him up the aisle between the pews. Relief as keen as pain surged through him. Madelina was alive, and the sight of her was all he and Greydrake needed. Even now, with the surety of where they held her, Lefthook would be setting her free.

Clementine had kept her word, for now.

Jasper clenched his fists, wishing he could run to Madelina, help free her. He trusted Greydrake, but if any harm befell Madelina, surely Jasper's heart would cease its beat.

Even at a distance, she was the stuff of dreams. Seeing her up there on the balcony, white, gauzy gown wind-pressed to her lithe form, silken, waist-length locks dancing about her, his heart suffused with joy.

Greydrake had promised that the moment he had her free, Dodger would enter the church and interrupt the wedding.

They reached the front of the church and halted before the vicar. Jasper eyed the frail old man, hoping he spoke slowly. The vicar gestured for them to kneel. Jasper bowed his head.

"Jasper," Clementine whispered, voice so low only he could hear.

He cast a look at her askance, head bowed. Above them, the vicar droned.

"You will marry me," Clementine breathed, words barely audible. "I let the girls at the Aspen go to Second Hope. I signed over my finances. I will have you." She shifted, ever so slightly, and the tip of a pistol appeared at a fold of her gown. "Understand?"

He dipped his head in the slightest nod. He understood her, but that did not mean he'd obey. The moment he had confirmation that Madelina was safe, he would leave. He didn't care if Clementine shot him. His life was worthless married to her.

The vicar bade them stand, then continued to speak. Time ticked by, every moment without word from Greydrake ratcheting up the beat of Jasper's heart until he grew dizzy.

Jasper's every sense muted. He could focus on one thought only, hearing Greydrake's adopted son enter the church and announce Madelina's freedom. All other sounds were no more than a dull hum. His vison dimmed, as if the world were painted over in gray. The flowers decorating the church were insipid colors that emitted no scent. Nothing was real, nothing mattered, except news of Madelina's safety.

"I can," his mother's voice rang out somewhere behind him.

"You can?" the vicar asked, voice squeaking in surprise.

"Yes. I know a reason why these two may not be wed."

"Jasper," Clementine hissed.

Jasper fought back into the moment and half-turned to his mother. She stood. Everyone else sat. They all looked at her, but her attention focused on him.

"My son cannot marry that woman," his mother declared. "Not a month ago, he came to me and told me of his love for another. I believe that love to be true." Her arm raised. She pointed at Clementine. "I don't know what evil you've done, Miss White, but you cannot have Jasper."

"Jasper," Clementine's voice was low and sharp. "I still have your precious Madelina. If you do not marry me here and now, she dies."

Jasper opened his mouth. Sound stuck in his throat. He cleared it and tried again. "Mother, I am marrying Miss White." Where the devil was Greydrake's assurance?

"But you love another. I know you do." His mother leveled a glare on Clementine. "And even though you've been avoiding me, refusing to tell me what is going on, I know this woman is somehow forcing you to wed her."

A gasp rippled through the assemblage.

Jasper met his mother's gaze squarely. "Mother, I marry Miss White for the sake of love. I swear that to you."

"You do?" his mother's tone beseeched.

"I do."

"There, that's settled." Clementine took his arm and swiveled him back to the vicar. "Please continue."

The vicar shifted from foot to foot, cast a look over the crowd, then returned to his drone. A sick, suffocating feeling grew in Jasper. Where was word from Greydrake? Had ill befallen Madelina?

Far too soon for Jasper, the vicar reached the question, "Jasper Arthur Wendell Mclintock, wilt thou have this woman to thy wedded wife, to live together after God's ordinance in the holy estate of matrimony? Wilt thou love her, comfort her, honor, and keep her in sickness and in health, and, forsaking all others, keep thee only unto her, so long as ye both shall live?"

Jasper swallowed against the dryness in his throat. Behind them, parishioners shifted. Sibilant murmurs of doubt sounded.

Clementine leaned near, a smile on her lips. "I will shoot your mother," she whispered.

Jasper didn't believe her. She wanted him, yes, but not badly enough to hang for him. But word from Greydrake still hadn't come. Jasper didn't know what signal Clementine might give, what parishioners might secretly be her men, but he didn't doubt she would have her men kill Madelina.

He mustered his voice and said, "I will."

The words rang in his ears. He cast over his shoulder, but no one burst through the door. No one halted the wedding as the vicar began speaking again.

In a numb haze, Jasper found himself saying, "With this ring I thee wed, with my body I thee worship, and with all my worldly goods I thee endow. In the name of the Father, and of the Son, and of the Holy Ghost. Amen." He slid a golden band about Clementine's finger.

The vicar once more began to speak. Bile balled in the back of Jasper's throat. Yes, he'd told Greydrake he'd go through with it to keep Madelina alive, and Jasper had meant that. But he'd hoped...he hadn't thought....

Clementine took his arm again. She turned him and walked him to the registry, then dipped the waiting pen in ink and held it out to him. Jasper's hand shook. He looked about the church again, but nothing had changed. Jasper signed and Clementine took back the pen to add her name.

Everything was done. The observances made. The blessings given. The words spoken. His bride tugged him back down the aisle. The people they passed looked at their hands or watched with pity in their eyes.

"Smile or I'll have her shot," Clementine whispered out the side of lips turned up at the corners.

Jasper tried to mimic the expression. The numbness enveloping him prevented him from knowing if he succeeded, but Clementine didn't reissue her threat.

They stepped free of the church. Jasper's gaze rivetted on the balcony at the far end of the street. It stood empty. Where was Greydrake? What had befallen Madelina? Clementine tugged Jasper down the steps to the waiting carriage.

He handed her inside, then climbed in after. He settled into the backward facing seat, across from her. His wife. A shudder ran through him.

One of his footmen came to the door. After watching Jasper for a moment, Clementine gave directions to his London house. They would go there together. He would introduce her to the staff. She would live in his home. Nausea stirred in his gut. The carriage jerked into motion.

A wide smile curved Clementine's lips. She switched seats, coming to sit beside him. Her form pressed his arm. She wrapped a leg across his lap. A smooth hand caressed his cheek, her touch barely felt through his shroud of haze.

"I've waited for this day for so long," she murmured against his ear. She trailed kisses down his neck, each one a stab of pain. "To take you not as your mistress, but as your wife."

Bile rose in the back of his throat. He squeezed his eyes closed.

"Kiss me," she whispered.

Jasper jerked free. He switched seats. "No."

"What do you mean, no?" Clementine asked, gaze narrow.

"You forced this union on me, Clementine. I've no desire to consummate it."

She pushed her lips into a pout. "You're still dreaming of your little virgin? She's beyond your reach now, Jasper. Unless you want to treat her like your father did your mother. I'd permit that."

Rage scorched his numb cocoon, set it ablaze in sparks of light that swam before his eyes. "That will never be Madelina's fate."

"No?" Clementine smirked. "It was a fate good enough for your mother."

"Leave my mother out of this."

"Why? She interrupted our wedding." Clementine tossed her head. "I told you she hates me. Don't think I'll forget what she did."

Jasper's fists balled. Heaven help him, he'd never struck a woman. Never considered that he might, but the creature before him...wasn't even human. What a role she'd played, for years. How great of a fool he was.

Her look morphed into a familiar, lazy smile. A smile that used to make his pulse sing. Now, his pulse hammered with impotent rage.

Clementine leaned across the small space that separated the seats. Her bosom strained against the overly modest cut of her gown, bulging out the top. Jasper grimaced and angled his face at the curtained window. Could she not see that knowledge of the evils she'd done made every inch of her repulsive?

"Dearest, you'll never be able to forget about her if you don't try." Clementine's tone was eminently reasonable now. A hand settled on his knee. "I can help. Together, we can put her behind you. Things can go back to the way they were before you met that waspish little beanpole."

"Things can never go back to the way they were," he said, voice low. "I know you're Madam Dequenne. I know the things you've done, the lives you've ruined. Madelina or no Madelina, I will never get past how evil you are."

"Well then." Clementine yanked her hand away. "No matter. If that's the way you see me, I may as well continue my operation and—"

Jasper's head whipped around. He stared at her, incredulous she'd admit her intention outright. "You swore that if I married you, you would stop abducting young women."

She folded her arms across her chest. "But I am a villain and a liar. Irredeemable. You only now said as much. Why should I keep my promise?"

A desperate rage flared in him. "What do you want from me, Clementine?"

"I want us to go back to the way we were," she cried. "We were happy, you and me, before that chit and her ridiculous Little Hook disguise and that accursed Aubrey Saint Lawrence came to London. Back when you wanted me for your wife. Don't you remember, Jasper? We had fun together."

"We were living a lie, only, you knew as much and I did not."

Clementine turned to the window and yanked back the curtain, then crossed her arms under her bosom. Familiar buildings crawled by. As always after services, the streets were crowded with people, horses, and conveyances.

Jasper turned to his own window and tugged open that curtain, as well. A breeze wafted through the carriage. He could open the door. Jump out. Run back to that balcony.

But what good would it do? He and Clementine were wed, before man and in the eyes of God. Even if he had her declared mad, which he just might do, he would still be wed. The only way out now was for Clementine to die.

He closed his eyes. Sunlight danced against his lids. Gray, black, gray, black, as buildings and trees blocked the sun where it hung, climbing higher. Warming rays pressed his cold flesh.

Greydrake's revelations came back to him. His father, the late marquess, a man who could and did murder at least one bride, and Jasper suspected, two. Jasper couldn't become that man. Even assuming he could, would Madelina want him then? A man who murdered the women he married, like the father she'd trained to kill? No, he was stuck with Clementine as his wife.

"We're nearly there," Clementine said.

Jasper could tell from her even tone that she'd decided to be reasonable again or, at least, present a façade of equanimity.

"When we get there," she continued, "you will alight and hand me down. You will give me your arm and walk me up the steps, and you will smile. Then, you shall introduce me to each member of your staff. I am mistress of the house now. I require their respect. Don't undermine me in this, Jasper."

Jasper kept his eyes closed, his face angled to catch any stray rays of sunlight.

"You won't like how I gain their respect if I'm forced to work for it, dearest," Clementine said. "I'm afraid my upbringing lacked sophistication. My methods can be rather...rough."

"I'll properly introduce you to the staff, Clementine, although they already know you."

"Thank you. See how easy agreeing with me is?"

He let that hang between them, aware she wished for a reply. Petty, he knew. Maybe petty was all he had left.

"Furthermore, this evening we will consummate our union."

His eyes opened. They were on his street. "I will not."

"Jasper," her tone was silken-sweet. "I still have your precious Madelina."

He turned to her. Anger seemed almost to shimmer in the air between them. "You said that when we married, you would let her go."

"I did say that." Clementine folded her hands in her lap. "I fully admit that I promised to free her once we wed." She held up a hand, raised a finger. "However, I do not believe the union to be official until it's consummated."

Jasper ground his teeth together. "How do I know that you won't keep holding her? That this is the final stipulation?" What the devil had happened to Greydrake?

Clementine refolded her hands. "I suppose you will have to take my word for that."

Jasper let out a bark of humorless laughter. "Why would I ever take your word for anything again?"

Clementine offered her sweetest, most innocent smile. "Obviously, I can't simply ask for your trust, dearest." Her smile grew, turning vicious, smug. "However, I can offer you this truth. If you do not come to my bed tonight and take me in your arms and make me believe I am your wife, I'll have Lady Madelina's throat slit from ear to ear."

He'd been wrong. He could kill her. A tightness coiled within, born of the desire to leap across the carriage and throttle the life from her.

Clementine held up a finger again. "Oh, and in case I forget again to mention it, I've left orders for just that. If my men don't hear from me by midnight, your precious Madelina dies." She let out a little laugh. "I almost forgot that part. How silly of me."

She lied. She would have used that ploy earlier. She said it now only because she saw murder in his eyes.

Clementine cocked an eyebrow at him, daring him to gamble Madelina's life.

Jasper uncoiled fists he didn't recall making. He turned back to the window. The home that let rooms on the top floor sailed past. He closed his eyes again, recalling his elation when he learned that Madelina was having him watched. That she had enough interest in him to spy on him. The carriage slowed.

"We're here, dearest," Clementine said. "Remember to be on your best behavior."

Jasper didn't reply as he slid across his seat to open the door.

CHAPTER 19

THE HANDS RESTRAINING MADELINA HEAVED. SHE FLEW THROUGH the air, hit the tile floor, and skidded until she crashed against the tub. The door to the room slammed closed. The lock turned with a click.

She lay for a moment, gasping, then thrashed against her chains. Sighting the end of the one they'd wrapped about her, she rolled away. Chain unraveled across the floor behind her. She'd no doubt they could hear the racket through the door. Hands still clamped behind her, she wiggled her way to a wall and levered to her feet, shoulders braced against the cold tile. As she stood, she could see that someone had emptied the dirty water from the tub. Only a few of the candles had burned out.

She shuffled to the dressing table and used it to tug her skirt askew until she could reach the hairpins she'd hidden in her dress. Getting one in each hand, she started the arduous task of picking the lock on the right manacle. The angle made her wrists seize with pain. She forced her fingers to keep working. There was no way to know how long they would leave her unattended. She struggled to balance haste, judicious movement, and fear.

Another candle guttered out, and another. Time ticked by. It felt

188

like more than enough time had passed for Jasper to say his vows, but with tension thrumming through her, Madelina doubted her grasp on the passage of time. Her wrist screamed in pain. Still, she kept working. There was nothing else she could do.

Finally, with a click so loud it elicited a wince, the manacle on her right wrist fell open. She brought her arms around front and shook her hands. She rubbed her aching wrist, then tried to massage feeling back into her fingers before starting on the left manacle.

The second manacle came off in moments. She sat on the floor to unshackle her ankles. Three more candles guttered out before the final band fell free.

She surged to her feet and hurried about the room, extinguishing all but two candles. Each time one went out, she would light one she'd extinguished.

Candles saved, she hurried to the door and pressed her ear to the wood. Two men spoke in low voices, but that didn't mean only two waited without. As she had earlier, she got the chair from the dressing table and quietly braced it against the door. She'd have a little extra time if they tried to enter.

She collected a candle and returned to the door, bending low to examine the lock. Through the keyhole, she saw one of the men but not the far door. If more men remained, they likely guarded the door to the bathing room and the door to the hall.

A crash sounded somewhere in the house, followed by what she thought were pistol reports. Two guards came into view as they stepped away from the walls beside the bathing room door. They crossed to speak with the man in the middle of the room.

Taking advantage of their distraction, Madelina set the candle down and stuck her makeshift lockpicks into the lock. Not designed to imprison, the lock readily gave way. In hast, she looped her hair into a tight bun and put the pins to their natural use, then put her eye back to the keyhole. Three men still stood in the middle of the room. She wished she could see the far door, to know how many guarded there. One of her candles went out.

She lit another and set it aside to return to the pile of chain she'd left on the floor. She extracted the section that strung shackles and manacles together. A nice, heavy length of chain. Not as good as a pistol, but greater reach than a knife.

Holding the chain away from her so it wouldn't brush her skirt and rattle, she returned to the door. A peek through the keyhole showed four men in the center of the room now, all facing away from her. Somewhere deeper in the house, a shot sounded, nearer this time. A man yelled.

One of the candles sputtered out. She straightened and squared her shoulders. Silently, she slid the chair away, put a hand on the knob, turned, and cracked open the door.

A quick glance showed only the four men, backs to her, arrayed in the middle of the room. Another shot came from the hall. Slowly, Madelina pushed the door open wider.

"Go see what's the matter," one of the men ordered.

"You go. No one you sent has come back," another replied.

"I said go," the first speaker growled. "Don't you get it? If you fail Madam Dequenne, she won't stop with punishing you. She'll kill your mum, your pop, your sisters. Anyone you care about. Now go."

The man who spoke grabbed another and shoved him at the door on the far side of the room. The momentum of the shove didn't carry him far but once in motion, he kept walking. He pulled a pistol from his belt as he crept to the hall door.

The remaining three had pistols, as well, none drawn. Madelina slipped from the bathing room and crept nearer to them while their attention remained riveted on the guard sneaking toward the hallway. Slowly, she passed the chain to her off hand. A shout sounded in the hall. A thud. The men flinched.

Madelina halted just behind them. She drew in a deep, silent breath. The man crossing the room reached the doorway and passed through. One of the men in front of her started to turn.

She yanked his pistol from his belt, cocked it, and fired at his thigh. He yowled as she reversed the spent weapon and slammed the hilt into the face of a man who whirled. He cursed, dropping the pistol he'd pulled free. The weapon struck the floor and an earsplitting bang filled the room as it went off.

The man she'd hit jumped back. The one she'd shot writhed on the floor, screaming, smearing blood. The third one had his pistol pointed at Madelina.

She dropped the spent gun. Tossing the chain to her dominant hand, she ducked. A pistol ball flew over her head. She lashed the chain at the man's ankles, tangled him, yanked. He toppled with a shout.

Before she could free the chain, the one she'd hit with the pistol butt charged. She released the chain and dodged. He skidded in the first man's blood. Madelina pivoted back and stuck out a leg, sweeping his. He smashed face-first into the floor.

A chain dropped over her head. She got her hands up before it tighten about her neck. Grabbing the man's wrists, she ducked and twisted.

She came up facing him and slammed the top of her head into his chin. Bone cracked. Clasping her hands, she drove an elbow into his ribs. He staggered back.

She grabbed the chain and whirled. The first man appeared to have passed out in a pool of blood, but the one she'd hit in the face staggered to his feet. Behind her, the third man cursed and groaned.

Madelina swung the chain over her head. It smashed the face of the man in front of her before he could fully regain his stance. He crumpled. She yanked the chain back and spun.

The remaining man backed to the door, hands held before him, palms out. Blood streamed down his chin. Madelina looked past him to see a lean, black-clad form in the doorway. When Madam Dequenne's man reached the door, the black-clad man hit him on the back of the head. He slumped to the floor. The man in the doorway bowed, his face obscured by a mask.

"Lord Lefthook," Madelina said.

"Little Hook," he replied, his voice instantly familiar. "You fight well."

The chain slid from Madelina's hand to clatter to the floor.

"William," she cried, and ran to her brother, skirting unconscious bodies. He wrapped his arms about her. She pulled back to look up at him. "How can you be Lord Lefthook? How could you not tell me?" She shook her head, retracting her questions with the gesture. "No, never mind. We must go. We cannot let Jasper marry that woman."

William let her step back but, even with a mask covering half his face, she read his grave expression. "It's too late. It's done."

Madelina staggered. She caught the wall with one hand. "No. We can't be too late."

William shook his head. "Dodger came in before I reached this hallway and told me they left the church together. There's nothing we can do now."

Pain surged through her. "There's something I can do," she cried. "I can kill her."

Keen hazel eyes met hers. "Can you?" William's sweeping gesture took in the room.

Madelina turned back. Three men lay on the floor. Likely, they would never be the same again, but all should live. She could have killed them. Aunt Aubrey would deliver an hour-long lecture when she learned Madelina had shot a man in the thigh when she could have shot him through the heart.

"No, I cannot," she admitted, misery eating its way up her throat to choke the admission. She didn't bother to ask William if he could. There was a reason Lord Lefthook didn't carry a gun. "But I can do something. I can go to him. We can run away together. Cross the ocean. Make a new life."

Pain darkened William's eyes. "You can. If that is what you wish, what he wishes."

"I must at least see him. Please."

"He doesn't wish to see you."

Madelina squared her shoulders. "I don't care. I wish to see him."

Silence drew out. Finally, William nodded. "Dodger is outside. He'll know where they're headed, although I suspect they go to Mclintock's London house." William entered the hall and turned right.

Madelina followed. They passed several still forms. They rounded a corner to a hall littered with more bodies. Decorative tables were overturned. Paintings hung askew. Bullet holes punctuated the walls. A wall sconce lay on the floor, wax sprayed about it and a hole in the plaster where it once graced the wall.

They followed the destruction to the front door. William knocked out a rhythm. The door cracked open and a boy slipped in. William's adopted son, Dodger, who said he was fourteen but might have been ten.

"Your ladyship." Dodger offered a bow.

"It's Aunt Madelina," she corrected, mustering a smile despite the pounding urgency in her heart. She had to get to Jasper. She couldn't allow him to settle on a life with Miss White.

"Where did Mister Mclintock go?" William asked.

"He went home," Dodger reported. "Took the witch with him."

"Normally, I'd correct you for speaking that way about a lady," William said.

"If she were a lady, I wouldn't speak that way about her," Dodger countered.

William shook his head. He turned back to Madelina. "I'll go with you. The rooftops will be the quickest way, but you'll have to work not to be seen. It's midday."

"I can manage, and I know the way. Please, could you go to my aunt? She's bound to be worried."

"I don't want you to go alone. Not with that woman there."

"I won't go inside," she said. "What can she do to me on a busy street at midday?"

"You realize, people saw you on the balcony, and more will in the street," William said. "If you go there alone, your reputation will be ruined beyond what even our standing can withstand."

Madelina shrugged. "I didn't deserve it anyway."

William clasped her arm. "You did. You do," he said, voice quiet.

William knew, she realized. He knew she was a bastard. Like Jasper. "You always maintained Jasper is good. I should have listened to you."

"Then listen to me now. Let me come with you."

"Somebody best go somewhere," Dodger said, peering out a window. "The watch just turned onto the street and they're coming this way. Probably on account of all the gunshots. I could hear 'um outside."

"Let's go," Madelina said.

"An upstairs window," William suggested. "Dodger, you'll be well?"

Dodger winked. He turned and ran down the hall toward the back of the building.

Madelina watched him go, impressed by the boy's speed. She turned to the staircase and tried to emulate him, William a step behind.

They took the steps up, then up again to the third floor. Recalling the height of the other buildings, Madelina ran down the hall. As expected, a narrow servants' stair led up to little rooms under the roof. She ducked into the first one and pushed open a small window. Kicking off her slippers with their smooth, slippery soles, she climbed through. William followed her out.

Climbing and leaping were more difficult in a dress. More than once, she wished she'd abandoned her reputation and commandeered a horse. As it was, they stayed to the back side of rooftops and rarely descended to the street. She had good reason to hope that few people saw her, and none had time to recognize her.

They came to the back side of Jasper's London home. Madelina scampered up the roof to the peak. Her heart pounded, her breath coming in short gasps. She'd never run so hard in all her life. She could barely hear over the pulse pounding in her ears. She drew in steadying breaths. William came up beside her.

"Do you think they're already inside?" she asked. The glimpses she'd had of the streets below, and looking down now, showed unusual numbers of travelers. A carriage would crawl through all that.

William shook his head. "We may have beat them."

As if in confirmation, Jasper's carriage turned onto the street. Joy shot through her. She made to climb over the peak.

"This way," William said.

She turned back to find he'd pulled off his mask and was tying the material into a cravat. He reached under his coat. In moments, he pulled free the edges of a gray waistcoat and buttoned them in front. He started down the roof, tugging off and reversing each glove as he went. Madelina followed, bemused. His hat, too, he turned inside out and patted into a nearly normal shape. Pausing at the edge of the rooftop, he unpinned tails from under his coat, letting them fall free. In moments, he would pass casual inspection. The choice of so much black would seem a bit eccentric, but then, the Marquess of Westlock was known for being his own man.

William swung down onto a garden-facing balcony. Madelina followed. They climbed over the edge, dangled from the bottom, and dropped to the soft earth. William dusted off his clothing. Madelina straightened her hair and dress. William offered his arm.

Madelina placed her hand there, wishing she had slippers and gloves. Her split, reddened knuckles belied their appearance of near normalcy, as did her bare feet. They reached the garden gate and entered a small alley between Jasper's home and the next. At the end of the alley, Jasper's carriage rolled by, slowing. In silent accord, Madelina and William lengthened their strides to burst from the alley just as the carriage stopped.

Before either footman or the driver could climb down, Jasper sprang from the carriage, expression livid. They headed up the side-walk to intercept him. He went still, as if sensing them. Slowly, he pivoted. His eyes widened as his gaze met hers. Dimly noted behind him, a footman reached into the carriage to hand Miss White down.

Releasing her brother's arm, Madelina ran to Jasper. He caught her, held her close, his arms strong about her. She felt every frantic pound of his heart. He buried his face in her hair.

"You're alive. You're well," he said, squeezing tighter. "Thank God."

"Jasper." She tipped her head back so she could speak, words tumbling out. "I know you aren't in league with her. I know you're a good man. I am a fool. A hundred times over. I should never have refused you." A sob threatened. "I wish I hadn't refused you."

"Jasper," Miss White's voice snapped somewhere behind him. "Come away from her."

Jasper stiffened. "She has a pistol," he whispered, releasing Madelina. "She'll shoot you." Pain infused his tone. He stepped back.

Madelina reached out to him. "Run away with me."

William drew alongside her, gaze locked on Miss White. "Careful," he warned, voice low.

Jasper met Madelina's gaze, a flash of joy lighting his eyes. "You would run away with me?"

"Yes. I love you."

"I said come away from her," Miss White screeched.

Madelina looked past Jasper to see his new wife standing in the street beside the carriage. A gaggle of people gathered about. Conveyances stopped in the street, occupants leaning out their windows. People murmured, pointed, stared, but none of them mattered. Only Jasper mattered, and the gun Miss White pointed at his back.

Madelina stepped to his side, then around him, firmly between him and the gun. He caught her arm and pulled her behind him. She yanked free and came to his side. He clasped her hand.

Miss White's full lips curled down in disgust. "Heaven above, you two sicken me."

"Let us go, Clementine," Jasper said. "You'll never make me stop loving her. Keep my name. Keep this life you wished for so much and let us go."

"I don't think so." Miss White's gaze narrowed.

The pistol swayed from side to side, pointing at Jasper, then Madelina, then Jasper again. William came to stand on Madelina's other side.

"Someone is going to die today," Miss White hissed. "If I can't have Jasper, no one will get what they want."

William lunged forward. Madelina dove for Miss White, Jasper alongside her. A sound like thunder rent the air.

EPILOGUE

JASPER STARED AT THE HEADSTONE BEFORE HIS FEET. SEVEN MONTHS ago, he and Clementine had wed, an act that once would have fulfilled him. There'd been a time, before his father died, when Jasper's greatest dream was a life with Clementine beside him. He took in the headstone sadly, recalling the Clementine of those days. A woman who'd never been more than a dream.

His life changed the day he'd married her. Unintentionally, he'd made himself an exceedingly wealthy man. He wasn't the only one she'd spent years bleeding of coin. She'd made a very successful Madam Dequenne. Not only through her abductions and auctions. It turned out, she also owned over a dozen brothels throughout London.

They were all closed now, the women in them sent to Second Hope, which Jasper had expanded. He'd also joined Greydrake in rehabilitating several streets at the edge of Lefthook's borough. Not so the gentry could move in, but so the residents could live better, could cultivate hope. If the change proved successful, they would expand their efforts.

Then there was the Aspen. Jasper had converted it into a gentle-men's club. No more women. Less gambling. So far as he could ascertain, a similar amount of drinking. The rooms above were rented to club members now. They were for business, or sleeping off a night of too much excess, not gilded cages for women with nowhere else to turn.

He'd thought he'd lose money. He didn't. A whole new sort of gentleman was on the rise in London. The nouveau riche, as the French dubbed them. Men fortunate enough in business to reach the ranks of the wealthy, but without the lineage to gain membership to clubs like White's. They flocked to The Black Aspen, where Jasper cared only for the quality of a man's actions, not the prestige of his forefathers.

"Mister," a voice said behind him.

Jasper turned to find Dodger, hat in hand, as he looked about the cemetery.

"Yes?"

"Her ladyship asked me to fetch you."

"How did you know where to find me?" Jasper asked, bemused. He was due at church soon. He'd stopped on his way to say one final goodbye to a woman he once loved. Ultimately, not in the way she wished, and not the true her, but still, for a time, he'd cared for Miss Clementine White more than anyone else in the world.

Dodger shrugged. "I always know where to find people, 'cept when they took her ladyship." He pointed. "She's in that carriage."

Jasper followed the boy's outstretched arm. A carriage with the Westlock emblem waited in the street outside the cemetery, behind his own.

"That one doesn't deserve to be buried here," Dodger muttered, glaring at Clementine's headstone.

"She wanted to be part of respectable society," Jasper said. "Now, she's among them, and no one will ever know she doesn't belong." He cast a quick look at the boy. "Any new information about who shot her?"

Dodger shook his head. "Only the same. Someone rented one of those rooms near your house and shot her from the window. Was a fine shot," he added.

Jasper nodded. A very fine shot. The ball had taken Clementine through the heart. Jasper, Madelina and Greydrake had strong suspicions as to who'd wielded the gun, but no proof whatsoever.

And if they couldn't find anything, the watch certainly couldn't.

Jasper shook his head. It didn't matter now. The time had come to put the past well and truly behind him. Leaving Clementine where she lay, he headed for the waiting carriage. Dodger fell in step at his side and shoved his misshapen hat down on his head.

"You know," Jasper said with a slight smile. "After today, I'll be your uncle."

Dodger cast him a quick look. "I never had an uncle before."

"Nor I, a nephew." As he said it, he wondered when his half-brother would wed. Would Jasper know Matthew's children? In the past months, they'd spoken twice. Not much, but for them, a rather large step.

Jasper caught sight of Madelina as they drew near. His heart stuttered in his chest, the way it always did, no matter how often they met. In the days to come, when he had the privilege of waking beside her every morning, would his heart still skip? He hoped so.

She smiled, quicksilver eyes alight as they met his gaze. Jasper didn't restrain an answering grin. They'd waited six long months for this day, for him to be properly out of deep mourning and for London to somewhat forget about the scene they'd made in the street.

"Dodger, could you tell my driver to meet us at the church?" Jasper asked. "I think I'll go with Madelina. You can ride in my carriage, if you like."

"Is that proper like?"

"Do you really care?" Jasper asked.

Dodger grinned. He trotted away to Jasper's carriage. Jasper climbed in with Madelina.

"My lady," he said, settling into the seat beside her.

Her smile faltered.

"What is it?" Jasper captured her hand.

"We're to wed today."

He tried not to let the tone of those words dampen his joy. "And that makes you frown?"

"I have one more secret."

Jasper's brow furrowed. "Another secret?"

The carriage rumbled forward, headed to the church.

Madelina bit her lip and nodded. "I know I've had months to tell you. It never seems like the right moment. It's difficult to bring up, because I don't wish you to think I'm ashamed, or there is anything wrong with it, but it is...." She shrugged. "There's no shame," she reiterated firmly.

He shook his head. "In what?"

Madelina drew in a deep breath. She met his eyes. "I was born out of wedlock. I am not a lady."

Jasper blinked. "So?"

"So, I thought you should know before you marry me."

He squeezed her hand tighter and slumped against the seatback. "You frightened me. I thought something was amiss."

"No, not amiss. Just...I thought you should know. In case."

He studied her, eyebrows raised. "In case what?"

She flushed. "In case you no longer wanted me." She bit her lip again, looking down.

He used gentle fingers to tip her chin up. "And if that made me no longer want you, would you still want me?"

She let out a sigh. "I'd like to say no, but I cannot."

He grinned.

"That's not very nice," she muttered. "Grinning at me."

"You said you would love me even if I were undeserving. That's worth grinning over."

"Well, stop it," she said, but the corners of her mouth twitched.

"Make me."

As he'd hoped, she flung her arms about his neck and kissed him. He tried to keep his hands from her person, aware of her carefully arranged tresses and gown. They were, after all, on their way to church for their wedding.

Or some such. Certainly, they were in a carriage, with curtains open. They were somewhere.

Or were they only there, together, in each other's arms, her skin soft beneath his fingers, her mouth warm and seeking?

A whiff of smoke reached his nose. The carriage bounced. Jasper dragged his lips from hers. "Do you smell smoke?"

She blinked at him, expression dazed. She let out a long sigh. "Oh dear, your cravat," she said and set to fluffing the crumpled garment. "Yes, this morning I burned something. I'm sorry. I thought I stood far enough back. I'm afraid I may have damaged the red parlor."

"I hate that room," he said. Only Madelina's presence could make any part of the late marquess's home bearable. "What did you burn?" He reached out to tuck up a curl. Somehow, he'd pulled it loose.

Her eyes took on a flinty look. She patted his cravat a final time and folded her hands in her lap. "This morning, I walked down the staircase, past my father's portrait, then I went back up and took him down, and threw him in the fire."

"Did it make you feel better?" he asked, wondering if she would ever shed her anger.

"Yes. It did."

He caught one of her hands again. "We haven't discussed, once we're wed, what will happen with that house."

"The Westlock family home. I don't have much right to it. William doesn't want it."

"Do you?" He hoped she would say no.

She turned to him, tension easing from her expression. "I'm coming to live with you. Why would I want two homes? William should sell it, or have it torn down. London would be the better for another garden, with some trees."

Jasper smiled again, relieved. "You like gardens and trees, then?"

"I do. I miss them. It seems like a long while now that I've been in London."

"I have a country estate, you know. Father left it to me and my mother." He said it with feigned ease, for that was another topic on which he never dared touch, whether Madelina liked his mother. She was always unfailingly polite, but then, she treated everyone that way.

"Maybe we can go there. Do you think your mother would care to join us?"

Jasper put an arm about his soon-to-be wife. "I think she would, and we'll also go there on our own. We have plenty of time to do both."

"Even though you and my brother are busy with your projects?"

"And even though you still sneak out at night and haunt the streets with him?" Jasper countered, but he didn't modulate his tone of contentment.

"Everyone has hobbies."

"Maybe, when we visit the country, you could grow roses."

Madelina smiled. "Maybe. I like roses. They're so pretty, but they have thorns."

"Petals for the country, thorns for the city?" he suggested.

"I like that idea, because I shall never be without thorns, and there is much to do to help set London right."

Jasper nodded, for that was a thing they had discussed. Madelina was not ready to give up Little Hook. While he worried for her, he loved her too much, understood too well the shadow she nightly fought, to try to stop her.

"And when we're in the country, with all this time we're to have, what will you do, while I trim roses?" she asked softly.

He squeezed her shoulder. "I'll be in the garden, too, because all the time in the world will never be enough time with you."

Madelina snuggled against him. The carriage rumbled onward, carrying them to the church where their family and friends waited. Where they would have their wedding and begin the rest of their lives together.

OTHER BOOKS IN THE UNDER THE
SHADOW OF THE MARQUESS SERIES

The Archaeologist's Daughter
The Duke's Widow

EXTENDED EXCERPT

Ballad of Discord

TARAH SCOTT AND SUMMER HANFORD

BALLAD OF DISCORD

Extended excerpt from Ballad of Discord, Book One in the
Songs of Rebellion series
by Tarah Scott and Summer Hanford

CHAPTER 1

GIGGLES AND RAPID FOOTFALLS SOUNDED IN THE CORRIDOR outside the sunny parlor. Elizbeth smoothed a stitch in her needlework while she waited for the bittersweet prick of tears to subside. It had been two years since their mother died. Laughter and joy were long overdue in their household.

"You know we ought to chide her for running," Aunt Davina said.

Elizbeth glanced at Davina, who sat across the parlor.

"She's nineteen," Davina went on. "A child no longer. When the two of you come out this autumn, we can hardly have her running about in company."

Elizbeth nodded as her strawberry-haired little sister charged into the room. Elizbeth wouldn't reprimand Margarette, and she doubted their aunt would, either. Only four years Elizbeth's senior, Aunt Davina was more an older sister than a matronly aunt and was as apt to join in their schemes as curtail them.

"The mail came," Margarette cried. She slid to a halt in the center of the Kidderminster carpet and waved a handful of letters.

Aunt Davina smiled down at her book, her bowlike lips pressed closed, her only censure to ignore the display.

"Oh?" Elizbeth looked up with feigned disinterest even as she tried to discern familiar handwriting on the flapping envelopes.

Her dear friend, Mister Robert McFarlan, was away on business for their father. Their three-week separation was the longest they'd been apart since...she fought down a blush...since he'd kissed her a month past. Although writing her was inappropriate—they weren't officially engaged—she considered a letter far less scandalous than his single, decidedly unchaste, embrace. So, she'd wheedled from him a promise to write. Though he was due to return that evening and she'd searched the mail for such a letter every day, he had been remiss thus far.

Smile wide, Margarette twirled on her toes, letters held aloft. Somehow, she'd noticed Elizbeth's recent interest in the mail and was determined to tease.

"Margarette, dear, shouldn't you be at your lessons?" Aunt Davina asked sweetly.

With a final spin, Margarette twirled over to the settee and plunked down beside their aunt. "After I see who's written." She began shuffling the envelopes. "Father," she said, and tossed two in a pile. "Father again." Another followed. "And again."

Elizbeth returned to her stitching. Attempts to contain her sister would only fuel her teasing. Perhaps Aunt Davina was correct and they should try to instill more decorum in Margarette. What man wanted a wife who ran giggling up and down the corridors of his home?

An intelligent one, she decided, who wanted a home full of joy. Not the same sort of man who would marry their aunt, but similar. She suppressed a grin. Little did Aunt Davina know, but as Elizbeth had already settled on a suitor, she planned to use her delayed season to find a man for Davina. It wasn't right that one disastrous romance, undertaken nearly a decade ago when Davina was just seventeen, should prejudice her against all gentlemen.

Margarette's sudden silence caused Elizbeth to look up. Her sister's blue eyes sparkled, her grin full of mischief. She'd finished her sorting and held two letters back from the pile for their father. Seeing she had captured Elizbeth's attention, Margarette pried one open and unfolded the pages within.

"Now, this one is interesting," Margarette drawled. "Great Aunt Saundra writes that she's returned from Italy for another visit."

"Has she?" Aunt Davina raised one delicate brow. "What is she now, eighty? I am surprised she made the journey."

"She says she wishes to see us, when we can." Some of the joy left Margarette. "She's of the opinion this will be her final visit to Scotland." Margarette blinked rapidly. "She means then to return, to die in Italy and be laid to rest there."

Aunt Davina plucked the letter from Margarette and scanned the page. "I know she's pious, but I will never understand how a good Scottish noblewoman grew so enamored of Italy."

"She is not even our real great aunt," Margarette said with a sniff. "It's not as if we will lose a real family member." Margarette's unspoken words echoed through the room: *as we did when mother died*.

"True enough, but our families were close, and she has never forgotten that." Aunt Davina folded the letter. "She's been Great Aunt Saundra since before I was born, and we shall visit her as she asks."

"Yes, of course, we shall," Elizbeth said. "What is the final letter, Margarette?"

As hoped, her sister's frown disappeared and mischief lit her eyes. "This?" Margarette held up the envelope, careful not to reveal the handwriting. "This letter must be an error. I shall have it returned. After all, only an engaged miss would receive a letter such as this one."

Elizbeth smiled before she could stop herself. Robert had written? Her soon-to-be betrothed cared more for her than for propriety, and more than he feared her father's wrath. Not that Father had ever indicated displeasure in their courtship...assuming he'd noticed.

Margarette popped to her feet. The pile of letters for their father toppled in her wake and spilled across the settee toward Davina. "In fact, such a letter as this is so scandalous, could do such harm to a lady's reputation, that I say we must burn it."

Margarette whirled toward the tall fireplace at the far end of the room.

"Margarette," Elizbeth cried before she could help herself.

Her sister turned back with a victorious grin. She thrust the letter behind her back and took two steps backward toward the hearth. Elizbeth didn't know if she should laugh or shriek. She felt caught between the girl she was at twelve, tormented by her little sister, and the woman she'd become at twenty-two.

"For Heaven's sake." Aunt Davina laughed, her chocolate-colored curls a jumble as she shook her head. "Give me that letter and take yourself off to your lessons, Miss. I believe 'tis Italian today."

"French," Margarette said, then clamped her lips closed with a grimace. She crossed to their aunt and proffered the envelope, which Davina accepted with a smile.

Although she still didn't have her letter, Elizbeth couldn't contain a smirk. Margarette hated French.

"Well, off you go to the library." Aunt Davina made a shooing gesture. "I will quiz you later."

"Yes, Aunt Davina." Margarette made a great show of becoming somber before she smiled and skipped from the room.

Aunt Davina gathered the scattered letters, placed Elizbeth's on top, and held out the stack. "Will you take these to your father? He likely wishes to have his mail."

Elizbeth set aside her needlepoint and stood. Eyes on the top envelope, she took the pile and hurried from the parlor. She reached her father's office to find the door closed. The thick wood panel shutting him away meant he didn't wish to be disturbed, so Elizbeth deposited his mail on the small table outside his office door. She couldn't help but recall a time when their golden-haired mother had been alive and his door was always open. Elizbeth sighed. Mother was not alive, and their father's office door was nearly always closed.

She turned from the door to find Mary hurrying toward her. The maid took in the closed office and proffered a card. "There is a Frenchman here to see your father, Miss. Claims he's a lord of some sort, or I wouldn't have let him in."

Elizbeth took the card. Etched on the surface was simply *Seigneur Faucon*.

Lord Hawk, she thought, her French considerably better than Margarette's.

She looked at the maid. "Do you think he truly is a French lord?" A lord would be worth disturbing her father.

"Well, Miss, he seems quite fancy, to be sure, and very French." This last, Mary delivered with a wrinkle of her nose.

"Show him to my office," came her father's clipped voice behind the closed door.

Elizbeth winced. She'd forgotten about her father's keen hearing. She offered the card back to Mary. "Bring him to Father."

"Yes, Miss." Mary took the card and scuttled away.

Elizbeth stood for a moment, gaze on the door. Should she ask her father if he needed anything? He had a bell pull, and servants to fetch for him, but since their mother's death, he'd taken to skipping breakfast. Now, they rarely saw him outside the dinner table, if then. She shook her head. He knew she was there. If he wanted to see her, he would ask her in. Besides, she had Robert's letter to read.

Elizbeth turned on her heels. Though guilt assailed her, she went to the little room that had been her mother's office. She withdrew the key from her bodice—a key none knew she possessed—opened the door, and slipped inside.

Stuffy heat warmed her arms. Her mother had kept the window open nearly year-round. Elizbeth preferred the fresh air, as well. Today, however, she dared open the curtains and beveled panes just enough for a sliver of light and a flicker of breeze. She couldn't risk being caught. Her father, who thought he had the only key, would be livid.

Elizbeth understood his feelings. He wished this room, where Mother was once so often found, to remain undisturbed, in some fruitless hope to preserve a glimmer of her spirit. But it didn't. When mother was alive, light poured in through the open window. Her household notes and correspondences lay scattered about the desk and the second table, which overcrowded the little room. Father had pressed her to take one of the parlors for her office, but Mother liked her cramped little space with its lavender walls and flowery upholsteries.

Now, desk and table were bare, their papers long since sorted by Aunt Davina. After Mother's death, Aunt Davina arrived with their wayward, unpredictable Uncle Graham, and she'd taken over running the household. While Elizbeth appreciated Aunt Davina and was daily grateful for her competence, she had no real notion why Uncle Graham was there. All he did was soak up Father's whisky—when he could pry himself away from his harlots long enough to come home.

Shrugging off her now-grim mood, Elizbeth settled into the armchair by the window. She ran a finger along Robert's concise handwriting then, carefully, she opened the envelope. This was her first letter from Robert and she wished to cherish every word.

Elizbeth:

As promised, I am writing. I comply only because I abhor breaking a promise. However, I must remind you how inappropriate it was for you to ask me to write. Your father would be displeased not only that you asked me, but that I allowed you to extract my promise to write. Be warned, in the future, I will not give in to your pleading.

Elizbeth rolled her eyes. If there was one little flaw in Robert, it was that he was too serious, but that was also what she cherished about him. His seriousness drew her in. To call forth his laughter made her heart sing, and she knew, when Robert spoke, he meant each word. Still, he could stand to be a touch less severe.

Her eyes went to the final line.

With the very greatest affection, yours always, Robert.

Elizbeth pressed the letter to her chest. Those words made the rest of the letter worthwhile. Her gaze caught on the quill sitting on the desk. The quill had been her mother's favorite. Tears unexpectedly pricked. It was terribly unfair that she had died without seeing

Elizbeth fall in love. Elizbeth recalled the delight in her father's eyes whenever her mother walked into the room. Elizbeth wanted a love like that. She'd found a love like that.

"You would have loved him as much as I do, Mother," she whispered.

Elizbeth held the page back in the line of sunlight to reread the short missive.

"This request to speak in the garden is ridiculous," her father's voice, speaking French, emanated from somewhere outside, near the window.

Elizbeth snapped her head up.

"Not ridiculous, but necessary," a man replied in the same tongue. "The manor has ears."

"I assure you, none of my staff speak your language," her father snapped back. "Half of them barely speak English."

Movements slow, least the chair creak, Elizbeth grasped the window and drew it back toward the sill. Father would not appreciate being made a liar of.

"Humor me, *Seigneur*, for my news is life shaking," the Frenchman said. "Any who hear it will face mortal danger."

The window clicked quietly closed, muting her father's reply into unintelligibility.

Face mortal danger? Elizbeth would have laughed had *Seigneur* Faucon's tone not been deadly serious. What news could possibly be of such importance? Her fingers tightened on the latch. She hesitated a heartbeat, then drew her hand back.

Eavesdropping was unacceptable. Doubly so when the two men were going to great lengths not to be overheard, and especially if the information they shared was truly somehow dangerous. If the Frenchman's words were for Father's ears alone, Father alone should hear them.

A thought struck. The library windows also opened onto the garden. Margarette!

Elizbeth surged to her feet. She folded and tucked Robert's letter into her skirt pocket as she crossed the room. She poked her head into the corridor—empty, as hoped. She slipped from the room and hurried down the hall.

Halfway to the library, she came up short. Lord, she'd forgotten to lock the door. Elizbeth hurried back and secured her mother's office, then again headed toward the library. She pushed the door open, stepped in, and nearly collided with Margarette. Elizbeth stumbled back.

Her sister recoiled. "Elizbeth," she cried. "You cannot believe what I heard."

Elizbeth contained a sigh. She leveled a frown on her sister. "You listened in on Father's private conversation."

Margarette gaped. "How do you know?"

"I heard them talking and came to stop you." Elizbeth grasped her sister's arm and pulled her into the center of the large room, away from windows or door, then realized the Frenchman's words had truly rattled her. "It is wrong to eavesdrop."

Margarette yanked free. "I do not care. 'Tis a good thing I heard. I don't want to go." Margarette's voice broke off in anguished tears.

Elizbeth stared. "Go where?"

"To France," Margarette cried.

"Why would you be going to France?" Elizbeth asked, unable to follow Margarette's tearful declarations.

"The Frenchman said we must." Margarette rubbed at her eyes. "He said we are to marry Frenchmen so Father can have an army."

"What under Heaven are you talking about?" Elizbeth demanded. "What do you mean, 'we'?"

"You, me and Aunt Davina," Margarette said. "Father is going to send us to France so they will send back an army to help him become king of Scotland."

"Margarette," Elizbeth hissed. "Do not say such things. That is treason. Stop making up stories."

Margarette lifted her chin. "It is not a story. The Frenchman said Father is the secret descendent of the Jacobite kings, and so we are princesses—which would be great fun—except that France sent him with a ship to take us away."

Elizbeth planted her hands on her hips. "Did you fall asleep over your lessons?"

Margarette grimaced. "Aye, because French is so boring, but that is *not* the point."

"It is exactly the point," Elizbeth corrected. "That is what you get for eavesdropping—and for not studying properly. Your French is terrible, which is why you so badly misunderstood their conversation."

Despite her admonition, a thread of unease wound through Elizbeth. Margarette might not speak French well, but Elizbeth did, and she hadn't misunderstood the Frenchman's warning about mortal danger.

Margarette's gaze sharpened. "You heard something, too."

Elizbeth groaned inwardly. Margarette eschewed books, but she was too intelligent for her own good.

"If I am wrong, why were they talking in the garden rather than Father's office?" Margarette demanded.

"There could be many reasons," Elizbeth said, but doubt persisted. While Margarette's story was obviously a mad mixture of dream and miscomprehension, the meeting was odd. Why was a French lord speaking with their father to begin with?

"My French may be atrocious, but I comprehend much more than I speak," Margarette said. "I know what I heard. We cannot let Father send us away to France. Especially you. What about Robert?"

"Mister McFarlan," Elizbeth corrected absently as she sought to make sense of Margarette's story.

"We must warn Aunt Davina," her sister urged. "The Frenchman said they want her, too." Elizbeth shook her head and started to tell Margarette to return to her French lesson, but Margarette grasped her hand. "Please, we must tell Aunt Davina."

The fear in Margarette's eyes stopped the refusal that leapt to Elizbeth's lips. Margarette feared nothing.

Elizbeth gave her hand a gentle squeeze. "You must try to see that you dreamed up this silly story."

Margarette stubbornly shook her head. "Aunt Davina can decide."

Elizbeth bit her lip. Their aunt was forgiving, but eavesdropping on Father's private conversation was a graver transgression than running down a hallway.

Margarette's hand clutched harder. "Elizbeth, I am afraid."

"We may have to tell Aunt Davina," Elizbeth allowed. "Or we may be able to keep your misbehavior between us. Tell me everything you think you heard, as near the original as you can, in French, and I will decide."

Margarette hesitated, then nodded and launched into her tale.

CHAPTER 2

Davina closed Debrett's *The New Peerage*. She weighed the etiquette book in her hands. Debrett's, and all of Britain, agreed that a proper chaperone must be wedded or widowed.

Due to Bhradain's betrayal, Davina was neither.

Mister Haywood, she corrected. He never should have been Bhradain to her. After nine years, some other woman must have the honor of addressing Mister Haywood by his Christian name.

She rubbed eyes tired of reading Debrett's dry, restrictive words. Across the room, the mantle clock ticked off slow minutes. The dinner hour approached, and Elizbeth hadn't returned. Margarette wouldn't. She would hide from a French exam for as long as possible. If the girl devoted as much effort to learning the language as she did to avoiding her lessons, she would be fluent.

Elizbeth, though, should have returned to her sewing. The envelope from Mister McFarlan had been thin. How many words could the page contain, and how many times could Elizbeth possibly read them? Davina considered fetching her niece.

A smile flittered across her lips. Elizbeth, as conscientious a young woman as Davina had ever met, thought no one knew where she hid when she wished to be alone. Sweet Elizbeth had no idea Davina—

who had never been very well behaved—routinely followed, snooped, and spied on her nieces. In their best interests, of course.

She drummed her fingers on the book in her lap. Nae, Debrett would never condone her as a chaperone. But she was all her nieces had, and she was determined to safeguard their wellbeing.

Which brought her to Mister McFarlan. A kind man. Intelligent. An attorney. Not a true gentleman, though from a genteel family. Born the same year as Davina, so not too old for Elizbeth, nor so young as to be foolish. In truth, she felt him a good match for her niece. There would be no trouble there, except that Davina had no idea how her eldest brother felt about the notion of his daughter wedding one of his attorneys.

One might assume, as James permitted the courtship to continue, he was pleased. That would be, if one didn't know James. Or rather, the man he'd become since Maryanne's death. With his wife's passing, James had lost all attachment to the world. Like as not, he hadn't noticed the glaringly obvious affection between his daughter and the attorney.

Hurried footfalls, growing in volume, sounded in the hall without. Davina stilled her fingers. The footsteps were too heavy to be Elizbeth or Margarette. Her brother James burst into the parlor. His gaze darted about the small room, minnow-like. A strange pallor had leached all color from his face and his normally neat brown hair was wind tossed, as if he'd been outdoors. Of late, James never went outdoors.

"Whatever is the matter?" She set the book aside and rose. "James?"

"Where are my daughters?" he barked.

"Not here, as you can see. Is something amiss?" In view of his distress, she tried to keep a check on her temper, a thing more easily accomplished were it not the case that James was continually brusque these days. "James?" she repeated.

"What? Nae. Nothing is amiss." He raked long fingers through his dark hair.

At forty, James was still a handsome man. Only a hint of gray touched his temples and his broad shoulders and arms were well muscled. Unlike many other men his age, he had no paunch. She saw the way women looked at him, even young women. He could find happiness again. If only he would try.

He looked about the room again. "Where did you say they are?"

"Margarette is most likely in the library." She would not betray Elizbeth's secret. He would be furious should he learn his daughter possessed a key to her mother's office. "I have no notion where Elizbeth is."

James's mouth thinned. "Is not your one purpose in this household to know where my daughters are?"

She tamped down harder on her anger. "Indeed. Shall I launch a search, or would you rather wait an hour and see if they join us for dinner?"

His frown deepened into a scowl. "A husband would have curbed your tongue years ago. But I suppose it's better this way." He turned on his heel and stomped from the room.

Davina stared at the empty doorway. "That was rude even for James," she murmured.

Should she go after him? Was something truly amiss, aside from his self-absorbed sorrow over Maryanne? Before she could decide, new footsteps filled the corridor. Recognizing both sets, Davina retook her place on the settee. Perhaps the answers were on their way to her.

"Aunt Davina." Much as her father had, Margarette hurtled into the room.

Behind her, Elizbeth entered, her lovely face marred by worry and her steps considerably more graceful. Instead of sitting, they stopped before Davina. She looked up at them, expectant.

"Aunt Davina, Margarette has overheard something that concerns us," Elizbeth's voice was grave.

"Overheard?" Davina cocked a brow. "How did you manage that, dear?" Davina understood all too well how one *overheard* things.

Margarette had the grace to blush. "I did not do it on purpose. I was in the library, studying French. I truly was."

Davina nodded.

"The window was open, and Father and that Frenchman started talking in the garden."

"Frenchman?" Davina asked.

"Yes," Elizbeth said. "He arrived shortly after we left you, and asked to speak with Father. He gave the name Seigneur Faucon."

"Lord Hawk?" Davina didn't like the sound of that. The name was obviously false. She turned back to Margarette. "What did this Lord Hawk have to say to your father, and how does it concern you both?"

"It concerns you as well." Margarette popped up on her toes as she spoke, hands clasped before her. She shot Elizbeth a look.

"Tell her," Elizbeth ordered. "Only, do try to make sense."

"He said it all in French." Margarette scrunched her nose. "Elizbeth says I must repeat it as nearly as I heard, so you may interpret the words for yourself, since my French is abominable." This last, she accompanied with a supplicative glance upward.

Davina didn't know if she should be amused or alarmed. James's harried visage came to the forefront of her thoughts. "Let's have it, then."

Margarette embarked on a monologue. She used two voices, one apparently her idea of her father and the other the Frenchman. Some of the syllables that left her mouth resembled no language.

As Davina took in the half-intelligible babble, her pulse quickened with each word. Lord Hawk had told James he was the descendent of Henry Benedict Stuart, Cardinal-Duke of York, and the last of the Jacobite kings? Davina clenched her hands in her lap, for the tale grew even stranger. Seigneur Faucon had asked, and James agreed, to be given custody of her, Elizbeth and Margarette. He planned to take them and their considerable dowries to France and marry them to men of power. Their new husbands would raise an army, and return with it to Scotland, to fight for James, the Jacobite king. Davina stared up at her nieces. Tall, lovely young women whose hands would be a prize for any man but...princesses?

"And then they went deeper into the garden," Margarette concluded.

Davina looked at Elizbeth. "You heard none of this?"

She shook her head. "Nae, but I did hear the Frenchman say they must discuss something very secret and dangerous."

Margarette stared, her blue eyes filled with uncharacteristic worry. "Aunt Davina, what are we going to do?"

Davina shook her head, dazed. She had no idea. "You are sure that is what they said? You weren't dreaming? I know how French puts you to sleep."

Margarette blew out a frustrated breath. "I repeated the words to you—badly, I might add. How could I have dreamt all that? I don't even know some of those words. Please, I do not want to go off to marry some horrible French lord."

Davina scrubbed at her forehead. It couldn't be true. They were not royalty, not even gentry, though possessed of considerable wealth. Even if Margarette had heard correctly, it simply couldn't be true. The most shocking part was that James might believe any of the tale. His frantic eyes, his pallor, rose in her memory.

"Let me think on this. Please," she murmured.

"Yes, of course," Elizbeth said.

"But, what if Father tries to send us away?" Margarette demanded.

"He will hardly have us abducted," Davina soothed. "Go ready for dinner. We will see how your father is then. Like as not, he'll tell us the tale of this strange Frenchman and his bizarre ideas, and we will all laugh together. Tomorrow, Seigneur Faucon will be but a memory."

Elizbeth smiled. "You are quite correct, of course." Margarette looked mutinous, but Elizbeth caught her arm and tugged her toward the door. "We'll see you at dinner, Aunt Davina."

"Yes," Davina murmured absently as they stepped from the room into the hall.

She hadn't wanted to further alarm her nieces by speaking of their father's odd behavior, but there was someone to whom she could report the entire series of events. Her brother, Graham. Davina rose and went in search of him.

Davina found her brother sprawled face down and shirtless atop his bed. Beside him, curled to one side and, blessedly, fully clothed, though grass clippings decorated slippers and hem, lay a blonde woman Davina had never before seen. Nor, if she knew Graham, would she ever see the woman again.

Nose wrinkled at the stale sweat that permeated the chamber, Davinia crossed the room to the window. She yanked back the curtains and unlatched the windows. As fading daylight and fresh air spilled in, a groan sounded behind her.

"Davinia, what the devil are you doing?"

She turned to find Graham seated on the edge of his bed. The blonde, snoring softly, didn't stir. Graham blinked rapidly, eyes blood-shot in a face still striking, despite his lack of sleep and what had undoubtedly been an abundance of whisky. Bare chested as he was, Davinia was reminded why her brother remained a favorite of the ladies. She would have thrown a shirt at him, but the one discarded on the floor looked too sweat-infused to touch.

"What am I doing?" she repeated. "I am here to tell you to ready for dinner. You have avoided consciousness long enough for today."

He pushed a hand through tangled brown locks, then cast a look over his shoulder. When he turned back, he wore a perplexed frown, as if he didn't quite know what to make of the unconscious blonde.

"Consider me told, sister dearest."

"That is not all," she said in clipped tones. "I must also, though Heaven knows why I bother, ask your opinion on a matter that may be significant."

Graham groaned and fell backward onto the bed. He fumbled for a pillow, found one, and pulled it over his face.

Davinia hurried back to the bed and kicked him in the shin. "Graham, this is important."

He lifted one half of the pillow. "I'm listening." He dropped the down-stuffed fabric back into place.

"I cannot very well discuss this in front of her." Davinia waved at the woman on the bed.

Graham lifted the pillow and craned his neck. Again, that perplexed look crossed his face.

"You *do* know her?" Davinia's voice dripped sarcasm.

"I suppose I must." He stretched out an arm and poked the slumbering woman in the shoulder.

Thick lashes fluttered open. Blue eyes focused on Davinia. "Hello."

With one word, the woman revealed her English origins. Davinia grimaced. Leave it to Graham to bring home an Englishwoman. Offering Davinia a shrug, he tucked the pillow under his head. The Englishwoman sat up and looked about, appearing just as perplexed as Graham.

"Hello, Miss…" Davinia let her voice trail off in question.

"Ingram." She offered a bright smile. "Anastacia Ingram. And you are?"

Davinia bit back a sharp retort. "Miss McKinley. If you could excuse my brother and me, Miss Ingram, I should like to speak with Graham alone."

Miss Ingram's head snapped toward Graham. "*You* are Graham McKinley?" She frowned. "I was told to stay away from you. You're a terrible rake."

"Posh." Graham smiled his most charming smile and tucked his clasped hands behind his head. "If I am such a rake, why are we clothed?"

Miss Ingram looked about again. "If you aren't a rake, why am I in this bed?"

"I haven't the foggiest." Graham shrugged. "But if you would care to remain, I can think of several ways to test my fortitude. We must put this rake business to rest."

"Graham," Davinia snapped. Between James's half-madness since losing Maryanne and Graham's devotion to sin, Davinia sometimes felt as if she were responsible for the entirety of their family's well-being—and sanity.

Graham pointed toward the door across from the bed, leading to an antechamber. "Go in there, sweetheart, and ring for a servant to ready you a bath. I will come to you shortly."

Miss Ingram stood. She tugged her skirt straight and squared her shoulders. She was tall for a woman, her build slender. "I will give you your privacy, but you will not find me waiting for you in the bath." Her blue eyes snapped. "Just because we ended up in this bed, does not mean I am here for your frivolous pleasure, sir." She cocked her chin in the air and marched from the room.

Graham watched. A slow smile stretched across his face.

"You have no idea who she is or how you both ended up here?" Davinia asked once the door clicked shut behind the woman.

"You heard her. She's Miss Anastacia Ingram."

Davina had a few choice things to say about that, on the heels of which, she launched into the details of both their nieces' story and her encounter with James. Halfway through, Graham's brow furrowed. By the time she finished, he sat upright on the edge of the bed, his features hard with thought.

"I suppose it is possible," he murmured.

"That we are decedents of the Stuart family and James is a Jacobite king?" Davinia snorted. "Hardly. My only fear is James might believe the mad tale and turn our nieces over to some strange Frenchman. Likely, this is some sort of ransom plot to get at his wealth."

Graham regarded her with worried eyes. "And you."

"Me what?"

"If he really believes the Frenchman's tale, he could turn you over as well."

"I am six and twenty. I am no more subject to James's will than I am to that of a random passerby." *Unlike Elizbeth and Margarette.*

Graham shook his head. He levered himself to his feet, towering over her. "I cannot imagine James being taken in by some Frenchman's tale. Besides, Margarette likely dreamt the whole thing."

Davinia nodded. For all his debauchery, Graham was dependable when it came to family, and he, if anyone, knew their older brother well. "Of course, you are correct. I am going to prepare for dinner." She glanced toward the door through which Miss Ingram had departed. "Do not let your English harlot keep you."

"She is not a harlot. She is Miss Anastacia Ingram."

Davinia raised her brows. "Graham, I found her asleep in your bed. She is a harlot." Without another word, she left the room.

CHAPTER 3

ELIZBETH ENTERED THE DINING ROOM ARM IN ARM WITH Margarette. As with every informal meal, Aunt Davina sat at her place to the right of their father's seat, which, as usual, stood empty. A small measure of relief loosened the knot in Elizbeth's stomach at sight of her Uncle Graham. He occupied his place at the opposite end of the table. He met her gaze and gave a reassuring smile.

Elizbeth's pulse skipped a beat.

He knows.

Aunt Davina must have told him what Margarette heard. That meant Aunt Davina was worried. Was Uncle Graham there to ensure their father didn't send them to France? Elizbeth took her seat to the left of her father's chair. Was it really possible he might agree to marry them to strangers? What of Robert? Surely, her father wouldn't tear her from the man she loved. Robert would never permit it. Her stomach cinched tighter. Could he stop Father?

Margarette sat beside her. "Father isn't here," she said, tone relieved.

Elizbeth fought to keep her thoughts clear. His absence had to be a good sign, didn't it? She exchanged a glance with Davina. Her aunt smiled encouragingly.

Margarette leaned close to Elizbeth. "Do you think he has already ordered our trunks packed?" she whispered.

"Hush," Elizbeth hissed.

Three maids entered, each carrying platters of food, but Elizbeth scarcely paid attention as they filled her plate.

"You appear refreshed, Graham," Davina said.

He laughed. "I always appear refreshed."

Davina gave him a look Elizbeth couldn't interpret. Were they mentally communicating about Father?

"Aren't you hungry, Elizbeth?" Margarette asked.

"Are you ill?" Uncle Graham regarded Elizbeth.

He waited, expression gentle. He was a good uncle. He looked out for them, particularly since her mother's death and their father's retreat from the world. He would never allow Father to send them to a foreign country to marry strangers.

She shook her head. "Nae. I am just not particularly hungry tonight."

His eyes twinkled. "I smelled blueberry buns baking earlier. Surely, you want one? No one makes a better bun than our Missus Henderson."

She smiled. Uncle Graham always made her feel better. "I do love blueberry buns."

He winked. "I know. At least taste a bit of the pheasant. It is quite good."

"I will."

She was being silly. She'd allowed Margarette's dream to influence her reality. She forked a piece of pheasant and lifted it to her mouth, then halted when Father strode into the room.

"Well, this is a pleasant surprise." Uncle Graham lifted his glass of wine and downed a mouthful.

Ignoring his brother, James looked about the room. His gaze fell on the waiting servants. "Leave us, and ensure neither you nor any other stand outside these doors, on pain of death," he said, voice grim enough to send a shiver down Elizbeth's spine. "I will ring when you may return."

Eyes wide, the staff hurried out. Elizbeth watched them depart with mounting fear, a fear reflected in Margarette's eyes. Aunt Davina stared at their father through narrowed eyes. Uncle Graham leaned back in his chair, expression sober.

Her father went to the hall door, then to the servants' door, peering out each before closing them firmly. Finally, he took his seat. "I am glad everyone is here. That will save me the trouble of having to repeat this announcement."

Aunt Davina exchanged a look with Graham.

Elizbeth's uncle turned and met her father's gaze. "You look far too serious, James. Have some wine." Graham lifted his glass again and emptied its contents.

To many, the action would appear cavalier. Elizbeth knew better. Her uncle's keen mind seldom dulled, even with great quantities of liquor.

Her father reached for a nearby platter of potatoes and spooned some onto his plate. "You could use with a dose of responsibility, Graham," he said. "But that will come soon enough." He reached for the decanter of wine.

"Responsibility?" Graham repeated. "It's rather too late for that, don't you think?"

Her father slowed in filling his glass and flicked a glance at his brother. "You had best hope not." He set the decanter down, stabbed a slice of pheasant, and transferred it to his plate. He began cutting the meat. "What I am about to tell you, remains between us." He flicked a glance at Graham.

"Surely, you are not accusing me of being a gossip monger?" Graham laughed.

"No man can be assured of keeping his own counsel when he drinks too much."

Uncle Graham laughed again. "I heartily agree. Luckily, I never drink too much." He reached for the decanter and refilled his glass.

Aunt Davina shot him a warning look.

James forked pheasant into his mouth. "I will get straight to the heart of the matter. Our great Aunt Saundra is not truly our aunt."

"If that is your big announcement, then it is you who have been drinking too much," Uncle Graham said.

Her father didn't so much as glance at him. "In fact, Saundra is our" —he pointed his knife at Davina, Graham and himself— "grandmother, and you girls' great-grandmother." The knife darted menacingly toward Elizbeth and Margarette.

Aunt Davina gasped in unison with Margarette's cry of surprise. Elizbeth could only stare. What they'd overheard indicated nothing like *this*.

"What could possibly give you that idea?" Graham asked.

"I have seen the ledgers, records of marriages, of real names and births," her father replied.

Graham regarded him. "Why are we only learning of this now?"

Her father ate more pheasant. "Because her husband, Henry Benedict Stuart, Cardinal Duke of York, was still living."

Even Elizbeth couldn't refrain from a loud gasp this time.

"*James*," Davina breathed, "Henry Stuart never married. He was a priest, sworn to celibacy."

"Davina is correct," Graham said.

"She might be naïve enough to believe that would stop a man, but not you, Graham," Elizbeth's father said, his attention on his food. "He would not be the first priest to marry in secret."

Elizbeth's mind raced. Henry Benedict Stuart was the last legitimate descendant of James VIII, and younger brother to Charles. What year had Charles Stuart last tried to take the throne? Her thoughts muddled. 1759. Yes. To the Jacobites, he had been the Young Chevalier. Dear God, Margarette hadn't dreamed the conversation between their father and the Frenchman. It was true. Nae, it wasn't true. It was ridiculous to think they were descendants of kings. But their father believed the Frenchman's story.

"Birth certificates can be forged, James," Graham said. "Where did you get this information?"

"That is not important at this time."

Graham snorted. "I beg to differ. Never has it been more important than now."

Her father took a drink of wine. "You may take my word. It is all true."

Elizbeth held her breath in anticipation of Graham's demand of proof.

Graham picked up his wine glass, leaned back in his chair, and studied her father. "What has Father to say of this?"

"He knows nothing of it," James replied.

Graham's brows rose. "I should think a man would like to know that the woman he called mother *isn't* his mother."

"He will be told when the time is right."

"When will that be?" Graham asked.

Under the table, Margarette's hand found and clasped Elizbeth's.

Their father laid down his utensils and looked at them. "Once I have laid claim to the Crown.

❧

AFTER DINNER, IN THE PARLOR, DAVINA TRIED TO MARSHAL HER thoughts, to plan out what she must say to reach through the madness engulfing James, but she couldn't think with Elizbeth pacing the parlor carpet. "Elizbeth, please sit down," she said, tone terse.

Elizbeth whirled to face where she sat on the divan. "Aunt Davina, this means everything Margarette heard is true."

Davina heard the tears in her niece's voice and jumped to her feet as Elizbeth sobbed. Margarette, too, sprang from her chair. Davina reached Elizbeth first and pulled her into a hug. Margarette threw her arms around Elizbeth's back and hugged them both.

"Shh," Davina soothed. "Graham will not let your father do anything foolish." Neither would she. "You know he hasn't been the same since your mother's death. He simply isn't himself, that is all." Perhaps Davina didn't need the perfect words. Maybe, while the gentlemen took their port, Graham was already reasserting reason.

"But Papa thinks he is the King of Scotland," Elizbeth said through another sob. "It is madness, pure madness."

She was right and that frightened Davina more than anything else

231

about the absurd tale. How could James believe such insanity? Worse, how could he possibly think he would succeed? England would crush him—and them along with him. In the meantime, however, he very well might try to ship the girls off to France.

Davina coaxed her nieces to the divan and sat between them. They each clasped one of her hands and laid their heads on her shoulders as they used to do as children.

"I will not go to France or marry some Frenchman," Margarette finally said.

"Of course you shall not go." Davina gave her hand a squeeze.

"If Papa tries to make me I'll... I'll jump off the ship," Margarette declared.

"You most certainly will not," Davina replied. "Besides which, there will be no ship from which to fling yourself. Your father is not sending anyone to France."

Elizbeth lifted her head from Davina's shoulder and swiped at her eyes with a finger. "But Father seemed so determined. I cannot leave Robert." Her voice cracked.

"Mister McFarlan," Davina corrected with mock severity.

A sad smile lifted a corner of Elizbeth's mouth.

"Neither of you need worry," Davina said. "Graham will know exactly what to do." She hoped.

Elizbeth shifted to face them, expression brightening. "Robert can help, as well."

Davina frowned. "I do not know—"

"Just consider, he is an attorney, so he knows the law." Elizbeth leaned forward, intent. "Not to mention, he is exceedingly intelligent."

Davina nodded. "Perhaps you are right," she said, more to humor her niece than out of any real belief in Mister McFarlan's abilities. "Between him and Graham, we are assured of a solution."

"Robert returns home this evening," Elizbeth said. "We could speak with him tomorrow."

Davina released a breath. "We will see what Graham learns from your father, then decide."

"Perhaps we should leave tonight," Margarette said.

"Leave tonight?" Elizbeth frowned. "Where would we go?"

"We will not leave tonight," Davina said. "Nothing can happen tonight." As the words left her mouth, Davina prayed she was right.

Elizbeth rose. "I would like to compose my thoughts." She smoothed the front of her gown.

Davina nodded. "Write nothing about your father." Elizbeth frowned, but Davina added, "Nae, Elizbeth. If anyone were to read your journal your father could hang."

The girls looked at each other, wide eyes bright with fear.

Elizbeth sucked in a deep breath and nodded. She turned toward the door.

Margarette jumped to her feet. "May I come, Elizbeth? Oh, please do not say no. I may not have a gentleman like you do, but I no more want to go off to France to marry a strange Frenchman than do you and I would like to organize my thoughts, as well."

Elizbeth looked at Davina. Davina gave a tiny nod of approval. She read the mutiny in her elder niece's features and realized Elizbeth had planned to sneak off to her mother's study, a place she wouldn't take her little sister. Davina raised her brows, all but daring Elizbeth to admit her secret.

"You may come," Elizbeth said and turned back toward the parlor door.

Margarette skipped across the room, but Davina recognized the worry in her eyes. She watched until the door closed behind her nieces and left her alone with her thoughts. Should she retire for the evening, as well? She glanced at the mantle clock. Eight thirty-five. Far too early to sleep, even if she weren't a bundle of nerves. What had happened to James to push him over the edge of delusion? She knew—everyone knew—a part of him died with Maryanne. But this... She shivered.

When the clock struck ten, Davina could no longer stand the suspense. She went to the dining room, where they'd left the men, but found the room empty and the table cleared. Her heart began to beat fast. Where had they gone? Her brother's study, perhaps? She checked but found the room empty.

Davina hurried up to the fourth floor where their private chambers were located and went to Graham's room. Her quiet knock brought no answer. She slipped inside and closed the door. She turned, then stopped short at sight of her brother's long legs stretched out in front of the chair before the hearth. Anger bubbled up. Had Graham retired to his room to drink himself to sleep? She marched toward the chair.

"He has gone quite mad."

Davina halted, alerted by his tone. "You do not mean..."

Graham gave a heavy sigh. "Aye."

Davina hurried across the room and sat in the chair opposite him. "James truly believes he is the King of Scotland?"

Graham's gaze shifted to her. "He may be right."

Davina gasped. "You cannot be serious. This-this is..."

"Treason?" He nodded. "I know."

"But you said he is mad."

He barked a humorless laugh. "Of course he is mad. Even if we are descendants of Henry, to lay claim to the Crown is the height of insanity. There isn't the slightest chance of success. Only the eventuality of the gallows."

"You are saying we are truly descendants of the Cardinal Duke of York—that great Aunt Saundra is really his wife?"

Graham shrugged. "The documentation certainly seems genuine. I would have to have it examined by an expert." He grunted. "Though where I would find one, I have not the foggiest idea."

"I know someone who might have an idea," Davina said. "Elizbeth suggested we enlist Mister McFarlan's aid."

"Robert McFarlan, James's attorney?" Graham's mouth thinned. "Is Elizbeth still pining after that pup?"

Davina frowned. "He is no pup, Graham. He is only five years your junior."

"Seems more like ten years. The man has no backbone. I would no more ask his help then I would a footman's."

"What do you suggest, then?"

His expression grew even more grim. Trepidation slithered in her belly.

"James truly intends to marry off all three of you."

Davina blinked. "He intends to marry off *me*?" She stiffened with indignation. "I am his sister, *not* his daughter. Not to mention, I am of age. He cannot force me to marry anyone."

His expression softened. "In fact, he can, and quite easily."

"But how?"

"Davina, he need only truss you up and toss you into a carriage with that fool Frenchman who has promised to launch the war that will win James the crown."

Davina stared. "He would take me by force?"

"What is the difference in taking you by force and sending his daughters against their wishes?"

He was right, of course, and she would no sooner see her nieces wed to strangers in another country than she would herself, but the idea galled her. "I pity the man who tries to force me into marriage, much less his bed," she said more to herself than Graham

A hint of the smile she was accustomed to seeing in Graham's eyes appeared, then vanished. "Such a man would not be kind, Davina."

She hated that he was right. "We must save the girls."

He nodded. "Unfortunately, there is only one way to secure their safety, and yours."

Unfortunately? A dread unlike any she'd ever known took root in her heart.

"Forgive me," he whispered. "But you three must wed."

www.scarsdalepublishing.com